Elysian Dreams

"Where the Past Meets the Present"

by

B.J. Neblett

Published by

Brighton Publishing LLC

501 W. Ray Rd.

Suite 4

Chandler, Arizona 85225

www.BrightonPublishing.com

Elysian Dreams

"Where the Past Meets the Present"

by

B.J. Neblett

Published by
Brighton Publishing LLC
501 W. Ray Rd.
Suite 4
Chandler, AZ 85225
BrightonPublishing.com

Copyright 2011

ISBN13: 978-1-936587-73-5
ISBN 10: 1-936-58773-4

First Edition

Printed in the United States of America

Cover Design by Tom Rodriquez

Cover Illustration by Carol Ruzicka

All rights reserved. No part of this publication may be reproduced or transmitted in any form or by any means, electronic or mechanical, including photocopy, recording, or any information storage retrieval system, without permission in writing from the copyright owner.

❧ *Dedication* ☙

For Mom.

And for Carol Stoker who had the dreams.

"It was a miracle of rare device, a sunny pleasure dome with caves of ice."

Kubla Khan

Elysian Dreams – B.J. Neblett

Mr. History

Chapter One

The Stutz Blackhawk is a wonderful car. With its one hundred seventeen horsepower six cylinder motor; smooth shifting three speed transmission; demountable spoke rims; balloon tires, and shiny nickel plated trim, it is the cutting edge of automotive technology. Quick and nimble, it is perfectly suited for the recently paved Paoli Pike.

Not very long ago, this picturesque length of road was little more than a harden clay and gravel wagon path. But now, two lanes of fine poured concrete, stretching from Philadelphia to the tiny hamlet of Paoli, Pennsylvania, run parallel to the railroad tracks.

It is a clear, sunny day early in September. Traffic is light along Philadelphia's quaint suburban main line. Leaves on the oak and maple trees which line the sleepy business district remain green, waiting for autumn's chilly breath to signal their colorful demise.

An ice wagon sits idle along the side of the road, the single roan mare waiting calmly for the return of the driver, unaware of her impending fate. Soon, the Wayne Ice and Coal Company will utilize its fleet of modern Dodge Brothers trucks and begin delivery of their winter product.

The bright red Stutz roadster moves effortlessly at thirty five miles per hour, with a soft whoosh of air, the result of open cockpit motoring. The lone occupant hums merrily, a wide brimmed white leather driving cap pulled low across his sun tanned forehead. His easterly route takes him past the Rosemont train station. People scurry about, crowding the raised wood platform, as a distant whistle announces the approaching local. Reaching into his vest, the car's driver pops open the cover of his grandfather's gold pocket watch, a gift from President Grant.

"Twelve-ten," he says aloud, "right on time."

Collin Calvin Crowly arrived on the twelve-ten from Philadelphia's 30th Street Station just one week earlier. He was returning from a month long vacation on the overcrowded beaches of Atlantic City. It feels good to be home, though he wishes he could have remained longer.

Aaoogah!

A phaeton, its tan canvas top folded, appears from the opposite direction. It is a blue Ford with black fenders and boards, a 1928, one of Henry's new Model A's.

"Rah! Rah! Go Villanova!" The occupants of the overloaded car scream and wave. "Go team, go!" Young men in blue v-necked sweaters raise hip flasks; apple cheeked young women shake blue and white pom-poms, and the Ford sways and lurches about.

Aaoogha!

Collin waves and shouts. "Go Wildcats!" But inside he bemoans the fact that soon he must leave. "If only things could always be like this," he sighs. "Then again, nothing ever remains the same."

Or does it?

"The more things change the more they remain the same." That's what the portly philosophy professor said at this year's commencement party. "We must look to the past," he continued, "to secure our future." Collin isn't sure if it was experience or red sangria giving the professor his insight. Collin has certainly seen a lot of change, not all of it good. Still, there is a lot of truth in the professor's words.

He brakes sharply, allowing a woman to cross the street. "Good afternoon, Mr. Crowly," she calls. Collin doffs his cap to the pretty red head and she smiles coyly. The roadster's clutch engages with a squeaky protest. Collin shifts into second and the car gains speed.

On his right, overall clad workers are relaxing in the shade of a three story brick and masonry building. Lunch pails are scattered about and the group of men talk and smoke and eat sandwiches. The Durham Coach Works specializes in fitting custom bodies to rolling chassis' from Peerless, Pierce Arrow, Lincoln and other fine names. Like all carriage makers, Durham found itself in a position of either change or perish as the automobile replaced the horse and buggy. The Durham Company manufactures some of the prettiest and most sophisticated car bodies for the country's rich and elite. Many movie stars drive Durham built cars.

Collin's eyes glaze and a thoughtful grin marks his proud countenance at the sight of a richly appointed Imperial formal limousine, recently bodied by the coach builder. "Art on wheels," he mutters dreamily. He deeply admires anything produced by the labor, sweat and talent of the human hand. Collin loves the flowing lines and sumptuous curves of the worker's creations. "It's a pity," he continues to the air, "how the factory assembly line depersonalizes and cheapens most products. Take the automobile industry. One example in which I'm afraid you are wrong, my dear professor. Sometimes the more things change the worse it becomes for all of us. *Vestigial resrtorsum,*" he sighs. "Look to the past. Maybe I'll have the Packard re-fitted." It is a thought he has each time he motors past the Durham works.

Collin Crowly is a direct descendant of the Middletown, Connecticut, Crowlys. Perhaps, not a proud, but certainly an ambitious lot, his ancestors paid for their passage aboard the Mayflower by scrubbing decks and washing Pilgrim clothes. Upon arriving at Plymouth Rock and establishing a settlement, the Pilgrims promptly and unceremoniously banished the Crowlys from the colony. Clathrob Crowly immediately laid a curse upon the ungrateful group and headed his small band west. He made his fortune in questionable trading with the natives.

During the French and Indian War, the Crowlys sold arms and provisions to both sides of the conflict, a fact not lost on the British. The family was rescued by a band of pacifist Algonquin Indians. When they couldn't deliver the promised *acres to the sun* to the friendly, naïve natives it was time to move on. Unable to stay out of trouble long, several Crowlys were later run out of Connecticut during the other New England witch trials.

Collin spends his money freely. He does not work as such and no one is quite sure where his fortune comes from; old money is the usual assessment. However, it is well known Collin is a sporting man, a gambler who picks and chooses his wagers carefully, and never loses. Sporting events and thoroughbreds are his main passion. He also has a keen eye for spotting good investments, particularly in the burgeoning automotive field. Collin was one of Walter P Chrysler's first investors. Recently though, it had been noted he was slowly divesting his stock portfolio. "What goes up must come down," he is often heard to remark.

During the war Collin flew with the élite American volunteers La Fayette Escadrille. Decorated by French Premier Clemenceau and President Wilson, he is said to have shot down nine German planes.

Collin's close friends include race car driver turned air ace Eddie Rickenbacker and Charles Lucky Lindy Lindberg.

Collin Crowly is the last of the Philadelphia Crowlys, a fact he seems oblivious to. Known about town as a bit of a playboy, a gadabout he has escaped the well laid snares of several marriage minded socialites. To friends he often japes that he is a bachelor, a person who never made the same mistake once. Actually desirous of a wife and family, Collin is painfully aware his peculiar and precarious situation makes such a union dangerous.

If Collin does have one weakness it is for beautiful, breezy Bunny Callison. Born Maria Concessa Teresa Franzesee, the free spirited young flapper is the daughter of Philip Sonny Franzesee, Philadelphia's notorious and feared mob boss. Bunny, who's relationship with her overprotective father is volatile at best, has managed to keep her identity hidden from the good natured, unsuspecting Collin.

Entering the town of Ardmore, Collin sticks out his arm signaling a left turn. He steers the Stutz into a space in front of a large, two story red brick building. Switching off the ignition, he steps out of the car and stretches. The sun shines warm and bright, glistening off the clean white pavement. But the distinctive scent of a crisp northern breeze reminds Collin that autumn is only a couple of weeks away.

Collin removes the leather driving cap and scrums back his dusty blonde hair. Hooking the cap over the Stutz's shift lever, he dons a brown derby matching his tweed suit. Smoothing a pant leg, he retrieves a paper sack from the car and crosses to the building's entrance. Overhead a hand painted oval sign hangs from an iron mast. It reads:

Macillvain Photographic Emporium

Angus T Macillvain Proprietor

Presley Scott Macillvain worked as an apprentice to famed photographer Alexander Gardner. Under Gardner's tutelage, the boy grew to become a renowned photographer in his own right. *Scotty* Macillvain was once commissioned to photograph President Grover Cleveland. Now his son, Angus Thomason Macillvain, runs the family business.

A bell attached to the shop door announces Collin's arrival. Inside, a wood and glass counter displays the latest Kodak and Roliflex cameras. There is even an expensive German made Leica and a 4x5 Speed Graflex. 8x10 and 11x14 framed black and white photos of Philadelphia landmarks; stuffy businessmen in high starched collars; sweeping landscapes, and Civil War encampments clutter the walls. One wall is given over to sepia toned family portraits. Collin wrinkles his nose as the sharp odor of developing chemicals wafts from the rear of the store.

"Good afternoon, Mr. Crowly. A fine day is it not?" An unlit cigar twirls in the corner of the big Scotsman's mouth, ruffling an unkempt mustache. He leans across the counter on muscular arms shrouded in protective sleeve-lets. The ubiquitous black bowler is cocked arrogantly to one side. To Collin, Angus Macillvain looks more like a bare-knuckled prize fighter than a shopkeeper.

Collin smiles, "That it be, Angus," he says, trying his best to imitate his friend's thick accent. He sets the bag on the counter as Angus is opening a box.

"You got some great shots this time, Collin. You should be considering moving up from that little box camera of yours."

"I'll think about it. I like the Brownie," Collin replies. He examines the vacation photos he took over the past month, holding one up to the light, "And the negatives?"

"All there individually numbered and sleeved, just the way you like. I took extra care in cleaning and preparing them, as always." Angus' chest expands as he speaks. He takes particular pride in his work and it shows. Never acquiring the artful touch with the camera of his father, Angus is well known for his darkroom and printing skills.

Collin is pleased. He carefully returns the negatives and photos to the box.

"Three rolls, 110 film, develop and print. That's twelve bits," Angus announces.

Collin counts out the exact amount, handing it over to the shopkeeper, and then slides the paper sack across the counter. "And this is for the misses and the kids, my friend."

Angus grins widely as he peers into the bag of sweet salt water taffy from James' Candies in Atlantic City. Collin knows his friend well. The bulging bag of taffy will be considerably lighter by the time it finds its way to the Macillvain family home on the second floor.

"Any tips today?" Angus calls as Collin reaches the door.

"Keep that dollar and fifty cents and the rest of your money stashed in your mattress. And while you're at it stay out of the stock market, no matter how good it looks!" Collin pauses in the doorway and winks. "The only sure thing is the Yankees in four over St. Louis in the World Series."

Back outside, Collin tucks the box of photos and his derby on the seat of the Stutz. Donning his driving cap, he works the throttle and spark adjust as his foot presses the starter. The Stutz cranks but doesn't catch. He tries again. Sometimes the updraft carburetor can be stubborn. On the third try the engine starts. Collin enjoys the feel of the Stutz shaking itself to life. He re-adjusts the spark lever to its mid-point, releases the handbrake and backs out into the street.

As he drives, Collin thinks of the day he can trade-in the old Blackhawk. He yearns to own an Auburn one of the sleek boat tail roadsters with large pontoon fenders and the powerful, throaty Lycoming motor. But he'll have to wait. Collin knows the Auburn Company won't be building the eye catching future classic for a couple of more years. The red roadster will do till then.

Chapter Two

Minutes later Collin slows and signals a right turn. The grass and gravel driveway of Casa di Tempo is nearly hidden from the street among the flourishing shrubbery. Collin motors past the impressive front lawn and imposing mansion on his left, pulling the Stutz up to an ivy covered two story wood and brick carriage house at the rear of the property. While the motor idles with the rhythmic tick of its valves, he opens the two barn type doors. In minutes the Stutz is inside, sleeping peacefully under a soft fleece cover. Slumbering next to the Stutz is a magnificent Packard Twin-Six touring sedan. Sadly, Collin realizes it is time to retire the sporty vehicle for the winter. "Well, maybe after one more jaunt," he declares, patting the Stutz's fender. With a satisfied sigh, he closes and locks the carriage house doors and heads across the meticulously trimmed lawn.

Fumbling in his trousers for keys, Collin unlocks one of the double doors at the center of the rear portico. He enters the house, carefully re-locking the door. Taking the box of photos with him, Collin does something most would consider odd. Something he does often.

A grand central marble stairway leads to the second and third floors. Hidden to the rear of the staircase, lies a small disguised door. Collin retrieves an odd looking gold key with a pentagon shaped head from atop the mahogany molding. Unlocking the door, steeping through, and then re-locking it, Collin disappears into the house's cavernous cellar. Moments later he emerges, carefully locks the cellar door, and returns the strange key to its resting place.

A soft, sad smile registers beneath the well trimmed moustache. Collin wanders through the expansive house to the foyer. He unlocks one of the large double doors, steeping out onto the front porch. Across the vast lawn a line of tightly knit trees muffles the din of traffic.

The air is warm, heavy with a mixture of diesel fuel and pitch. A work crew, wielding jack hammers and blacktop, is busy filling pot holes. Collin stands arms akimbo surveying the rich acreage with its thick, weed free grass, towering oaks and wall of evergreens. He notes the shrubs need trimming.

Satisfied, he steps inside being careful to lock the doors behind him. It's not burglars Collin is worried about.

Upstairs, he undresses, depositing his clothes into a linen hamper. After a leisurely shower and shave, Collin opens his impressive walk in closet. He dresses in sweat socks, Nikes, a burgundy Polo shirt, Eddie Bauer jeans and a grey suede sports jacket.

In the manly bedroom hangs an oil painting of Collin's grandmother. The striking woman's stern, mysterious eyes are those of a cat, appearing to follow as a person moves about the room. "You're looking well today, Donna Rose." Collin moves the painting aside, revealing a hidden wall safe. He places his billfold, keys, gold pocket watch, and loose change on the safe's bottom shelf. From the top shelf he collects a wallet, key chain and gold Omega wrist watch.

Collin takes time to count the neatly arrayed stacks of fives, tens, twenties, and hundred dollar bills: five thousand, six hundred, and fifty eight dollars on the bottom shelf; twelve hundred, and seventy five on the top. He makes a mental note to check his accounts. "Banks are certainly more reliable these days, if less friendly," he says to the picture, re-positioning it on the wall. He studies the image of the woman carefully. "Oh, Donna Rose, I'm afraid I'm getting a bit too old for this. Your wisdom and gift have left me but a prisoner...trapped in two worlds, in which neither I feel very comfortable. The fun, the excitement, even the danger no longer can fill this ever widening void inside me. Where is my Daisy? Well, *numin sustinet*...providence sustains." He takes a quick survey of the bedroom and heads downstairs.

In the sturdy, Collin carefully selects a number of his vacation photos and negatives, slipping them into a manila envelope. He locks the remainder in the bottom drawer of an antique roll top desk. With the envelope and a brown paper sack in hand, Collin Crowly locks the double doors at the rear of the manor and crosses the lawn to an old carriage house which has been converted into a three car garage.

Chrysler's remarkably popular Le Baron Convertible is a wonderful car. The catchy squared off body and computer controlled, fuel injected, turbo charged, four cylinder motor efficiently and attractively blend edgy styling and modern technology. Top down, the sporty bright red car motors effortlessly, the only sound a pleasant whoosh of wind as it nimbly picks its way through traffic.

The repair crew has finished but traffic on route 30 is heavier than usual. The wide modern four-lane, sometimes referred to by old timers as Paoli Pike, is lined with cars and station wagons and vans, many with out of state plates. It is like this every year as thousands of students head back to the two large and several smaller colleges in the area.

Collin sings along cheerfully to a song on the F.M. radio as he patiently waits for a red light to change. "Hey there, Professor," a young woman calls as she crosses in front of the car. Collin tips his white driving cap to the pretty blonde and she flashes a dazzling smile. The light blinks green and soon Collin is motoring along in traffic at twenty-five miles per hour. "The more things change..." he says to the sporty dashboard.

Beep! Beep!

From the opposite direction a large blue convertible appears. It sways about under its cargo of excited young men and cheering young women. "Go Wildcats!" Collin calls as it passes. He smiles to himself. "Well, some things don't change, do they?"

Collin passes from the collegiate bustle of Villanova, into sleepy Rosemont. On the right, several men in spotless mechanic's uniforms linger in the shade of a three story stucco building, smoking and talking. Two massive ground floor windows on the building's street side reveal a yellow Lamborghini, a red Ferrari Dino, and a convertible Bentley parked inside. The former Durham Coach Works is now home to Main Line Motors: Discriminating Automobiles for Discriminating Tastes. Collin finds the dealership's description, as well as its ugly, over priced cars pretentious.

Philadelphia's suburban main line's busy business district is a clamorous non-stop jungle of gas stations and art galleries; theatres and night spots; expensive boutiques and discount houses; chic, trendy eateries and fast food restaurants. It takes almost twenty minutes in traffic to cover the few miles from Villanova to Ardmore. Finally, Collin flips on his left blinker and steers the Chrysler into an el-shaped strip center. Finding a parking spot, he leaves the driving cap on the shift lever, retrieves the envelope and paper sack, and heads to a large store at one end of the complex. Overhead a fancy, lighted plastic sign declares:

Macillvain Photo and Video

On the display window, gilded lettering proudly announces:

Serving the Main Line for 90 Years

Thomas A Macillvain, Owner

Inside, an electric eye senses movement and broadcasts Collin's arrival with an electronic chime.

"Good afternoon, Mr. Crowly. Fine day is it not?" the handsome man behind the glass counter calls, without a hint of accent.

"That it is, Tommy," Collin replies with a poor Scottish drawl.

The brightly lit shop is crowded with glass shelves and counters lined with the latest Nikon, Cannon, and Minolta photographic equipment. One shelf holds expensive Hasablans and Leicas. Modern audio and video equipment is on display in a separate room. The walls are covered with vivid color photos of kids, and cars, and sunsets. One wall is given over to vintage black and white photographs of Philadelphia landmarks no longer standing; dour looking men in stiff collars, and grim family portraits. Behind Tommy hangs a large blow-up photo of the store's original building, Scotty Macillvain posed proudly on the front step. Soft rock music and the scent of orange fill the air.

"How was your vacation, sir?" Tommy Macillvain is the image of his grandfather Angus. He has the same muscular build, square jaw, and squinting eyes. But he doesn't smoke and has never been able to grow much of a moustache.

"It was just fine, Tommy. Thanks. How's your father?"

The store keeper's chest expands as he speaks. "Dad's great, Mr. Crowly. He and mom are in Washington, D.C. Dad's been asked to photograph President and Mrs. Reagan."

Collin eyes the large photo hanging behind the counter. "You've quite a family, Tommy." He places the paper sack and envelope on the counter, removing a few photos. Tommy's eyes grow wide.

"Been going through your family's photo albums again I see," Tommy says, examining the black and white pictures. "I swear I've never seen anyone take such meticulous care of their photos. They look as if they were printed yesterday! And your collection, Mr. Crowly, it must be worth a fortune."

Collin smiles, "Oh, I don't know. We Crowlys have always been a bunch of pack rats. Think you can have them ready for me by Monday?"

"No problem, sir, anytime Saturday." Tommy returns the photos and negatives to the envelope, attaching a work order to the outside, "The usual format?"

"Yes, please, as always, Tommy, and copies of the prints and negatives."

"Yes, sir, always good to have copies and keep the originals safe."

Collin slides the paper sack across the counter, "For the misses and the kids."

Tommy grins wide as he peers into the bag of sweet salt water taffy from James' Candies in Atlantic City. "Make sure you save some for them," Collin teases.

"Any tips today?" Tommy asks as Collin reaches the door.

"Hang on to your Microsoft stock no matter what. Dump the Ford and get a few shares of Cocoa Cola."

"Will do, sir."

He pauses in the doorway and winks. "My money is on it being Oakland and the Dodgers in the Series."

Chapter Three

"Ah, Professor Crowly, welcome back. It is good to see you. How have you been?"

"Good to see you, too, Dean Howard." Collin takes the older man's hand, shaking it warmly. "I'm fine, sir thank you, and yourself?"

"Oh, you know...first week of school...busy, busy, busy. I trust you had a good summer?" He peers down his pointed nose at Collin, "Haven't seen much of you around campus."

Collin sighs to himself; he knows where this conversation is going. "I've been keeping kind of busy myself, sir. You know..."

"Yes, I do, Collin," Dean Howard chides, interrupting his friend, shaking a finger accusingly. "I do know...I know you need to settle down. Find yourself a good wife, someone who will keep you home nights. The way a department head should behave."

"You mean someone for my arm at social functions. The way the *board* thinks a department head should behave."

Both men smile and nod. There is a soft knock and the administrator's door opens. A tall, alluring young woman enters. She carries books and a writing tablet, a pen protruding from folds of cascading hair the color of a legal pad. "Excuse me, Dean. I was told to come right in..."

"Well...speaking of the devil..." the dean chuckles. "So to speak...please, come in. Your arrival is most fortuitous," he quips, giving Collin a quick wink. Collin turns to find himself face to face with the stunning woman. "Professor Crowly, I'd like you to meet Miss. Moira. Or is it *Ms*. Moira?" He snorts his private laugh again. "No matter, here at university we're all family. Miss. Moira, this is Professor Crowly, head of our History Department."

Collin accepts her delicate, manicured hand. He isn't sure if the trembling he senses is her or his own. The significance of the woman's name isn't lost. "It is very nice to meet you, Miss. Moira."

"Thank you, Professor. But please, it's Angelina." Her pretty heart shaped face is alive, considerate, and genial. Collin is drawn to the young woman immediately. It's been a long time since he has felt this way.

Dean Howard drapes an arm around Collin's shoulder. The expression is uncharacteristic and surprises Collin. "Miss. Moira here is our new associate English teacher. She's also working on her Masters degree in Literature. As a matter of fact she'll be taking some of your classes, Professor."

Collin gives the other man a wry, sagacious smile. "Well...how fortuitous."

"I've heard many wonderful things about you, Professor Crowly. Dean Howard tells me you are known around campus as Mr. History."

"Yes...well..." Collin manages to extract himself from the embarrassing embrace. "Dean Howard is too kind."

"Oh, come now, Collin, let's not feign false modesty. The students love you...err...your classes. They are the most popular on campus. It took some fancy scheduling to accommodate Miss. Moira."

Collin does his best to ignore the dean's ebullience. "Anyway, you will be a lovely, welcome addition to my class, Ms. Moira...Angelina. I only hope I can live up to the billing."

"I have no doubt, Professor," Angelina replies. Collin can't help but notice her ears. Small and dainty, they are beginning to redden. Soon, they are an incredible shade of plum which Collin finds sexy. Angelina feels herself blushing and demurely diverts her lush eyes. There is an awkward silence.

"Well...I'm sure you two kids have much to attend to...you know, first week and all." The dean again places a hand on Collin's shoulder. Taking Angelina by the elbow, he guides them to the door. "Once again welcome to Villanova, Miss. Moira. 1988 should be a banner year. Professor, why don't you show the little woman over to the English Department? I believe it is on your way."

Now it is Collin's turn to blush, "If Ms. Moira has no bjections."

Rolling her emerald eyes at the dean's jingoism, she casts Collin a sideways glance and smile, "Of course not."

Grinning broadly, Dean Jerry Howard stands with his arms behind his back as the pair disappears down the carpeted hall. He feels like a proud father watching his daughter walk down the aisle with her new husband.

※

"But what exactly *is* history, yesterday; the day before? Can what happened say two thousand years ago be considered history? More importantly, is it…can it be…relevant to today? Should we even care? Or is it just…history?"

Collin paces slowly before the capacity classroom. He chooses his words carefully, speaking not only from knowledge, but also wisdom, experience. This is his arena, and his passion. It is where he feels most at home.

The eager pupils in Collin's charge include Angelina Moira. Collin presses a button on the remote control he holds and the image on the large screen behind him changes to a great stone elephant. There are muted giggles among the students. "Ah…the famous, historic Elephant Hotel, a lost icon of the Jersey shore. Indeed, it is, or rather was an icon. And you may call it historic. But is it history…compared to say the Pyramids?"

"Of course it is," an enthusiastic student calls out.

"Ok, but why?

There is silence.

A timid female voice advances, "Because it no longer exists."

Collin scratches his moustache, "Not an all together incorrect assertion. But there must be more to it than." He pauses, giving his words a chance to roost. "How do we know a hotel constructed to resemble a multi-story elephant actually existed?"

"Because you have a picture of it right there," another student replies.

"I also have your grades from last year, Mr. Dinges," the professor fires back playfully. "And judging from them I'd be hard pressed to believe *you* ever existed."

The class erupts in laughter. As the din subsides, Collin continues. "The point is photographs can be faked; scientific methods of dating are suspect at best. We have chards of pottery; famous paintings; crude stick figures on cave walls, all good for corroborative evidence. Alone, however, none would stand up in a court of law. Fortunately, we have something else, something much more substantial and, usually reliable. We have the word of eye witnesses. And, more importantly," he raises a thick book, "we have the written word of eye witnesses." Collin presses another button. The class room lights come up. "When you have the written word, it becomes your truth…your history."

"That's all for today. You have your assignments. Thank you."

As the students file out, Angelina lingers behind. "That was quite a lecture, Professor." She collects her books and moves to the desk where Collin is carefully filing his slides. "You manage to answer a million questions yet evoke a million more new ones, all at the same time. No wonder your students love your classes."

"Thank you, Ms. Moira." Collin pauses for a second to reflect. "It's easy when you are blessed to be able to do what you love." He places the last slide in its holder, assembles some papers, and snaps his briefcase shut, noting Angelina's look of admiration. Together they make their way out into the bright October day. "And what questions did I evoke in you today, Ms. Moira?"

"There are so many. I hardly know where to begin."

Collin turns and faces his pretty student. "Perhaps you'd care to discuss some of them over a bite of lunch? Or is it improper for a professor to be seen with one of his students? We wouldn't want to start a scandal. I don't think Dean Howard's old ticker could handle the stress."

Angelina's downy laughter is a feather in the breeze. She looks off, her jade eyes slits. Finally, she nods towards the stone and granite building. "Inside I am your student," she says. "But out here I'm just plain old Angelina, a girl with exactly two cans of diet soda and a pint of moldy yogurt in her 'fridge. I'd love to dine with you Professor."

"As you said…outside the class room we are friends. So you must call me Collin. And we won't limit the conversation strictly to history."

Angelina's infectious smile is encouraging. "Deal and I wouldn't worry too much about old Dean Howard."

They both laugh and head across the sprawling campus.

Chapter Four

Along the Paoli Pike, a short walk from the campus of Villanova University, sits a most peculiar house. To the undiscerning eye it is easily overlooked as one motors past, towards the concrete congestion of Philadelphia to the east, or seeks the pastoral peacefulness of the western country side.

Turning into the narrow gravel and grass driveway discreetly nestled among dense shrubbery, you are greeted by an expanse of blue green lawn. Peppered liberally with towering oaks, sturdy maples, and hauntingly beautiful weeping willows, the yard stretches a verdant carpet to the main house.

Setting foot upon the meticulously maintained estate transports the visitor into another era, to a time when life was simpler, unhurried; genteel. Here, visions of bustled ladies and mustachioed gentlemen picnicking, riding high wheeled bicycles, or engaged in lawn croquet spring to mind. However, sixteen cylinder automobiles and argyle sweaters feel equally at home here, as do ponytailed and dungaree youths with yo-yos and hula-hoops. Casa di Tempo is timeless.

It must be pointed out that while the manor, a curious mix of old English mansion and medieval castle, is indeed grand, a bit of clever architectural trickery is at play here. The massive hand hewn building stones; a sweeping full width portico, and two grand rectangular windows yawning out from either side of the oversized arched mahogany and brass double doors, conspire to make the building appear much larger than its modest three stories.

A pair of regal reclining griffons, each holding a lantern of green light in a raised paw, flank three broad Italian marble steps. These lead to a front porch sporting a polished Brazilian wood floor which is girded by a low stone wall. Winged gargoyles simper down from their posts atop four smooth, white granite columns supporting the porch's canted roof. Gracefully curved window turrets project from the rounded corner battlements. They are capped by steeply sloping orange Spanish tile spires, while the main roof is of dark slate. Delicate, over square windows line the upper floors. Topping the entry, a tall amber, leaded glass casement filters the sun's rays into a grand central hall and stairwell. As befitting any fine estate, the side walls team with lush clinging ivy.

At the apex of the façade sits a gleaming white Italian marble pentagram capstone. Upon it is engraved 1868 – the year the house was completed – and the cryptic inscription, *ecce cinque dimensiones,* 'behold five dimensions'.

To the acute eye, a curious feature comes to light while taking in the serene grounds: the mansion's peculiar orientation. Squared neither to the road, nor its own property, the home sits askew, facing south by southeast. This is not a flaw in planning anymore than a mistake in construction. The most obvious, and therefore accepted, reasoning for the alignment is that the clever placement affords maximum exposure to sunlight, while providing perfect natural ventilation from the regular northeast and easterly breezes. Considering the pure stone structure, and the abundance of protective trees, even on the most scorching of August afternoons, inside, Casa di Tempo remains cool and comfortable.

However, convenience and aesthetics aside, a more complex reasoning lies behind the home's curious alignment and singular appearance. Upon investigation, a remarkable coincidence comes to light.

Or is it a coincidence?

Drawing a line of longitude from compass – that is magnetic – north directly through the middle of Casa di Tempo and continuing south, one finds himself in the heart of the Bermuda Triangle. It has been noted that during occasions of strong magnetic and electrical activity such as thunderstorms, compasses and watches alike tend to sway and vary noticeably, within the confines of the house's grand central hall.

While the powers and mysteries of the infamous triangle are well documented, this local anomaly has never been explored or studied. Nor is it likely to be. The builders of Casa di Tempo understood the intricate, furtive forces at play here and harnessed them for personal use. The key lies beyond Collin's secret locked door.

Chapter Five

"Take good care of her, Johnny." Collin is resplendent in his fine camel hair coat, blue pinstripe suit, and gleaming white spats. A cream colored fedora is pulled rakishly low, partially concealing his features. He tips the young man handsomely.

"Yes, sir, Mr. Crowly," the attendant replies, climbing behind the wheel of the stately Packard.

Collin crosses the deserted street to a non-descript brownstone. Down six curving steps, he comes to an unadorned wooden door neatly hidden beneath the building's main entrance. The tranquility of the clear night belies what lies beyond.

Collin knocks three times. A pair of cruel steel grey eyes considers him critically through the door's narrow Judas hole. In seconds the questioning gaze softens, several bolts are moved aside, and a beam of harsh yellow light splits the darkness. "Evening, sir. Nice to see you again."

Inside the sparse foyer the crisp night air is shut out. Ignoring the simple door on his right, Collin curtly nods to the large tuxedoed doorman. At the touch of a well concealed button, a section of wall slides effortlessly to one side, revealing a flight of steep, well lit steps. Collin nods again, passes through the secret passage, and heads down the steps as the wall returns to its position.

During the descent, the sound of music and voices steadily increases. The clamor blasts forth full force as a door at the bottom of the stairwell is thrown open. Collin pauses, allowing his ears and eyes to adjust to the rousing din and thick blue smoke. He smiles and steps inside, removing his hat and overcoat. They are whisked away by a scantily clad young woman who winks at Collin seductively, slipping a claim check into his palm.

There are some three hundred speakeasies in the metropolitan Philadelphia area, illegally and unabashedly doing business under the relaxed scrutiny of the local authorities. Prohibition has had quite the opposite affect its optimistic supporters intended. If anything, sales of alcoholic drinks and beverages, prohibited in the U.S. since 1920, have increased. Some say as much as two fold. The healthy state of the American economy has given rise to a jaunty, live for today attitude settling like a blanket, comforting yet blinding, over the populace. Life is good in 1928, a non-stop festival of flivvers and flappers; jazz and gin. At the center of this celebration is the secretive speakeasy. And Sharkey's is Philadelphia's best known secret among the nightlife.

Crossing the crowded club, Collin wanders to a small serving bar. The barista behind the counter adjusts his gartered shirtsleeves and winks. "'Bin a wh'ils, Mr. Crowly. 'Tis good to sees ya. Withs or withouts 'night, sir?"

"Thank you, Patrick, with…a double, please."

Patrick produces an oversize coffee mug. Filling it half way with smoky, amber liquor from a non-descript bottle, he watches Collin accept the beverage and sip deeply. He smiles at Collin's mixed reaction. "Guts in dis 'morn. Right offs 'de boot."

Collin blinks several times, examining the cup's contents. "Yes, but which boat, the Mayflower or the Santa Maria?"

Patrick responds with a puzzled stare. "'Ows 'dat, sir?"

"Never mind, is Big Mike in tonight?" Collin asks, adjusting his glasses, scanning the room.

"'Es jist arrived, sir. Usual booth." Patrick nods to the far corner. Overhead a glistening mirror ball paints the room and its occupants with swirling soft pink dots.

"Thanks, Patrick." Leaving a saw buck – a ten dollar bill – and the disagreeable drink on the counter, Collin skirts the emptying dance floor, making his way across the club as the house lights dim. In moments every seat is occupied and an excited murmur comes over the room. The nine piece orchestra strikes an agitato chord and half a dozen dancers appear in the smoky beam of two oval spotlights. Costumed identically in black thigh high shorts, matching V-necked blouses, black gloves and heels, the bob haired sextet begin a lively tap number to an infectious version of *You're The Cream In My Coffee*. Collin watches the performance for a moment and then sidles over to the corner booth.

Lumpy muscles and custom cut five hundred dollar suits do little to conceal obvious bulges. Two armed goons on either side of Big

Mike's private booth eyeball Collin's movements with expressionless distain. As he approaches, one leans to the ear of the dapperly dressed Don seated in the crook of the curved booth. A china tea cup and saucer are perched atop the white linen covered table, and a three dollar cigar smolders forlorn in a crystal ashtray. Big Mike nods, the goon frowns, steps aside and casts his partner a worrisome look.

Glancing up from his table, Big Mike acknowledges Collin who grins derisively at the two body guards, allowing them to rudely and roughly frisk him.

"Easy, boys…easy." Big Mike's voice is strong, powerful, rising over the roar of the band now breaking into its second number. "Mr. Crowly is our guest."

Adjusting his rumpled suit, Collin slides into the booth. "'Evening, Mike, I see you still haven't house broken Punch and Judy here." Mike ignores the wisecrack.

Big Mike Shannon runs the largest book in Philadelphia. A tough as nails mobster, he is also first lieutenant to Frank Mc Ginny the owner of Sharkey's and undisputed boss of Philly's second largest gang. The two grew up together in the tough Irish-Italian neighborhood. Mc Ginny entrusts the gambling and protection arms of his illicit empire to the no-nonsense Big Mike Shannon.

The gangster smiles pleasantly across the table, sizing up Collin. The pair exchange stares as Shannon exhales a long pull from the re-fired Perfecto, filling the booth with grey smoke. Collin lets out a stifled cough and Big Mike grins. "Reigh Count in the derby; Gene Tunny KO's Heeney in the twelfth," he points to Collin with his cigar, punctuating his words, *"then he retires!* And now the Yankees sweep 'dem bum Cardinals…four games straight!"

Collin shrugs timidly as Big Mike continues to stare. "Sometimes you get lucky."

Shannon spits out a rough expletive. "Luck is Louis Meyer taking the flag at Indy by half a second on shredded tires." He leans across the table, lowering his voice to a whisper. "Luck is canceling opening night theatre tickets to *The Front Page* at the last minute, without knowing someone's put a hit on you." His gaze makes Collin uncomfortable. Suddenly Big Mike erupts, half in riotous laughter, half in strained fits of coughing. With redden cheeks, he reaches into his jacket. Collin stiffens in his seat as Shannon pulls out a wad of C-notes – hundred dollar bills – tossing the bundle on the table. "Four games to nothin'…against the Gas House Gang…'dem bums," he manages, still laughing.

Collin's breathe returns as he scoops up the money, stashing it in his coat pocket. "Thanks, Mike," he says, sliding from the booth. "Take care."

Big Mike's expression turns serious again, "You too, cowboy."

A waitress intercepts Collin and escorts him to a private table at the edge of the dance floor. She smiles flirtatiously and leaves a coffee mug. Collin frowns at the liquid then realizes it is black coffee. He takes a sip and settles into his seat.

On the dance floor, the chorus girls have finished their numbers and exited. An upright piano now sits to one side, a tuxedoed pianist, as black and shiny as his instrument, poised at the keyboard. He begins to play and a lilting voice fills the darken room. The revolving mirror ball has changed its mood to blue. An indigo filtered spotlight slowly blooms revealing a lissome blonde. Dressed in a sleek spaghetti strapped cerulean gown and an electric blue boa, she stands center stage warbling a breathy version of *Am I Blue*.

Bunny Callison is the star of Frank Mc Ginny's Sharkey's Club. She is also the girlfriend of Collin Crowly. Mc Ginny is the sworn enemy of Bunny's father Don Franzesee. The two mob bosses are rivals for control of Philadelphia's affluent Main Line. Because of Bunny, they have called an uneasy truce. Collin, who is a distant relative of Mc Ginny, is blissfully unaware of his precarious position.

Chapter Six

"What did you think, Snookums?"

Bunny hugs Collin's neck and kisses him. Pale red lipstick marks the spot. Returning the spirited embrace, Collin wipes his cheek with his handkerchief. "Very nice, Bunny, very nice, is it new?"

She wiggles into the chair next to Collin's and he returns to his seat. Her voice is as squeaky as a hinge and as perky as her modest breasts. "New? Oh, Colli, don't you ever read *Variety*? Am I Blue is socko!" Collin stares blankly at his bubbly companion. "You know… it's just the biggest song out today!" Bunny giggles. Bunny Callison is always giggling. She playfully drapes the silky boa around Collin's neck. Collin endures the affection. "Goodness, sometimes I wonder where my Snookum's head is at. You just don't seem to be able to keep up with the times." Her bottom lip juts, her eyes sadden like spaniels'. "You even missed Buggy's big Halloween bash."

"I'm sure I wasn't missed among the multitudes of guests."

"You know somethin', Colli?" She is unable to maintain the feigned petulance and giggles again. "I didn't even know you weren't there 'til after midnight." She leans close, batting her long lashed hazel eyes. "But I missed you… when I realized you weren't there. Did you miss your little Bunny?"

"Yes, yes I did. And I'm sorry I couldn't make the party. How have you been, sweetheart?"

They kiss sweetly, and she giggles. "Oh, you know… well, if you were around more you'd know."

Collin's had enough of the slinky wrap, folding the uncooperative boa best he can onto the back of Bunny's chair. "Did you read the material I left for you?"

This time the singer's pouty face is sincere. "Do we have to talk about that stuff now? Don't you wanna have some fun?"

"Of course I do, sweetheart. But this is important. It's Election Day. You should know a little about what goes on in the world."

A waitress appears with two mugs of imported champagne. Bunny slouches back into her chair in thought. As the waitress leaves, Bunny looks at Collin, her moist lips pursed. "Do you think they'll repel prohibition, Colli?"

Collin smiles, "Repeal, Bunny, you mean repeal prohibition. So…you have been reading."

"Of course, Snookums, you wanted me to…I mean…sometimes I'm not real sure about what I'm reading…" She looks to Collin like a chastised school girl. "But you did say you wanted me to read it…"

Collin kisses her cheek. "Good for you." He pauses to think, choosing his words carefully, something he must do often. "Well, let's see…that depends…if Smith is elected…"

Bunny perks up, smiling broadly. "You mean Al Smith. He's the one who wants to do away with the prohibition." She is proud of herself.

"Why, yes, Bunny. That's right. Al Smith is the democrat and he says if he is elected he'll end prohibition. Of course, he must be elected first. Then we'll just have to see. Anyway, we should know who won in a little while."

Bunny props an elbow on the table, her delicate pointed chin resting in her palm. Her expression grows serious. "I hope he doesn't win. I like the way things are. I like working here…it's so much fun…I mean, you know, having to be so secret and all." Despite herself she titters gleefully at the thought. "Besides, I don't like that Smith guy's voice. It reminds me of…"

"Of what, Bunny?"

"Just never you mind." She picks up her drink and they clink mugs. Collin watches the young flapper as they both sip their champagne. Suddenly, the band breaks into a hot rendition of the Lindy. Bunny's eyes dart wide open. Setting her cup down, Bunny pops up. "C'mon, Snookums, let's dance." Collin reluctantly allows himself to be led onto the dance floor.

Elysian Dreams – B.J. Neblett

The big maroon Packard sedan with dual side mounts and plush mohair upholstery rolls to a stop in front of a posh Bala Cynwyd high rise. The only sounds are from a squeaky rear brake spring and the muffled baritone exhaust note of the car's powerful twelve cylinders. The cry of a newspaper boy, his applejack cap pulled low, breaks the still, pre-dawn air. "Extra...extra...Hoover sweeps in! Extra...read all about it!"

"I already have," Collin says to himself, yawning. He lowers the driver's glass. "Here, boy..." Accepting the Wednesday, November seventh early edition of the *Philadelphia Inquirer*, Collin hands the youngster a new fin – a five dollar note. "Keep it," he calls, raising the window.

"Gee, mister thanks!"

"Let's see..." Collin scans the front page as Bunny snuggles close. "It seems prohibition may be with us for sometime...Hoover has won."

"That's the old guy, isn't it?"

Collin laughs. "Yes, the old guy."

A worried look crosses Bunny's sleepy, thoughtful face. "What does that mean?"

"It means, sweetheart, that Sharkey's stays open; you get to keep on singing, and everyone gets to keep having fun, drinking illegal gin and making easy money in the stock market." He sighs and folds the paper, "For a while longer, anyway."

Bunny couldn't be happier. "Goodie, goodie!" she squeals.

"That really makes you happy, doesn't it, Bunny?" he asks, turning in his seat.

"Well, sure, Snookums. Who wouldn't want things to stay the way they are?"

"But don't you ever...ever..." Collin struggles for words. "What about the future? Wouldn't you like to be...married someday...raise a family?"

Bunny's cheeks glow a soft pink. "Gee, Colli, if you're proposing...well...I'm flattered and all. And I sure do like you." She gazes into his steady brown eyes. "An awful lot...you're really swell...I mean you're sweet and fun and all...even if you are forgetful at times. But all that other stuff...well, sure...of course...like you say, someday...in the future."

Collin strokes her pixie platinum hair. "Ok, sweetheart...you're right...in the future."

They kiss and Bunny giggles. She always giggles when they kiss. "You wanna come up, Snookums?"

"No, sweetheart, I can't."

"Ok, Colli..." With an unrestrained laugh, Bunny accepts the doorman's hand and exits the Packard. "See ya around, Snookums." She blows him a kiss and hurries into the apartment.

Collin watches the first streaks of dawn unfold over the Schuylkill River and the city beyond. He places the elegant touring car in gear and drives into the waking day.

The Packard tucked safely away in the carriage house, Collin enters Casa di Tempo through the rear doors. He makes a quick visual survey of his home. Satisfied, Collin uses the strange key hidden above the ledge to unlock his secret door beneath the stair case. He passes through and locks it behind him, then descends down a dimly lit flight of ancient stone steps. The basement is spacious and, like most, cluttered with storage boxes, trunks and unused furniture. In a far corner, partially obscured behind a stack of barrels and crates, there is a small, unassuming metal door. Its darkened patina blends in with the slate grey walls, making it nearly invisible to the undiscerning eye.

Using the same oddly shaped key, Collin unlocks and opens the iron door. Before him, stretches a narrow access hewn out of the earth and rock. The portal predates Casa di Tempo by thousands of years. At its end lies an iron door identical to the one Collin has just passed through and locked.

There is no light or electricity, yet the corridor walls, adorned with strange markings and glyphs etched into the rock, glow an eerie greenish blue. The atmosphere is gelid and Collin can see his breath. Covering the fifteen foot passage, Collin uses his key, steps across the threshold, and relocks the second door. He finds himself back in his basement where he started. Mounting the well worn stone steps, the secret door is open, entered and secured; the strange key returned to its hiding place.

Upstairs, Collin laboriously kicks off his shoes and spats; sheds his hat, overcoat, jacket and tie, and wearily flops down on the bed. Locating the remote control, the modern twenty seven inch television blinks to life, and an authoritative male voice is heard: "Good morning, America. Today is Monday, November seventh, 1988. According to the latest polls, heading into tomorrow's election, Vice-President George Bush holds a commanding lead over democratic presidential hopeful Michael Dukakis. While the congressional races remain hotly contested, it would appear the White House will remain in republican control for another four years."

Collin lowers the set's volume, stretches and yawns. "The more things change…" he mutters aloud, "the more they remain the same. Isn't that right, Donna Rose?" The iconic painting stares down at him mutely.

Checking the settings on his digital clock radio, he yawns again and is immediately asleep. Professor Collin Calvin Crowly has an early afternoon class.

Chapter Seven

"Oh, Collin, it's…it's…"

"Yes, I know," Collin admits. "It is something else, isn't it?" He parks the Chrysler on the front drive.

"No, no, silly." Angelina eagerly exits the convertible, her eyes growing wide as she surveys the estate. "I mean it's…it's magnificent, beautiful!"

Collin blinks, smoothing his moustache. "Casa di Tempo has been called a lot of things but never beautiful."

Kicking off her shoes, Angelina rushes into the dewy grass of the front lawn. She dances and twirls, a ballerina, in the jealous moonlight. "Don't you see it, Collin?" she calls. "Look…I'm Catherine…'Oh, Heathcliff, you *are* such a feral creature'…I'm Garbo," she mugs, throwing an arm dramatically across her forehead. "'*And I vant to ve alone!*'" Angelina cavorts gaily, affectionately petting a stone griffon. "I'm Daisy, hosting an elegant soiree while poor Gatsby stares forlorn at the intangible green light."

Collin feels his heart melt for the beautiful, beguiling woman before him. It is a cool Thanksgiving evening, and this is their fourth date. Earlier, Collin and Angelina dined on Beef Wellington and yams and a rich Merlot at the historic General Wayne Inn. Now, after much anguished soul searching, he has brought her to see his home. Except for a modest social Collin holds on the back lawn each spring for his graduating students, Casa di Tempo rarely sees visitors. Watching Angelina now, Collin is glad he made the decision.

Moving to her side, Collin glances up at the building absently. "A house is just a house…"

"What's that?"

She touches his hand. He touches her cheek. A ghostly breeze stirs the trees, an encouraging hand urging him on. Hesitantly, Collin pulls her to him. She permits his advance. Without a word they kiss.

An eternity later their lips reluctantly part. Both are breathless and flushed. Collin is the first to speak. "Well, it seems Casa di Tempo has cast its spell." He holds her at arm's length savoring her beauty.

Angelina's eyes twinkle like fireflies. "I don't think it's the house." She takes in the mansion again. "Casa di Tempo," she whispers to the night, "House of Time. How perfectly mysterious, just like its owner." Her smile warms the evening. Hand in hand they stroll up the front steps.

Collin and Angelina sit close on a beautiful velvet Queen Anne sofa. A crystal decanter containing Napoleon brandy rests on a polished mahogany ball and claw coffee table. There are a pair of eloquent Victorian chairs and a delicately hand carved curio cabinet. Carefully framed vintage photos and some original oil paintings line the walls. The rest of the house is furnished with equally exquisite antiques. Nearby, blue and yellow flames engulf the pyramid of logs in a large stone fireplace, warming the ample living room.

"That is Donna Rose."

The woman in the picture is the same as in the painting in Collin's bedroom. She is accompanied by a distinguished, lanky man in full dress civil war officer's uniform. The large photograph hangs above the fireplace mantle.

"Who is the serious looking gentleman?" Angelina asks.

"Major Calvert Conlin Crowly, Donna Rose's husband."

Studying Collin's face, Angelina turns her attention back to the framed photo. "You look like him. Same jaw, same puppy dog eyes…same moustache. And just a handsome! I must say, they make a striking couple."

"Oh, from what I understand they really were something. Donna Rose was a black eyed gypsy girl from a tiny village in central Sardinia. She was barely sixteen when they married. Calvert, twelve years her senior, lost his right leg at Gettysburg. He was personally decorated by General Ulysses S Grant. I still have Cal's gold pocket watch the general gave him on his birthday. Casa di Tempo was Calvert's wedding present to Donna Rose."

"Wow, some wedding gift!"

"Oh, they loved each other very much. It was actually Donna Rose who chose this location, based on some secret family tradition or superstition. She also designed and oversaw building of the house. Construction took several years due to the war."

Angelina is impressed. "She must have been some woman."

"Yes," Collin replies with great affection for the strong woman. "Yes, she was. In 1869 president Grant asked his old friend Calvert Crowly to accompany John Wesley Powell on an expedition to explore and map the Colorado River and Grand Canyon. Their party was the first white men to navigate the dangerous river. Calvert was killed during a brief skirmish with some Indians. Widowed at twenty four, Donna Rose Maria Visconti Crowly became the matriarch of the Crowly Family."

Together Collin and Angelina explore the expansive first floor of the mansion. "You know," Collin says seriously, "the top floor has been closed for many years. But still…sometimes…late at night, when the moon is a gelid ghost…you can hear the clomp, clomp, clomp of Calvert's wooden stump as he paces back and forth…alone…up in his third floor study."

An icy finger runs down Angelina's spine. The lovely English teacher jumps. Then her laughter fills the lonely rooms of Casa di Tempo. "Oh, Collin, you had me going there for a minute."

"Well, I'm sure old Calvert would be glad to know he can still get a rise from a beautiful young woman."

They both laugh. "You have such a rich family history, Collin. Tell me more."

Returning to the living room, Collin refreshes their drinks. "Calvert and Donna Rose had only one child, a son named Conlin. Do you know all the males in the Crowly family were born in leap years?"

"Really, you also?"

"Oh, I went them all one better. I was born on leap day, February 29," he answers proudly.

"I've heard it said people born on that day are ageless," Angelina replies.

Collin tastes the irony in her words. "Sadly, Conlin, his wife Bessie and Donna Rose were on a trip to Ireland aboard the Lusitania when it was sunk by Germany in 1915." His heart saddens at the private memory. He takes a long pull from his glass. "The estate and Crowly fortune, such as it was, fell to Conlin and Bessie's only child, Collin."

"Is that for whom you were named?"

The question pulls Collin from his thoughts. "Humm...yes...yes, sort of."

"It must be wonderful knowing all about your family, having pictures, mementos, and such vivid and colorful stories." There is sadness in Angelina's words.

"Oh, I don't know. We Crowly's have our share of skeletons."

"What," Angelina teases, "no family curses?"

"I don't know if you would call it a curse..." Collin looks deep into Angelina's mystical jade eyes, "and what about you?"

She sips her drink as memories fill her thoughts. "Me? Oh, gosh, there is really nothing much to tell. Honestly."

"How about your name, Moira. You are Greek, right?"

"Yes...well no...I mean..." Collin is bemused by her response. "I guess I better explain. I never knew my parents, my family. I was raised in a private orphanage. My earliest recollections are of a jovial, older, round faced nurse named Marina holding me and singing to me. She called me Caliopia, after the Greek muse Calliope. Marina loved mythology and said I had a, 'Beautiful little voice'." The memories are bitter sweet. "She'd tell me stories of gangsters and speakeasies and when she sang with a big band, and how she traveled with the U.S.O. She even taught me about guns and how to shoot. Marina was the closest thing to a mother I ever knew. She gave me the name Moira."

"Moira, it means fate...destiny, doesn't it?"

"Yes, that's right. Can you imagine...Caliopia Moira!"

"It's a beautiful name."

"Oh, I agree, Collin. Please don't get me wrong. But can you picture a shy, orphan kid going through school with such a handle? I added Angelina in the sixth grade." She sets her glass on the table and strolls over to the fireplace. "For some reason I was never adopted. Books were my friends, school my life. A lonely one I suppose…but…"

Angelina's voice trails off in reflection. A log cracks and splits open in the fireplace sending forth its warmth. She glances about the room then turns to Collin. "What about you, Collin? I can't believe you live here all alone. It must get terribly lonesome at times." Angelina feels her ears redden at the forwardness of the question. She thinks she may have drunk too much.

Collin smiles, feeling compelled to answer. "To be perfectly honest, Angelina, it does." His well oiled defense mechanism kicks in. "Of course I could never leave Casa di Tempo." He raises the stemmed snifter to his lips then hesitates. Realizing he, too, is feeling the effects of the strong liquor, Collin sets the nearly empty glass down. He has longed to share himself fully with someone. Gazing at his lovely companion, he wonders if perhaps he has found her.

They return to the sofa. She touches Collin's arm tenderly. "Don't be silly, Collin. Why would you wish to leave? Your house…your home…it's perfect, just perfect."

"Do you really think so?"

Angelina's tender young face waxes dreamy. "When I was a girl, Marina gave me a copy of *The Great Gatsby*. It was my first real book. It's long since gone, but it stirred in me a love of reading and an interest in literature. And, I'm afraid, awakened a hopeless romantic. In it there was an illustration of Gatsby's mansion, with its imposing façade, and ivory draped tower, and magnificent blue lawn. Very much like your home." She watches Collin's face as she speaks. He is deeply interested, his expression reassuring. "Every girl dreams of growing up and living in a grand mansion," she continues, "the Cinderella syndrome. I suppose I just never stopped dreaming."

Collin understands. "And, in a way I suppose I never grew up. You know, the Peter Pan syndrome, wanting to live a life of sandlot baseball and chasing fire trucks. Little has changed here since the house was built. It's as if I live at two different times, in two different worlds: that of the respected university professor, and the carefree existence of a well to do rake. It's my escape, I guess, from the realities of everyday life. Only, which is real and which the escape?" The ease of the near confession surprises him. "Like your Gatsby, acting the playboy, waiting for my Daisy."

Angelina relaxes back in the sofa. Raising her arms overhead, she stretches luxuriantly. "Oh, Collin, wouldn't it be wonderful to be able to live in that time, that carefree, crazy, reckless, exciting jazz age? A time before the Depression and inflation and war and atomic weapons; before cell phones and cable and computer this and techno that." There is excitement in Angelina's flashing green eyes tempered by frustration. "Sometimes I feel as if I were born into the wrong age."

"We all feel that way at times, Angelina. Is anyone every really content with the age into which they were born? Man is a malcontent; a disaffected sojourner, seeking out Elysium. Someday, when we can freely move in time, through space, even into the other dimensions, I'm afraid we will be disappointed. Like Alice, man, too, will discover life isn't any better – or worse – through the looking glass, only different." He pauses, trapped in the realities of his own words. "And here we are…pawns of the fates. What did Fitzgerald call it? That *orgiastic future* that eludes us…'No matter – tomorrow we'll run faster, stretching out our arms further…and one fine morning –.'"

Angelina knows the famous epilog well, "'so we beat on, boats against the current, born back ceaselessly into the past'."

Contemplating the words, Collin removes his glasses, cleaning them with a handkerchief. Bunny's faded red lip print catches his eye. He thinks of the effervescent singer as he adjusts the wire rim spectacles. "I suppose the most important thing is to find that certain someone, that special person to share your journey, your life."

"You mean like…soul mates…" Angelina whispers.

Their eyes touch.

"Yes…"

The kiss lingers. There is nothing more to say, or can be said. Fate has played its capricious game.

⇜ *Chapter Eight* ⇝

The school term drags on. The last brush of the sun's warming hand surrenders to winter's steely blast. Collin finds himself increasingly distracted. His relationship with Angelina is moving ahead, perhaps too quickly. Yet Bunny is never far from his thoughts.

"Or is it Bunny?" He broods as he steers the wine colored Packard onto bustling City Avenue. "Is it Bunny…or the life she embodies? What about Angelina? Do I even have the right to choose? Would it be fair to either to ask them to share my secret?"

Lost in his doubts, Collin finds himself stopped in front of the firm Rothschild and Greenspan – Philadelphia's Oldest and Finest Jewelers. With a sigh, he switches off the ignition and heads into the building.

An hour later, Collin steps out into the sharp winter day. As he starts towards the car, he is sidetracked by an alien sight. He is very familiar with the neighborhood, yet he has never noticed the tired wooden shop tucked in the corner of a side street. The hand scrawled sign in the window reads: Books - Rare, Unusual and First Editions. Collin is inexplicably drawn to the store. He finds himself milling about the over-stuffed, rickety shelves, lost in the rash aroma of the dusky, quaint shop.

"Something for a loved one?" the woman is ancient, with hair the color of smoke. Dressed in a simple grey frock and black shawl, she leans heavily on a carved ivory cane. Below its curved handle is a globe be-speckled with red, green, and blue stones. Her skin is much like the leather which binds the thousands of books filling every available space and corner. They are heaped in what seems no discernable order. A large black tom cat with deep yellow eyes lounges atop an open antique volume of *Canterbury Tales*.

"No…no need to tell me," she says with a dusty voice. "You aren't sure…you aren't even sure why you came in." Her face splinters as she casts a sardonic smile. A gold tooth flashes. "But then again who can be sure of anything these days?"

Collin unwittingly returns the woman's smile.

"It's here you know…all here…" Her black eyes cloud as she lovingly strokes the spine of several antiquated books. "Always has been…"

"I'm…I'm sorry…"

The cat yawns open one glass eye, studying Collin cautiously; stretches, and returns to his dreams. "Answers my lad…answers." She giggles. Placing a boney finger to her lips, she points to Collin with her cane. "You posses the key, young man…but not the answer. Do you know why?"

"No…" Collin hears himself reply.

The ironic smile returns. "You have the gift…but never learned to use it properly." Her voice is a whisper. "Take care, least you lose it…for you see only with your eyes." She lifts a large, heavy volume with ease. It is well used. But unlike the others, its red leather binding is clean and shiny. Finding the desired page, her fingers play across the gothic hand lettering. Collin thinks it might be Greek. She reads, yet her eyes remain on Collin's. "See with your mind. Speak with your heart. Touch with your eyes. Love with your entire being."

Collin considers the words. "I'm sorry…I'm not familiar with the passage."

She winks and closes the tome, "Exactly."

A prettily wrapped package with a red and green bow rests on the passenger seat of the Packard. Collin's route takes him through the graceful community of Wynnewood. His mind preoccupied, he hasn't noticed the black Duesenberg all weather phaeton following him closely. As the road widens, the Duesenberg suddenly speeds up, its massive eight cylinders throbbing deeply. In seconds it has overtaken Collin. With a skillful jerk of the steering wheel, the driver veers the mammoth car directly into the path of Collin's Packard. Both cars skid to a stop against the curb.

Two men spring out of the Duesenberg. The inimical pair produce sub-machine guns from beneath their heavy overcoats. They casually level the weapons at the Packard. Collin's first thoughts run to the expensive ring he purchased earlier. His hand automatically pats his coat pocket where the gem rests in a polished wooden box.

No, that's not it. Collin realizes these men are gangsters, professionals; not simple hijackers. He timidly places his hands on the steering wheel, a sign of resignation. From the rear seat of the Duesenberg a large man in a camel overcoat and white brimmed fedora emerges. Even with the brim bent low, Collin recognizes him. He is one of Big Mike's personal thugs. Confidently, he sidles over to the Packard. Collin reluctantly lowers the window. A blast of winter air slaps Collin's face with its icy palm.

"Goin' somewhere, cowboy?" The gangster mouths through yellow teeth tightly clenching a toothpick. Collin doesn't answer. "Yer quite a cowboy…ya know 'dat? Yea, boy…wat ya got cowboy…a crystal ball?" Leaning one foot on the Packard's running board, he grins at the two machine gun toting mobsters. "Yous guys ever hear of a cowboy wit a crystal ball?" The pair stands expressionless. Toothpick turns back to Collin. "Georgia Tech over California in next month's Rose Bowl…ten G's…on the nose." He spits out a sarcastic laugh. "Yous is either stupid…or else yous knows somethin'." Collin shrugs nervously. The hired goon leans in the window, his breath oppressive. "Yous knows wat? I don't think yous is stupid…" The sneer sends shivers up Collin's spine. "Everybody loses sometime, cowboy," the gangster hisses, "one way or another."

The threatening hood grins. Then the trio returns to the waiting Duesenberg. With a roar it is gone. Despite the cold, sweat beads on Collin's forehead. As his hands slowly steady, he raises the window. Taking a deep breath, Collin tries to relax. He absently feels for the small box in his pocket. With all that has happened, Collin thinks of Bunny. A smile warms his face. Reaching for the shift leaver, the wrapped package on the passenger seat catches his eye. Thoughts of Angelina flood Collin's mind and he feels his heart catch in his chest.

Collin sighs and shakes his head to try and clear it. The old woman's words return to him: *You have the gift but have never learned to use it properly. Take care least you lose it.*

Chapter Nine

"Happy New Year, sweetheart."
"Happy New Year, darling."

Collin and Angelina kiss tenderly, passionately, lovingly as the 1989 ball slides to a stop, lighting the Times Square crowd on the flickering TV set.

The brassy sound of Guy Lombardo's paean *Auld Lang Syne* fills the air. Collin takes Angelina in his arms. The couple dance slowly, affectionately across Casa di Tempo's spacious living room.

"Are you sorry we left the party early?"

"No. No... not at all." Angelina accepts Collin's hand, permitting him to lead her to the sofa. She is radiant in her low cut, layered evening gown that mirrors her sparkling emerald eyes. A magnum of Rheims '66 awaits the couple, chilling in an antique silver ice bucket. Collin fills two stemmed crystal flutes half way with the blush bubbly liquid. Angelina sits close, taking the drink.

"If that's as exciting as faculty parties get I may have to rethink becoming an English professor."

"It was a bit stuffy, wasn't it?" Collin replies.

"Stuffy?" Angelina giggles at the thought of Dean Howard's idea of a New Years Eve blow out. "The cadavers in the medical lab are more animated! Everyone seemed so stiff and bored."

"Welcome to academia, Ms. Moira."

They laugh, clink glasses and drink deeply. Collin watches Angelina closely. Over the past month they have spent many hours together. He has found himself falling deeply in love with the beguiling beauty. Collin has tried to resist his feelings but to no avail. And yet, at the same time, he cannot ignore his strong affection for Bunny. Collin has spent sleepless nights with the two disparate women playing heavily on his mind. His thoughts are more than complicated by his Byzantine double life.

He thinks of the day Donna Rose first led him down the ancient hand hewn stone steps beneath Casa di Tempo. Collin was barely fifteen years old. They emerged into a warm, pellucid day, a magnificent Imperial Ghia chauffeured limousine awaiting them in the grass and gravel driveway. Wide eyed, Collin took in the fantastic sights and sounds of Philadelphia in the summer, as Donna Rose spoke.

"You are heir to a great power, Collin. It is a power which holds much responsibility as well as adventure and excitement. That responsibility must not be taken lightly.

"The passage way...portal...we passed through will carry you back and forth at will. It is tuned to a sector of the fifth dimension exactly sixty years advanced: as time progresses in one, so it progresses in the other. But do not be confused, Collin. Time does not exist...not as we commonly think of it. There are a great many of these sectors, planes, which exist simultaneously with-in the fifth dimension. And there are many portals, or gate ways, with which to past between these planes. The ancient ones who opened these portals placed them throughout this world and beyond. Some include the Hudson Valley of New York; the Arizona desert cliffs; in Peru; Central America; off the Bermuda coast; on Easter Island; Siberia; northern France; Egypt, and many other locations. There is one near my village on the island of Sardinia. Every portal is interconnected through a series of radiating lines of energy, forming a triangular grid across the planet. As you will learn, the night sky maps this grid. It is centered in the Pleiades. Remember your Bible, Collin? Job 38:31-33.

"Now, each portal is tuned to a different plane with-in the fifth dimension. In this way one may travel great distances through what we think of as time. A few of us have been honored with the task of guardians to this great power. The power may be revealed in time, if and when mankind becomes ready and worthy of such knowledge. Then the ancient ones will return and reveal themselves. Most believe this may occur early in the second decade of the twenty-first century."

Collin listened as he watched the magical world of 1963 glide past the smoke tinted windows of the limousine. And he understood. There was no question or amazement in the revelations he experienced. He understood this was his destiny, his place in the great scheme of the cosmos. How the almighty creator had set things in motion.

Collin and Donna Rose moved often through the mysterious, chilly portal after that. They took long rides in the limousine. The summer of 1963 became a classroom, teaching Collin of life in a more modern plane. Young Collin found himself enthralled by the politics and social issues of this exciting and perplexing sector of the fifth dimension. He saw parallels between what he knew as history and what he saw unfolding before him. But he couldn't understand why no one else seemed to be able to grasp the significance of these parallels: why the same mistakes continued to be repeated. It was then he decided to devote his time to studying and understanding history.

One day in the fall, Donna Rose and Collin passed into 1963. But instead of the usual learning excursions in the black limo, they remained in the great stone house. It was the first time they stayed overnight. While Collin immersed himself in the books in the home's extensive library, Donna Rose remained fixed before the television. She confided to Collin that as gatekeepers they were to operate on faith in their following and obeying the Almighty Creator. They had been sent on a mission.

"A day will come," Donna Rose explained, "when I, your mother and father will no longer be with you. At that time do not morn us. You must remember that no matter what you may hear, what circumstances may seem, we are simply following our destinies; moving on to another plane. I look forward to that day. I will miss you. But it is as it needs to be. Then you shall become gatekeeper. Follow your instincts and your heart, Collin. Allow the Almighty to guide you and you will know what to do."

The next afternoon, word came across the television that the president had been assassinated. Donna Rose and Collin remained by the TV as the incredible events of that portentous weekend unfolded. On Sunday, as they watched the late leader laid to rest, the chauffeur entered the room.

"Excuse me, Signora Rosa," the driver announced, "they have arrived."

A minute later two very serious looking tall men in black suits and sunglasses entered. They were accompanied by a third man with dark wavy hair and an engaging smile. Collin recognized him at once.

"It is an honor, sir," Donna Rose said, shaking the man's hand. "I am glad to see you are fine."

The warm smile widened. The Massachusetts accent was unmistakable. "Well, as Mark twain once noted, 'Reports of my death have been greatly exaggerated'."

Nothing further was spoken. The small party passed through the portal in silence, emerging back into 1903. It was the last time Collin ever saw the iconic gentleman, his two companions, or the chauffeur.

"Sometimes destiny needs a helping hand," Donna Rose had commented, giving Collin a smile and a wink. During the ensuing years, Collin had been called upon as an escort through the portal three times. The last time he had failed. No recourse or mention of the incident was ever made. But the memory haunted him.

"Hell-o…earth to Collin…"

"Huh? Oh, I'm sorry."

"Are you ok, sweetheart? It's like you were a million miles away."

Collin looks deep into Angelina's crystalline eyes. It's as if he is seeing her for the first time. His heart races. "No… not a million miles, just many, many years… a life time."

She moves close. "What are you talking about? Are you sure you are ok? You seem a bit flushed."

A warm smile crosses Collin's face. "I'm ok, perhaps just too much of this disappointing champagne." He takes her hand in his. "Tell me, Angelina, what are your plans?"

"Well, I don't know New Year and all. I haven't even thought about any resolutions. I pretty well have my hands full with school."

"No, my darling, I mean later. What would you like to be doing say five years from now? Where would you like to be?"

The question catches Angelina off guard. "Gosh, I don't know. I can't say that I've given it much thought. Why…why do you ask?"

Collin kisses her cheek then rises. Moving across the room, he opens the front leaf of a Victorian secretary. The small square wooden box from Rothschild and Greenspan is tucked in a cubby. Collin opens it, admiring the gleaming gem set atop a delicate gold band. The unusual six carat pentagon diamond is flanked by smaller stones, one red and one green. His conversation with Bunny outside her apartment returns. He thinks about the confrontation with Mc Ginny's hoods; about his life and the enigmatic portal. Donna Rose's chidings echo in his mind: *A power which holds much responsibility...that responsibility must not be taken lightly.*

Collin sighs, closes the box and places it back into the antique desk. Returning to Angelina, he hands her a prettily wrapped package with a red and green bow.

"What's this?" Angelina asks, accepting the gift.

"Just something I thought you might like."

Angelina blushes as she opens the package. Inside is a book beautifully bound in green leather. "Oh, Collin, *The Great Gatsby*... it's..." she opens the book to the title page. "Oh, my God, Collin...this is a first edition...signed by F. Scott Fitzgerald! Where on earth did you ever find it?"

"Let's just say it came a long way."

As she examines the rare volume, she notices an inscription below the iconic signature. She reads aloud: "'see with your mind. Speak with your heart. Touch with your eyes. Love with your entire being'. Why Collin, those are beautiful words."

Collin is at a loss. He cannot recall the inscription being there when he received the book from the mysterious old woman. "Yes, yes, they are, aren't they?"

Collin's mind is a cauldron of confusion as he takes Angelina into his arms and they kiss.

Chapter Ten

"I don't know, Jess. I just don't know." Angelina paces her apartment trying to sort things out. "The winter semester starts the day after tomorrow. I don't know what to say to him when I see him. Our last evening together was so wonderful. Yet he seemed distracted, like he wanted to tell me something, or maybe ask me something. And now I don't hear from him for over a week. It's all so very confusing."

"There's nothing confusing about it, you two are in love."

"Do you really think so, Jess?"

"Has he ever told you he loves you?"

Angelina turns to her friend. Frustration marks her soft features. "No...no, not in so many words..." She picks up the first edition *Great Gatsby*, eyeing it affectionately. "But I know he does, I can feel it."

"And have you ever told him?"

The question strikes a nerve. "Well, no...no, but..."

"But you are sure he knows...that he can *feel* it." Jess smiles and shakes her head. "We've been friends for some time now, Angelina. I know you. And I know how stubborn and independent you can be. As your roommate and your friend I have a responsibility to see you don't get hurt. And that includes keeping you from hurting yourself." She takes Angelina and sits her down directly in front of her. "Now listen to me. Men like Collin are a great catch. He's a warm, wonderful man, if a bit eccentric at times. And that's exactly what you have to do...catch him. Alright, you've done that...time to reel him in!" Angelina opens her mouth to protest but is cut off by a wave of Jess' hand. "Now don't you go innocent on me sister! You know exactly what I mean. I agree completely with you. I'm sure he loves you. But men like Collin often need reassuring. He's been a bachelor for so long he doesn't know exactly how to tell you, or even if he should. He's probably afraid he'll scare you off." She pats Angelina's shoulder. "It's up to you, kid. You need to make the first move."

Angelina considers her friend's words. She understands the folly of her restrained behavior. Jess is right. "You are right, Jess." With a determined smile her mind is made up and she jumps from her chair. Tucking the autographed book into her coat pocket, Angelina snatches up her car keys and hurries across the room. "Thanks Jess."

"Hey, it's pretty late. Where are you off to in such a rush?"

"To make the first move," she calls, and then disappears out the front door.

Sharkey's Club is a boisterous blend of music, dancing and drinking. The celebratory spirit has lost little of its verve in the days following New Years Eve. Collin and Bunny are cuddled in a private booth near the dance floor. Bathtub gin and smuggler's whiskey flow freely, as do confetti, streamers and jazz. With a new republican president about to take office, it is an especially euphoric celebration as prohibition remains the law of the land.

"You were right, Snookums," Bunny squeals into Collin's ear. "Everything's just as it should be."

1929 has started off with high hopes and wistful wishes of continued prosperity. Collin alone is aware of the dire changes that will take place before year's end. Black Tuesday is but a short ten months away. He smiles at his winsome companion. Bunny beams in her shimmering silver, fringe laden flapper dress. Her hazel eyes sparkle like diamonds and she titters gaily. Champagne and charm claim their toll. Collin fumbles in his suit pocket for the wooden box from Rothschild and Greenspan.

Collin has strong affections for the bewitching singer. But something is wrong, something is missing. Angelina dances in his mind. He tries to shake the confused thoughts. He needs to know Bunny's true feelings. "Maybe you are right, Bunny. Maybe, just maybe everything is as it should be."

"Of course, Colli." She giggles her engaging laugh. "This party will never end!"

As they kiss, the room is plunged into a deafening silence. The band halts in mid-chorus and a pall settles over the revelers. Startled, hushed comments begin to circulate. All heads turn to the baronial figure that has just entered the club.

"So...this is the *famous* Sharkey's." The voice is harsh, gruff, yet somehow familiar. "Hummm..."

The stranger is flanked by a pair of dangerous looking bodyguards. In a corner booth, Big Mike Shannon stirs, signaling his own men to monition.

Bunny jumps in her seat, nearly biting Collin's bottom lip. "That voice..."

"Al Smith?" Collin replies.

The pair turns in unison towards the entry.

"Daddy!" Bunny exclaims in surprise.

Collin blinks in disbelief. He has often seen newspaper photos of the imposing interloper. "Daddy!" he looks at Bunny befuddled, and then back to the trio now making their way across the club. The box with the expensive engagement ring drops back into his pocket. "Daddy?"

Don Franzesee stands an intimidating six foot three. Despite his years, he carries the trim, defined body of a man half his age, and the unforgiving bearing of a no-nonsense mob boss. Having fought his way to the top, he now controls Philly's largest and most infamous crime family.

Scrumming back his salt and pepper hair, Franzesee surveys the club. "Not so much," he says with a sarcastic laugh. His burley companions sneer in agreement. Big Mike Shannon, accompanied by his own pair of goons, strides across the club. The fearsome sextet meets in the middle of the dance floor as the crowd shuffles nervously.

Franzesee and Shannon stare at each other. Shannon is the first to break the icy silence. "Long time, Snuffy, what brings you to this side of town?"

"Slumming..." the Don replies. Shannon doesn't blink. Slowly, cautiously, like two pit bulls greeting one another, the pair shakes hands. "It has been a while, Mikey. How's the leg?"

"Still carrying the limp you gave me in the sixth grade." They exchange smiles, easing the room's tension. "Can I get you and the boys something?"

Just then Franzesee spots Bunny. He softens at the sight of his daughter. "No thanks, Mikey. I won't be staying. Give my regards to Helen."

Collin slinks back into the booth. "Daddy?" he repeats quietly.

"Daddy!" Bunny pops up as her father approaches the table. She gives him an affectionate embrace. "What...what are you doing here?"

"That was going to be my first question," he replies with a sober look. "You are supposed to be at your aunt's in Drexel Hill."

"Now, daddy, don't go getting all huffy! I'm just having some fun with my friends."

"Friends!" The mob chief scans the room, his steely stare landing on Colli. "And what's this?" he asks, brushing past Bunny, "one of your *friends*?"

"Oh, daddy, that's just Colli. Say Hell-o to daddy, Colli."

His mouth is suddenly dry. Swallowing hard, Collin can only manage a feeble finger wave.

Without removing his eyes from Collin, Franzesee snaps his fingers, "The car...now!"

"But..." Knowing it's useless to protest, Bunny shrugs, "Sorry, Colli." She giggles, blowing him a kiss. "See ya around, Snookums."

Bunny is escorted out of the club by one of her father's hoods. Collin manages to regain some of his composure. Rising and straightening his tie, he offers an unsure hand. "Collin...Mr. Fran...err...Don...err...Sir. The name is..."

"Names is for tombstones," Franzesee bellows. The room turns quiet as a graveyard at midnight. The Don stares Collin in the eye, while the specter of a smile shadows his stern face. In one swift, powerful move Franzesee wraps an arm around Collin's shoulder. "So..." He forces an ironic laugh, "You're the guy who's been keeping my little Maria's time!"

Collin tries in vain to escape the crushing one arm bear hug. "Well…I…yes…you see…"

Interrupting again, Franzesee half walks, half drags Collin around the dance floor. "I like this guy," he boasts aloud. "He doesn't say much. I like that."

The remaining retinue cracks a cagey smile to his boss. Bunny's father makes a wide sweeping motion with his arm. "But this…this is no place for a fine young man like you." He looks over at Big Mike, "No offense, Mikey." Shannon acknowledges the remark and Franzesee's manner turns serious. He sets Collin in front of him, wagging a threatening finger. "And it ain't no place for my daughter, either."

All Collin can do is smile thinly and nod.

Emoting with a flourish and wave befitting a vaudeville actor, the mob boss sweeps across the room with his bodyguard in tow. "Happy New Year," Franzesee calls to the crowd, "and Mikey, take care of that leg!" With a rowdy laugh he is gone.

Chapter Eleven

The house lights dim as the band strikes up the Charleston and the crowd returns to the orgy of dancing and drinking; but not everyone. Many, aware of the seriousness of the confrontation between the two mob bosses, have called it quits, at least for the night. Collin wanders across the filling dance floor, oblivious to the growing hoopla. He finds himself at Big Mike's private booth, returned to reality by the rude remarks of Mike's henchmen.

Shannon considers Collin carefully. "You're a lucky man, cowboy."

"What…how's that?"

"Luck-key…" he repeats, "messing around with the daughter of Don Franzesee." He laughs his hoarse laugh, shaking his head. "Right now you should be fish bait."

The image gives Collin a shiver. "Well…"

"Wha'da ya want, cowboy?"

"Ah, the Rose Bowl…"

Big Mike squints up at Collin, worrying the Cheroot clenched between his teeth. "Georgia Tech over California…ten G's…on the nose. Do you know how much that comes to?"

"I have an idea. Roughly…"

"I'll tell you *exactly* how much," Shannon interrupts, his demeanor souring. "It comes to what I'll lose in business once word gets around of your little scene here tonight. And now I have to find a new singer!"

"I don't want any trouble, Mike." Collin shifts nervously, avoiding the other man's eyes. "I just want my money."

Big Mike bristles in his seat. "Go home, cowboy," he barks. "Go back where you belong. And don't return. You're bad news for my business."

Collin is handed his hat and coat and roughly shown out the door. It is a cold, moonless night. A dreary grey snow dusts the lonely streets as the Packard shivers to life. Barely aware of the drive home, Collin is unaware he is being followed. A big black Marmon sedan paces his Packard.

Collin's mind is a ping pong ball, bouncing between two women; two times; two lives. The vanity of his cavalier lifestyle comes into focus. He is sure he is through with speakeasies, gambling and gangsters. He is not sure where it is he *belongs*. One thought persists: wherever it may be, he is sure he wants Angelina there beside him.

Arriving at Casa di Tempo, Collin's mind is made up. His only thoughts are for Angelina. Heading into the house, he bounds down the cellar steps, carelessly leaving the hidden door and the mysterious portal open. Jumping into the Le Baron, Collin speeds off into the late night hours of 1989.

The black Marmon rolls to a stop, the only sound the crunch of gravel beneath the tires.

Casa di Tempo is dark and quite. Noting Collin's Packard sitting idle in the drive, two shady figures smile and exit the Marmon.

"C'mon…" one whispers. "He's probably asleep."

Finding the rear doors unlocked, the two hoods enter the house. They split up, one searching the ground floor, the other stealthily making his way upstairs. Minutes later they meet in the central hall.

"No one's up there."

"He's not here," the other grumbles.

Just then both notice the open secret cellar door. They nod to one another and head down the ancient stone steps. A quick search of the basement reveals nothing.

"What now?"

A leering grin darkens the first hood's face as he spots a can of kerosene. Splashing the volatile liquid around the room, he looks to the other, "How about we teach 'dat dandy a lesson?"

"You said it."

As they set about their deadly business, one of the gangsters wanders through the open portal. A few minutes later he returns.

"What's in there?" the other asks.

"Nothin'…it's just another room like this one." A twinkle in his steely eyes, he holds up a make shift torch, "It's taken care of…"

Satisfied with their ruinous handiwork, the expansive basement already aglow with flames, the unsavory pair makes their escape up the basement steps.

ಞ

"Ok…ok…I'm coming! Did you forget your keys again, Angelina? Oh…"Opening the door, Jess is surprised to find Collin. She sizes him up, noting his dated clothes, "Where have you been, to a costume party?"

Ignoring the quip, Collin slips past her, scanning the modest apartment. "Angelina, where is she, Jess?"

Wiping sleep from her eyes, Jess closes the door, resting against it. "Gone," she says with a yawn. "She's not here."

"What do you mean?"

More awake now, the roommate gives Collin a puzzled look. "I thought she was with you."

"With me…"

"Yeah, she flew out of here not too long ago, said she was going to find you. You two must have passed on the road. She's probably at your place right now."

The news makes Collin's heart leap. "Thanks Jess." Grazing her cheek with a kiss, Collin hurries out the door. "You can dance at our wedding," he calls over his shoulder.

"Yeah, sure, whatever…" Jess mumbles and heads back to bed.

ಞ

Angelina raps on the rear portico's double doors. One swings open and she enters Casa di Tempo.

"Collin…Collin…"

There is no reply.

Moving deeper into the house, something catches her eye. A plume of smoke rises from the back of the marble staircase. Finding the secret door ajar, Angelina heads down the smoke filled steps. The fire has spread throughout the basement. Across the room, Angelina spies a shadowy figure darting into an open passage.

"Collin!" she franticly cries out.

Coughing from the thickening smoke, her eyes burning and tearing, Angelina carefully makes her way through the flames, disappearing into the portal.

Collin Crowly's heart races at the sight of Angelina's car. His joy soon turns to terror. Casa di Tempo is completely engulfed in flames. Managing to enter the house through the front door, Collin races down the main hall. His private cellar door is wide open.

"Angelina…Angelina!"

Several attempts to go further are thwarted by the intense heat and smoke.

"Angelina!"

Finally, driven back by the flames, Collin takes refuge on the front lawn, as Casa di Tempo succumbs to the fire. With a frightening groan, the once magnificent manor collapses into itself. But Collin's attention is elsewhere. He is desperately searching for Angelina.

Chapter Twelve

It is a month since the devastating fire. The rubble has been cleared, the scorched earth already beginning to heal itself. Like a recent grave, all that remains is a solemn, barren mound of dirt to mark where Casa di Tempo once stood. Buried deep beneath the ground lays the ruined aberrant portal.

The winter day is as gloomy and somber as Collin's mood. The cluttered office he once loved now seems a remote stranger. He snaps closed the new leather briefcase, a gift from Dean Howard. Wiping his glasses, Collin gazes at his old friend.

"I've got to find her, Jerry."

"She's gone," the older man replies.

"They never found a body."

"Collin, the house was completely destroyed, it and everything inside. There is nothing left."

"She's alive, dean."

Realizing the futility of continuing, Dean Jerry Howard sighs affectionately laying a hand on Collin's shoulder.

"So, what will you do now?"

Collin absently fondles the mysterious, oddly shaped gold key which once held so much adventure. As he slips it into his coat pocket, his thoughts are on Angelina and the enigmatic portal.

"Oh, I don't know. I have a lot of thinking to do. Travel is good for a restless soul."

"Where will you go?"

"I hear the pre-historic caves of northern France are interesting. Maybe see the Pyramids, Stone Henge." He permits himself a sagacious smile. "I have always wanted to visit the isle of Sardinia."

"You can't run away forever, Collin. You can't just leave yourself to the fates."

The dean's words give Collin reason to pause. "Would that be so bad? Oh, I'll be back, someday, when I am sure…"

"You'll always have a home here at Villanova." The two friends shake hands for the last time.

"Thanks, dean, but no. I'll find where I belong in this universe someday." Collin's affecting smile broadens instinctively. "I'm sure somewhere there is a nice small, quiet nothing of a high school in need of a tired old history teacher."

"I hope you find whatever it is you're looking for, Collin. I really do. Just remember…the past is a hotel. You can check in anytime; enjoy the view. But you can't live there. The cost is too high."

"…born back ceaselessly into the past…"

"How's that, Collin?"

Outside, a streak of yellow sunlight, the color of Angelina's hair, breaks through the battleship clouds. It warms the small office, casting its amber glow on Collin's thoughtful face. He recalls Donna Rose's words: *Follow your instincts and your heart, Collin. Allow the Almighty to guide you and you will know what to do.*

"I wonder, Jerry," Collin says quietly. "I wonder…"

"...Curiouser and curiouser..."
Alice

Alice's Adventures in Wonderland

"...the idea of fate as a force which can't be escaped seems to start with the Greeks..."
Ted Brautigan

Hearts in Atlantis

Angelina

⚘ *Chapter Thirteen* ⚘

The first awareness to reach the waking figure was that of being naked. Nothing more.

She tried to move.

A bolt of dizzying white pain shot through her alien body. A million nerve cells responded to a million pin pricks as feeling returned to her petrified limbs. Gingerly she tested each joint, flexed each muscle. Soon the tingling was replaced by more subtle sensations: warmth, comfort, and an uneasy stillness. She felt herself a chrysalis, emerging like Sleeping Beauty from a long deep spell.

Sleep leaden eyes fluttered open drinking in the dusky light. Something in the circadian rhythms of her drowsy body told her it was morning, early. Feckless fingers of night still grasped the air in a vain attempt to stave off the encroaching dayspring. Reluctantly, the jealous room revealed itself, slipping into a hazy tangerine cloak.

She lay between the folds of a cottony comforter. It nestled against her bare flesh like a cloud, cool, comforting. The stitching, delicately hand sewn, bound the fabric in a pleasing pattern. Its cerulean color, which was that of a contented mid-day sky, shimmered with a subdued sheen worried to its present luster by innumerable dreamers.

Stretching, the woman took a deep breath. Her lungs strained and she coughed hoarsely. Turning her head to one side, an acrid scent nipped at her kittenish nose. It entered her like a shot of adrenaline. The odor intensified as silky strands brushed her cheek. The delicate whips of hair smelled like burnt coffee.

Gently rising on one shaky elbow, she took in the unfamiliar surroundings. The room was ample, tidy and clean. There was a nightstand next to the large sleigh bed. A beautiful hand hewn cedar hope chest lay at its foot and to one side stood a tall wardrobe of highly lacquered mahogany. A matching ladies vanity and velvet cushioned settee sat opposite. Remaining space was taken up with a well worn overstuffed chair and rough shelving. Incongruous to the room's harmony the raw planks strained beneath the weight of dozens of books.

Egg shell walls held a stylish gold cross; framed sepia toned portraits, and crudely conceived paintings. The harsh figures and grossly distorted torsos of the abstract art work seemed that of a child's hand. The renderings were talented but undisciplined; pleasing, yet frightfully harsh and raw. The young woman forced herself to turn away.

A single square window, partially shrouded in lace, filtered the cool sunlight. Frost tapping at its panes proclaimed the season: winter.

Something flashed in a sequestered corner of her mind. Shapeless memories danced and teased, melting like spring snow, leaving in their wake only questions.

She tried to think.

Nothing.

No recollections. No recognition.

No murky images struggling to surface.

Nothing.

Her mind was an empty slate.

She eased back into the confines of her cozy cocoon. Tears traced the young woman's tender cheeks, as sleep once more claimed her.

The knock was soft, almost imperceptible. Or was it a dream? Bleary, confused images began to coalesce. An old witch floated overhead.

"Well, I see you've finally decided to join us." A gold tooth flashed from the jagged smile. "Good afternoon, Missy."

Fighting off the lingering drowsiness, the young woman blinked her eyes to clear them. The room seemed vaguely familiar.

"Where…where am…" Her throat burned with each painful word. Her parched mouth and lips felt like stiff leather. "Who…"

"Easy…easy…"The figure finally came into a fuzzy focus. It was an old woman with hair the color of smoke. She leaned upon an odd looking cane, bending close, gently stroking the woman's cheek. "Don't try to talk. You'll be fine, just fine. But you need to take it easy." The smile grew, lighting the ancient face. "Well, at least your fever has broken. Here, see if this helps." Pouring from a slim green bottle and letting out a restrained giggle, she passed over a glass of sparkling liquid. "Potter swears by this lemon-lime confection. He says Primo can cure anything. Maybe...who knows?"

Her dusty voice waned as she helped the woman to a sitting position. Slender, unsure hands received the simple glass, gingerly pressing it to her lips. Hesitantly she sipped. The bubbly fluid stung. A second later, her throat began to cool, open.

"Yes," she managed in a raspy tone, taking another sip. "That's better."

As she drank she had the opportunity to study her caring companion. The stiff, cracked face evidenced no secrets, speaking only of age. Her countenance was kind; the black eyes clear, sharp and mysterious; her smile sincere. "Do...do I know you?"

The old lady sat lightly on the edge of the bed. "Now, Missy, you mustn't try to speak too much. No, you must rest your throat...and your lungs. Potter says you'll be fine in a few days. But you must rest." She brushed back stray strands of the woman's hair. "Relax and finish that drink, it will help. I'll tell you what I can."

Leaning on her cane, she stared off across the room, her haunting eyes narrowed in thought. "My young grandson," she began, "found you wandering alone, very late the other night. He couldn't leave you to wend about in the cold. He said you seemed dazed, disoriented. He brought you here, to our home." She turned towards her comely patient. "Your clothes were blackened, carrying a strong odor. Let's see, that was what...two nights ago."

Absently, the woman sniffed at a strand of her hair. It smelled of smoke. The old woman nodded. "Potter – that's my grandson – Potter says he is sure you've been in a fire. You must have taken in quite a bit of smoke." She laid both hands atop the crook of the strange cane, resting her chin on them. "You are lucky to be alive."

The young woman considered what she heard. The words might have come from one of the many novels that lined the walls. She could remember nothing.

"By the way, my name is Lachesis." The genteel smile splintered the old woman's face. "Most just call me Nana."

Finishing the soothing drink, the young woman set the empty glass on the nightstand. Turning, she spied the curious cane. It was white and seemed to be hand carved, perhaps ivory. Below the curved handle was a strikingly beautiful gold and silver globe that mapped the earth. Tiny red, green and blue stones shone in locations, dotting the delicately embossed continents. In the middle of the Atlantic Ocean reposed an opulent diamond cut in the shape of a pentagon. The gem fascinated her. Something clicked in the vacant halls of her memory. She struggled to bring it forward.

Nana noticed the woman's troubled expression. She glanced down at the enigmatic cane, then back to her patient. "What is it, dear?"

She shook her head. "I...I..." Frustration shadowed her pretty face. Sinking back into the feathery pillow, a tear marked the woman's cheek. "Can't...I can't remember..."

With a gentle, mothering gesture, Nana wiped the tear. "There, there now, Missy. Easy...Potter said you could have amnesia. He knows these things. He says situations of great emotional stress can bring about a loss of memory."

Refilling the glass with more Primo lemon-lime soda, Lachesis stiffly rose from the bed. "Don't worry yourself about it. No, don't worry. You're safe now, Missy...you're safe," she whispered. "You're home."

That evening the young woman's dreams were troubled with stark, confusing images. She found herself walking through pleasant woods after a recent snow fall. A white diamond moon sparkled in the sky. It was pentagon shaped. Around it red, green and blue stars twinkled, forming cryptic patterns and signs. Then, without warning, the woods erupted in flames and thick grey smoke. She felt herself struggling to breathe. From a distance, a faintly familiar voice desperately cried out.

"Angelina...Angelina..."

A hand, gently shaking her arm, freed the woman from the nightmare. As her eyes adjusted to the scattered light, her body released its sleep induce tension. The voice was unknown, the smooth round face pressing close.

"There...there, that's better." Gently raising first one, then the other eyelid, the stranger studied each jade pupil in turn. His comforting touch helped her to relax. "Good," he announced, "no signs of a concussion."

"I'm feeling much better, actually." The words came with less pain, sounding more natural.

"Now, just a moment, please," He produced a wooden tongue depressor. "Let's have a look."

As he examined her still tender throat, she examined him. He seemed a kind man, his boyish face honest, considerate. The unkempt wavy hair was two shades darker than a raven. It spilled lazily across a furrowed brow prematurely ridged from hours of thought and study. His sausages like fingers were not unaccustomed to hard work. Yet his hands were gentle against her silken skin. She decided she trusted this man, although she couldn't exactly pinpoint why. Perhaps it was the way his thin lips twitched in nervous contemplation. It made her smile. At the same time she realized her position left her little choice.

"Humm... uh huh...yes, very good." Smiling down at her, he straightened. "First, you must use your voice sparingly." He wiggled a finger to punctuate his words. "I believe the heat and smoke caused no long term damage. But you will feel a bit raw for a few days." She nodded her understanding. "Next, other than a couple of minor scrapes and burns on your arms, and that nasty bruise on your forehead, I can find no injuries. Judging from the condition of your clothes, I'd say you were very lucky." The reassuring smile broadened, swallowing his handsome face.

Yes, she decided, she would place herself in the care of the funny, wrinkled old woman, and this agreeable gentleman. "Thank you, Doctor."

"You must call me Potter. I'm not a doctor, not yet anyway. I study at Villanova University, which is where I found you. Tell me, do you remember anything, anything at all?"

She tried to think. Her only memories were of the recent nightmare and waking in the strange room. She felt as if she were lost, lost inside a great, empty warehouse. Slowly she shook her head. "No...I'm sorry, nothing. You...you called me Angie...or Angel..." she said, her voice unsure, her emerald eyes pleading.

Potter nodded, "Angelina...An – ge – lina." Sliding open the night stand drawer, he retrieved a cream colored business card. "Do you recognize this?" he asked passing it to her.

Examining it carefully she read the raised black script: *Angelina Caliopia Moira*. There was nothing else. She looked to Potter.

"I believe it is the sort of keepsake one gives to friends and family members upon graduating from high school or college," he said.

Studying the puzzling artifact, her mind desperately raced from one dusty corner to another, searching.

It found nothing.

Finally she sighed. "No...I'm sorry..." She ran a finger across the unique name. "Is this...is this me?"

Potter reached again into the open drawer. "It would seem possible. It is such a lovely name, isn't it?" He produced a delicately bound book and handed it to her. "That card was found inside of this. These were the only things you had in your possession."

With trembling hands she accepted the volume. Its soft green leather smelled faintly of smoke. "*The Great Gatsby*," she said quietly, thumbing through the pages, "a first edition." The book felt oddly familiar in her hands. She found the title page, a hand scribed inscription catching her eye. "See with your mind. Speak with your heart. Touch with your eyes. Love with your entire being." The poetic lines touched something inside her. "Those are beautiful words."

"Yes, they are. Do you recognize them, or the book?"

She felt frustration return, settling over her like a shadowy shroud. "No, no... not really... It feels as if I should. Somehow I know this is mine. And yet..."

Potter's touch to her shoulder was soothing, his words sympathetic. "Don't try to force it, Angelina. You've been through a lot.

The mind is a funny thing. We barely understand it. Sometimes it just needs to shut down, take a vacation. Things will return."

"What if they don't?" she heard herself ask.

Potter folded back an ebony lock from his squinting grey eyes. "We'll worry about that if and when…rest now. I'll look in on you later."

"Thank you, Potter."

As the door closed, Angelina stared at all that remained of her life. "Angelina," she said aloud. "Angelina Caliopia Moira." For the first time she laughed. "What a mouthful."

She put the edition of *The Great Gatsby* to her nose, breathing the tart mix of leather and smoke. *Why can't I remember? What is it I'm trying to shut out?* She looked at her fingers, counting to herself: *one – two – three…one – two –three – four. Three plus four is seven. C – A – T spells cat.* She ran through the alphabet then the months of the year. She had trouble with September and November. *Thirty days hath September…April…and June…and November. My brain seems fine.* Her soft jade eyes narrowed. *The president of the United States is…is…*

Nothing.

Opening the book to the last page, she read quietly. "Tomorrow we'll run faster, stretching out our arms further…and one fine morning." She looked about the room. "One fine morning what, Sleeping Beauty awakening?" She thought of Potter's smiling face and laughed again. "But where's my Prince to break this spell? Why can't I remember? Why…"

Running her fingers over the supple leather binding, a sudden calm began to wash over her. At least she knew who she was – her name anyway. Placing the card into the fold of the page, Angelina tucked the book back into the drawer. She poured herself a glass of Primo. The cool liquid felt good, cheered her.

Potter was right. It was all going to be fine.

Unable to sleep, Angelina discovered a copy of the Philadelphia Bulletin newspaper on the night stand. She was drawn to a front page article.

"FIRE MAY BE ARSON"

Owner perishes.

The fire that destroyed the historic Crowly mansion late last Saturday is now thought to have been deliberately set.

Police investigators theorize the fire had originated in the house's basement. The sixty year old mansion, known as Casa di Tempo, was completely destroyed.

Owner Collin Calvin Crowly, whom authorities have been searching for, is believed to have perished in the overnight blaze. Crowly, a well known bachelor and man about town was 40.

The words and names were chillingly familiar to Angelina. Yet they remain just beyond memory's reach.

Studying the paper, Angelina froze. A frightening foreboding seized her in its gelid grasp.

The date on the morning edition read: Tuesday, January 8, 1929.

✐ *Chapter Fourteen* ✐

It had been snowing for two days. Nana's small herb and vegetable garden lay covered in white velvet. Normally bustling City Avenue was deserted, save for an occasional Mac truck, its chain wrapped solid tires furrowing a path through the lightly packed snow. Side streets remained the exclusive domain of rotund snow men and Fleetwing coaster sleds.

Angelina relaxed in a comfortable chair, reading Julia Peterkin's *Scarlet Sister Mary,* and savoring the best hot chocolate she was sure she ever tasted. It was Potter's special concoction. Gleaning the thick cream from atop a bottle of Abbots Dairy milk, he brought a large cupful to near boil. Adding two Hershey bars, the rich melting chocolate blended smoothly with the foamy cream. Finally, he floated in a tablespoon of honey. The golden brown elixir was ambrosia itself. It kissed the young woman's healing throat, and caused her bare toes to ball into fists on the plush Oriental rug.

The rug, like the rest of the modest apartment, was a study in contradiction; a contrast of emotions. Oddly conceived shapes in blue, burgundy, yellow and cream floated on a thick, deep red nap. Covering most of the quaint parlor's wood flooring, it captured the warmth of the potbelly wood stove.

As in the bedrooms, rough hewn shelving lined the room, bending and creaking with the weight of books. To one wall sat a small secretary, a delicate porcelain mantle clock resting on top. A pair of brass floor lamps, their tasseled shades yellowed with age provided reading light for a pair of matching mauve mohair chairs. Between them stood a new Philco radio-phonograph set, the genial glow of its dial adding to the room's homey atmosphere.

Setting aside the book, Angelina gazed out a snow painted window. A week had passed since Potter found her roaming alone in the cold pre-dawn hours. He and Nana were taking excellent care of her, as if she were kin. Potter even surprised her with an assortment of clothes. Red faced, he obstinately refused to reveal where the pretty but plain outfits came from. To Angelina's surprise and delight each fit her perfectly. She felt safe and comfortable in the tiny apartment, except for one thing.

Her memory hadn't returned.

Try as she may, Angelina couldn't recall anything about herself or her past. Basic thought and motor skills worked fine. But personal and social details still eluded her. It was as if Angelina Caliopia Moira never existed.

But what vexed her most was the date – 1929.

"Penny for your thoughts," it was Nana.

"You'd better hold on to that penny, and all your others. It's going to be a rough year, especially after October."

The two women stared at each other. Finally Nana spoke. "My, where did that come from, Missy?"

"I don't know. It wasn't like a premonition or anything; not like I *feel* something is *going* to happen." Angelina struggled for words. "It's more like knowledge, maybe even a memory, of something that has *already happened*. But I don't know why I know." Her pretty face twisted. "That doesn't make any sense."

"Maybe it does." Nana moved to the empty chair opposite Angelina. Her black eyes glinted with empathy. "Sometimes it's best not to question the gifts of the Fates. But then you know that, don't you, Missy?"

"What do you mean?"

Leaning forward, the old woman rested a boney hand on Angelina's knee. "Why, your name, my dear. Don't you know?" Leaning back in the chair, she brought her hand to her lips. "Oh, my, of course, you wouldn't. I'm sorry, Missy."

The younger woman smiled. "It's ok; I think I am learning what is meant by 'ignorance is bliss,' but what about my name?"

Though rusty, Lachesis' voice was steady, soothing. Angelina had come to enjoy talking with the interesting old lady. "Well, let's see now. Caliopia…I'm sure it's Greek." She giggled girlishly. "You certainly are as pretty as Aphrodite herself!"

Angelina could feel her ears begin to redden at the compliment. "Well..."

"No, no, Missy," Nana broke in, "you just take a good gander at yourself sometime in that tall mirror. You'll see...you'll see." She was tittering gaily now, rocking back and forth, pointing with the ivory cane. "You'll see. Why, you've even managed to turn 'ol Potter's head."

Angelina was now full a blush. She held great affection for the man who rescued her, possibly saved her life. And she perhaps even loved him for the deed. "I find Potter a most striking, unique man. But..."

Nana was enjoying watching her youthful companion squirm. Gathering herself, she held up a hand. "Now, now, Missy, don't fret yourself none. You don't have to worry about Potter. He only has eyes for the cadavers at that mortuary where he works part time." Her hand returned to her gaping mouth, as both women laughed out loud. "Oh, dear...but you know what I mean. He's too busy studying to be socializing and such. Anyway, now where was I..." She tapped her cane. "Oh, yes. I believe Caliopia is for Calliope. She is chief among the muses and rules over epic and heroic poetry."

Angelina considered the words.

"Oh, that's not all, my dear. Your last name Moira, now that *is* Greek."

"So then I'm Greek?"

"It would seem so. You wear no ring and there are no marks or signs as if you ever have."

She glanced down at her left hand. It hadn't occurred to her that she may have been married, had a family. She weighed this. No, no, it didn't feel right. She was a young, single woman. Satisfied, she looked back to Nana.

"Go on, please."

"Well, Moira means destiny, fate. The Moirae are three goddesses who determine the span or limit of a person's life. They also dispense good will and fortune to mortals. To be named for them is a great honor." The withered face melted, as if recalling fond memories. "There is Atropos – she's the oldest. Oh, she's the unbending one." Nana shook her head. "She's always so serious and obstinate. Then there is pretty little Clotho. They call her the spinner."

She paused.

"And then there's…"

"Lachesis…" Angelina looked at the Delphian cane then to Nana. She understood. "Lachesis…the assigner of lots…"

The ancient woman peered back, her expression impenetrable. She nodded. "Yes, yes, Missy. That's right. Are you remembering?"

"I'm not sure. Listening to you it was just there."

"Perhaps you read it somewhere," Nana suggested, probing. "Perhaps you were a scholar of some sort; a teacher or student…of mythology."

Angelina's brow wrinkled in thought. "No, no I don't think so, I mean, not mythology. But it does seem I have read. Many of the books here are familiar to me." Dozens of random thoughts filled her mind, like a gathering storm. She liked the fact that she was named for the muse of poetry, it seemed to fit her. Like the clothes Potter furnished. She felt her life was perhaps somehow connected to books, literature. Perhaps it was why she felt at home in the cozy apartment above a book shop.

Lachesis suddenly thumped her cane on the rug, stirring Angelina from her thoughts. "Oh, my, I nearly forgot. Potter wishes to see you, downstairs."

Outside, the snow had finally stopped. Several children delighted themselves with snow forts and snowballs. The sun was chipping away at the wall of concrete clouds, casting the book shop in its cheery golden glow. Potter stood behind a wooden counter, oblivious to the thick medical text book open before him. His elbows rested upon the seasoned surface, his chin resting in his experienced hands.

He is a handsome man, Angelina mused as she swept across the room, *in a funny sort of way*. Potter's husky frame was tucked neatly into a smart brown suit. His gold pocket watch and chain, dangling from the old fashioned waistcoat, reminded Angelina of the White Rabbit in *Alice's Adventures in Wonderland*. She laid a hand to Potter's muscular shoulder. "Find a cure for any major diseases today?"

"Oh, there you are, my dear. I have something for you." He produced a large black book, placing it on the counter.

Angelina noted the fancy gilded lettering. *"Who's Who in Philadelphia Society*, I already looked at this, I'm not in there."

"I know. If you were I would think somebody would be looking for you by now." He flipped open the book. Angelina considered the black and white photo in the corner of the page. A distinguished man wearing an expensive pinstriped suit and a neatly trimmed cookie duster peered from behind gold wire rim glasses. His dark sandy hair was wavy and carefully parted to one side.

"My, he's very handsome," she said after a time. "But not anyone I recognize." Her eyes moved to the detailed biography.

Crowly, Collin Calvin

B. February 29, 1888 Villanova, Pennsylvania

Graduate: St. Bonaventure Academy for Boys1906

Phi Beta Kappa University of Pennsylvania1913

Masters: History

Bachelor: Business

Devon – Main Line Polo and Racquet Club1910-1916

Philadelphia Club1915-

Lafayette Escadrille Luxeuil, France1916-1917

The Franklin Society1918-

Philadelphia Athletic Club1919-

Board of Trustees Chrysler Motor Company1924-1925

Philadelphia Sesquicentennial Committee1925-1926

Father: Conlin Collin Crowly Esq.

B. September 2, 1864 Philadelphia, Pennsylvania

D. May 7, 1915

Mother: Margaret 'Bessie' Mary Mc Ginny

B. May 30, 1868 Kilkenny, Ireland

D. May 7, 1915

Grandfather: Calvert Conlin Crowly Maj. U.S. Army Retired

B. July 13, 1832 Philadelphia, Pennsylvania

D. June 27, 1869

Grandmother: Donna Rosa Maria Visconti

B. October 31, 1845 Sardinia, Italy

D. May 17, 1915

"I must say, he has quite the pedigree, doesn't he? Interesting…did you notice both his parents and his grandmother died on the same day?"

"Yes," Potter replied. "That's the day Germany torpedoed the Lusitania. The ship's sinking brought the U.S. into the War."

"Oh, how tragic, but I don't know. Nothing rings a bell, should it?"

"How about the name Crowly?"

She thought. "Crowly…wasn't he the one in the newspapers the other day?"

Potter nodded. "Yes. The family home burnt down. It was not far from the campus of Villanova."

"But that's…that's where you found me!" Angelina felt as though she'd been kicked in the stomach. "Oh, Potter! You don't think that maybe I… I could have had something to do with his death, do you? The police say the fire was set!"

Potter placed a hand to Angelina's arm, trying to allay her fears. "Now dear, don't even think it. Of course not, but I do believe you were in the house."

"What do you mean?"

His expression turned thoughtful. "That book of yours, *The Great Gatsby*, Nana recognized it. She says this man, Crowly, came into the shop a few weeks back. He purchased the book. She remembers wrapping it for him."

Angelina could feel her knees start to buckle. She felt faint. She could recall nothing. Yet the book and her smoke stained clothes placed her in the burning house; possibly at the scene of a murder. Leaning on Potter's sturdy arm, she allowed him to lead her to a corner sofa.

"Don't trouble yourself over this," he said quietly. His smile eased her fears some. "You certainly don't seem the type to harm anyone." He patted her leg playfully. "But we never know, do we? And besides," Potter motioned to the open book in her lap, "no body was found. The police are only speculating. This Crowly could have set the fire himself then took off."

She looked at the photo again. "No... no, he didn't set the fire... he has kind, honest eyes. But still...there's something... and I must know him."

"It seems that way, yes."

"He's very handsome. But you said you thought me to be around twenty-five. Crowly was forty. I don't know. It's certainly not the age. But he seems so straight laced; maybe not my type." She sighed and rested back into the sofa. "Oh, Potter, I'm so confused. I don't even know what kind of man is my *type*."

Potter studied her moist green eyes, his voice reassuring. "You know what I think, Angelina? I think you knew Collin Crowly. Perhaps he was a friend; maybe you did date him. The book could have been a Christmas present. But from what I've been able to find out, Mr. Crowly enjoyed gambling. Why, I wouldn't be surprised if he got into some kind of trouble with gangsters. Perhaps he was one himself. It's as simple as that."

His words helped. "You're probably right." Then something occurred to her, something she hadn't thought of before. She turned in her seat, looking at Potter. "You said you found me on the campus of Villanova, right? Maybe I was a student... or worked there... in the library or a teacher."

Potter smiled thinly. "I'm sorry, Angelina. I checked. There's no record of you as a student or an employee. And no one in the area recognized your description." He stroked her long yellow hair tenderly. "And you are not exactly easy to forget."

Angelina cupped his hand in hers, kissing his palm. "Thank you, Potter, for everything. I mean it. If it wasn't for you I probably would have frozen to death."

"Don't worry about it, my dear. You've been given a rare opportunity, one many people only dream about. You've been given a second chance, a chance to start fresh. Enjoy this gift, Angelina. Use it wisely." The bell above the store's entrance chimed and Potter rose from the sofa. "In the meantime your home is here. Nana enjoys your company and you can help out in the store."

The idea that gangsters may have somehow been involved in her life left Angelina with mixed feelings. Later that night, in her cozy sleigh bed, she resolved to make the most of whatever Fate handed her.

✒ Chapter Fifteen ✑

The Rare and Used Book Shop occupied a hidden corner of a maple tree lined side street at the bottom of City Avenue. Located in a converted wood frame home, the second floor served as living quarters for its unique owner and her adopted grandson. Downstairs, recent offerings from Hemmingway, Faulkner, Fitzgerald, Lewis and other prominent authors lined the dozens of hastily constructed shelving. Rare and one of a kind editions competed for space with the latest detective and western pulp. The shop's collection of Civil War books and memoirs was unequaled. Reference tomes on everything from mythology to mysticism to occult sciences and the rising craze of spiritualism abounded. Anything from the new and popular genre of science fiction could be found. If it had been printed in the last hundred years, chances are it lay among the thousands of volumes.

Each semester the unassuming shop became a favorite stop for the college crowd. Used text books and required reading from the University of Pennsylvania, Penn State, Villanova, Temple and other local colleges were available at modest prices. To a quite, well lit corner, clustered around a large cheery brick fireplace sat an assortment of comfortable old chairs. Fresh hot coffee and tea were always available along with Biscotti and a complimentary bowl of homemade soup. The thoughtful offerings provided many a hungry collegian with needed nourishment.

Wannabe poets and struggling writers were always welcomed and encouraged. The store often became the scene of many an impromptu recitation or political debate. But what set the shop apart was its knowledgeable and mysterious caretaker.

No one could remember a time when the curious, cluttered little store wasn't around; or its even more curious owner. When asked about her age, the ancient proprietress would wink, flash a gold tooth and coyly reply, "I stopped counting at one hundred." Few doubted her.

Angelina Moira was busy dusting a tall shelf containing rare volumes of English poetry. She hummed happily to herself as she worked. The melody was familiar, but she didn't know why.

In the corner, Lachesis checked one of several tin canisters on a small counter. "Oh, dear, we're out of coffee again," she said. "I'd better fetch some. Thursday night is usually busy."

"Better stock up on Biscotti and Pittzelles, too," Angelina called. "You know how hungry that crowd gets once they start debating politics."

"Oh, don't I know it! My, you should have heard some of the heated discussions that went on just before the war. Maybe we should invite the new President to sit in some night."

The two women laughed, but Angelina held no doubts that if the remarkable old lady desired it to happen, then it would. "I doubt if it would do any good. Mr. Hoover will have plenty on his hands as soon as he takes office. More than he bargained for, I'm afraid." She paused as the cryptic thoughts formed. "Then again, he will need all of the advice he can get."

Nana looked up with a wry smile. "So, that oracular mind of yours is at work again. Good for you, Missy."

"I don't know... I just feel a long hard road ahead for the poor man."

"Don't fight the thoughts, the feelings; intuitions. Let them flow; come to fruition. And be sure to always write them down."

Though her memory remained lost, Angelina's imagination was working over time. At least that's to what she attributed the extrinsic thoughts and images that occurred to her with increasing frequency. Nana had another name for them: omens. At first Angelina downplayed the idea. But as the number and intensity of her visions grew, she was beginning to think perhaps Lachesis was right. The problem was her visions were vague and confusing.

"I think the Oracle of Delphi herself would be hard pressed to come up with messages more muddled than my own. But I do write them down, Nana, in that journal you gave me. I keep it by my bed. Good thing, too. Last night I had the most vivid dream."

"Come, my dear, tell me."

Moving to the corner reading area, they sat in adjoining chairs near the warming fireplace. "Well," the striking images returned to

Angelina. "I was in a house somewhere, I don't know where. It might have been in the country, a farm house. The house was pleasant, roomy. But it was deserted, emptied of furniture; the walls bare. It was as if it had been suddenly abandoned. I walked outside. It was mid-day, yet it was more like dusk. There was no sun. The sky was an angry brown; the air heavy. It was difficult to breath." She looked over to Nana. "That's about it. Except when I awoke I felt very, very hungry, like I hadn't eaten in a few days."

Nana continued to watch her young companion, measuring her words. She nodded and winked, "Well, we both know there's nothing wrong with your appetite. I believe your premonition concerned others." Her eyes touched Angelina's. "Remember what I told you, my dear. Don't worry yourself too much with trying to figure these things out, if the explanations come, all the better. I believe they will in time. If not, well perhaps it's not for you to know. You are the messenger, Missy. For now your job is to channel these visions, not to interpret them. And maybe you are to see to it that the proper persons are made aware. There's not much else you can do."

"I wonder, Nana, I wonder," Angelina replied, helping the other woman from the chair. "Oh, would you prefer I went to the store for you?"

"Oh, no, don't trouble yourself. The sun is shining, it's a pleasant day. And I can use some fresh air. Besides, I need to get some things. I think I'll make a big pot of potato soup for our guests. It's supposed to turn cold again tonight."

"I don't see how you and Potter do it, Nana. There is always plenty to go around. And now you've had me on your hands this past month."

"Faith, my dear. The store is doing well. We all need to do what we can. And, like the loaves and fishes, the Lord always provides. You just need faith." She slipped into a worn wool coat. "And you need to stay here and mind the store." Cane in hand, she ambled out the door.

Around noon the door chime rang and a chic young woman breezed into the store. She wore a posh grey coat lined with a fur collar, Italian leather gloves, and a stylish black silk cloche. Looking about, she made a cute, indecisive twitch with her painted lips, and then approached the sales counter. Considering the fancy wardrobe, Angelina thought she seemed out of place.

"May I help you?"

Her smile brightened the winter day. "Gee, I sure hope so, Sweetie," she chirped in a squeaky tone reminiscent of an angry cat. "Daddy's decided I need to learn some grace and manners; get some culture. I don't know why. I've done just fine so far. But he thinks I'm some silly fribble or something. He's dumping me in this school that's supposed to make me into a lady." She mugged dramatically, dipping in a poor curtsey, and then giggled. "Can you imagine, *me, a lady!* As if I'm not one! Like he'd know from a lady! It is costing daddy a bundle to get me in, middle of the year and all. He says he could build his own school for what he's spending. It serves him right, actually." She placed a thoughtful finger to her gracefully pointed chin. "You know, most of the girls there seem really nice, even if they are a bit snooty. That's what happens when you get too much breeding and culture and stuff. I tried to explain it to daddy." Her voice deepened and her mouth pursed like a prune. "He said, 'Get to that school or I'll pack you off to your aunt Isabella in Cosenza!' in that huffy tone of his, which mean you gotta do it or else. And everyone said this was the store to come to, so," she smiled, wrinkling her button nose, "here I am!" Casually unbuttoning her coat and removing her gloves, she stared bright eyed across the counter.

Angelina stared back, completely confounded. "So," she finally managed, "you need books?"

"Yeah!" the cheery customer replied, digging into her clutch purse. "I got everything, but the school bookshop was out of history books and I need this Frosty guy." She passed over a slip of paper.

Angelina regarded her quizzically then examined the hastily scribed note. "Oh, Robert Frost..."

"Yeah, that's him," she beamed back.

"And what school did you say?"

"Humm... you know... that girl's school out on the Main Line."

"You must mean Rosemont," Angelina replied, impressed. "Rosemont is a fine school. You said history... that should be Ford's *History of the United States Since the Compromise.*"

The engaging smile spread. "That's the one!"

Angelina searched several shelves, keeping an eye on her perky customer. Despite herself she smiled. She couldn't help liking the effervescent young woman right off. "Here we go." She placed the books on the counter top, "James Henry Ford's first two volumes and Robert Frost's *West Running Brook*."

The book of poetry brought about a look of uncertainty. "Gee, I don't know about this stuff..."

"Don't worry; I think you'll like Mr. Frost once you get to know him," Angelina encouraged, opening the stiff new volume. "His poetry is not difficult, and full of very beautiful images:

...Some say existence like a Pirouot

And pirouette, forever in one place,

Stands still and dances, but it runs away,

It seriously, sadly runs away,

To fill the abyss' void with emptiness."

A vacant stare met Angelina as she looked up from the book. "I'll tell you what. If you like you can come by the store and I'll tutor you. I know about English."

The expression grew earnest. "Gee, you'd do that for me? You know what? I like you. You seem really nice." She held out a finely manicured hand, "My names Bunny."

"Thank you, Bunny." They shook hands. "I'm Angelina Moira."

"Oh, that's a pretty name. Mine's really Maria Concessa Teressa Franzesee. That's some moniker, huh kid-o? But everyone just calls me Bunny. Bunny Callison, that's my stage name."

"Oh, are you an actress, Bunny?"

"Gosh, I wish. Wouldn't that be something, me, another Colleen More? No, I'm a singer. Well, I used to be, before daddy made me quit."

"Well, Bunny it's nice to meet you. I'm sure you'll do just fine at Rosemont. And I'm sure your father just wants what's best for you.

Who knows, maybe between the two of us we can show him just how much of a lady you are. Then maybe you can go back to singing."

"That'd be nice. But you know," Bunny raised a hand to her mouth, tittering girlishly, "I'm not really that good. I think Mr. Mc Ginny only hired me to spite daddy."

"I'll bet you have a fine voice." Angelina let out a long breath. "I only hope I can help you. You see, I have amnesia."

"You mean you have trouble breathing?"

The shop keeper couldn't help but smile. "No, Bunny. Amnesia means you can't remember. Some things are familiar to me. Others are kind of fuzzy. I'm just starting to discover who I might be. Most all of my personal history is gone."

The blank stare returned then Bunny flushed a rosy pink. "Oh, I'm sorry, Sweetie. I shouldn't stare. It's just I know some girls who have known some guys... and those girls would just as soon have this amnesia, if you know what I mean."

They both giggled.

"It's ok, Bunny. And yes, I believe I know what you mean."

Bunny's expressive eyes grew wide with excitement. "Hey, I got an idea. You're gonna help me with school, right? Well, I'm gonna help you! Daddy's work lets me meet all kinds of people. I'm gonna take you around and show you things you may have forgotten; introduce you to people. It'll help you remember." Her eager voice jumped an octave. "Who knows, maybe somebody will recognize you! What do you think, Sweetie? You will be my teacher and I'll be yours."

"I don't know what to say, Bunny. That would be so sweet of you."

"Yeah, sure... there isn't any place in this town I don't know, or anyone daddy doesn't know. We'll have lots of fun. I know... we can start Saturday night. A couple of guys from out of town are leaving and daddy's throwing a big bash for them. Everybody's gonna be there."

Angelina's heart sank. She eyed Bunny's expensive clothes. "Gee, I don't know... I..." Self-consciously her hand clutched the front of her simple dress.

"Are you worried about your clothes, Sweetie?"

"Well, to be perfectly honest, Bunny, my clothes were given to me, and this is the nicest dress I own." Her voice dropped and her ears reddened. "Don't tell anyone, but most of my clothes remind me of something you'd wear to be buried."

Now both women's laughter filled the store.

"Don't worry, Sweetie. I'll tell you what… I don't start classes until Monday. How 'bout I come by late tomorrow morning and we'll see what we can do?"

For the first time since awakening in the strange room, Angelina felt positive about her life. "Bunny, I think this is the beginning of a beautiful friendship."

"You said it Sweetie!"

☙ *Chapter Sixteen* ❧

Angelina stood naked in front of a full length dressing mirror. The figure before her was tone and fit. Her long, shapely legs were those of an athlete. Pretty, daffodil hair kissed strong shoulders. The thick tresses framed a smooth, attractive heart shaped face with striking jade eyes that smiled back from below wispy bangs.

"Nana was right," she said aloud, approving of what she saw.

But something was wrong.

She studied the image closer. The woman in the mirror was shapely with firm round breasts. Even in mid-winter, the flawless skin reflected a hint of healthy tan. Angelina thought of the cute coeds who came by the book store. Many were near her age. Yet their bodies were pale and thin, almost boyish. But it was their hair that inexplicably troubled Angelina. Most wore coifs that were short, bobbed and straight. Fashion ads in magazines featured rail thin models with flat chests and page boy hair styles. Even her new friend Bunny sported a fetching, short pixie cut, which barely reached her ears.

Angelina ran her fingers through the lush yellow locks then down her flat waist and curving hips. "Why am I so different?"

The question nagged at her as she dressed.

Angelina's stunning looks turned many heads the previous day. Bunny arrived at the shop in a big black Marmon, piloted by a handsome but rough looking man. Angelina noticed him constantly adjusting the rear view mirror. He seemed to be studying her.

The stately sedan carried them into downtown Philadelphia. It was the first time Angelina ventured more than a couple of blocks from the book store. Wide eyed, the two new friends spent the day shopping and exploring the expansive lingerie and women's sections of Gimbles' and Wannamaker's department stores. Over a late lunch at the Horn and Hardart Automat, the pair became closer acquainted.

"So, you really can't remember much, huh?"

"Actually I remember very little," Angelina replied, sipping a disappointing cup of cocoa. "Things like English and math and which fork to use and how to choose tomatoes remain intact for the most part. But I have no clue as to who I am or where I'm from; where I lived, who my friends and family are."

"Gee, that must be weird! It gives me the heebie-jeebies."

"Oh, it does me too, Bunny, if I think about it too much. I wasn't even aware of my own name when I first awoke at Nana's. It's like Angelina Moira never existed before January eight, 1989."

Bunny looked up from her tuna sandwich, "Twenty nine, Sweetie."

"Huh?"

"You mean 1929. You said 1989."

An icy shiver shot through the pretty blonde. "I did?"

"Yeah," Bunny replied, shrugging it off with a nose wrinkling giggle. "It's nothing. I do stuff like that all the time. It's probably just that amnesia thing."

"I guess so." Angelina's tone belied her words, "Yes, just my mixed up mind."

Pulling a small compact from her purse, Bunny began repairing her make-up. "Sure, that's what my boyfriend said about me, being mixed up. He said I'm really a lot smarter than I give myself credit for being. He was always giving me things to read and teaching me stuff."

"It sounds like he cares a great deal about you. When do I meet him?"

With a sigh, Bunny rested her chin in her palm. "He's not around anymore."

"Oh, I'm sorry, Bunny."

"It's ok. I kinda miss him. Actually, I miss him a lot. He was sweet and treated me like a lady." With a tilt of her head, she looked across the table. "And yet daddy didn't like him and thinks I'm *not* a lady. Ain't that a hoot?"

"Yes, it is, Bunny. Yes it is." Giving up on the now cold cocoa, Angelina set the half full cup aside. "I think I'll stick with Potter's hot chocolate from now on."

"C'mon, Sweetie, we still gotta find you a dress for tomorrow night. There'll be plenty of guys there for us."

The friends made their way out along the city's Main Line. An elite ladies shop in Brynmawr provided several stylish outfits for both women. At Bunny's request, the obliging owner gladly set up a credit account for Angelina. She returned to her room above the book store happily exhausted.

☙

The black Marmon drew up to the canopied entrance of a large, flashy white stucco building. This time Angelina was sure the driver was checking her out. She said nothing. Snapping to his duties, a bearded man, regally outfitted in Sheik's robes, bowed sharply and opened the shiny sedan's read door. Two bubbly women alighted into the cold night air. They caught the attention of several shivering couples awaiting admittance into the posh night spot. Arm in arm, the fashionable duo sailed past the murmuring line of impatient patrons, and through red leather clad doors.

"Good evening, ladies." The sounds of excited revilers echoed down high arched halls and mirror like marble floors. The club's manager, a tall, older gentleman with stiff manners and a glass eye, took Bunny's hand. "It is nice to see you again, Miss. Franzesee. Your father regrets he will be detained for some time."

Bunny's frown twisted her freshly painted face, as a costumed woman in harem garb accepted their wraps. "That's just like daddy not to be here. He's always too busy, even for his own daughter. But thanks Uncle Mario. It's good to be home."

Angelina looked at her friend, "Home?"

"Yeah, didn't I tell you? Daddy owns the joint."

Green eyes grew wide as they took in the rich, foreign furnishings. "Wow! What exactly does daddy do?"

With a giggle, Bunny took Angelina's elbow. They followed a scantily clad hostess down a private corridor. "Oh, you know... this and that. C'mon, I'm starved."

The Oasis lived up to its catchy name. The gaudy building was the pride of Sonny Franzesee. During an extended visit to Casablanca, the Don became enamored with the customs and architecture of North Africa. This was during a time that saw a bloody power struggle between Philadelphia mob factions. The feared Don's gang won control of the area's crime interests. Franzesee returned to build his criminal empire, and his chintzy edifice overlooking City Avenue.

The ostentatious alcazar was rumored to be rife with hidden panels, concealed rooms, secret passages, escape tunnels, and even a dungeon. An underground garage and drive way connected it to a secluded back alley a block away. The private palace doubled as Don Franzesee's headquarters, and one of the region's most popular night spots. Located just outside Philadelphia county limits, in mob friendly Merrion Township, the thinly veiled speakeasy operated openly in the face of prohibition. Here the city's most elite rubbed elbows with the city's most notorious.

Passing through heavy purple curtains, Angelina and Bunny entered the Oasis' main salon. Everywhere, imported ferns; date and palm trees added to the assumed ambience of a sheik's harem. High pitched stringed instruments filled the smoke tinged air. Enthusiastic customers watched awestruck as a belly dancer twisted and wiggled around the room. The lithe dancer's finger zills rang in perfect time to her hypnotic pulsating hips.

A make-shift dais spread across the head of the central dance floor. The long, linen covered table seated an even dozen street hardened men in hand stitched Italian suits and leather spats. Engaged in raucous conversation as they watched the risqué floor show, several smoked staunch cigars. A few savored plugs of Piper-Heidsieck, freely relieving themselves of the champagne flavored chewing tobacco into brass cuspidors. Bunny took note that the central seat of honor remained conspicuously vacant.

Bunny and Angelina were shown to a private booth to one side of the spacious room. An oversized basket of fresh flowers crowded the table top. Pushing them aside, Bunny slid into the plush seat. Angelina sized up the garish arrangement. "Wow! Who died?"

"Oh, that's just daddy. He thinks gifts will make up for his not being around. It's been that way all my life." Her expressive eyes turned inward. "After mom died he stuck me in a catholic boarding school. I had two private rooms just to hold all the junk he bought me. I hated it there; I ran away every chance I got." She suddenly broke out in fits of laughter. "One year for my birthday daddy bought me a pony. Can you imagine! They delivered it right to the school. That night I snuck out, saddled up and took off! They caught up to me riding down Haverford Avenue. But I think daddy finally got the message. I moved back home... of course daddy still wasn't around much."

Angelina shook her head, a clip of yellow hair falling out of place. "That must have been some sight!"

They watched intrigued as the belly dancer circled in front of them. Applause and whistles rang out as she finished her number, folding on the floor like a flower.

"That was quite a show."

"That? Just wait till later when the party really gets going." The young flapper motioned to the dais. "See that guy there, the one with the carnation on his lapel and the scar on his cheek?" Angelina watched as the older man signaled a waitress. A moment later he and the lissome dancer slipped into a secluded booth. "That's Uncle Guido," Bunny explained. "He's daddy's right hand man. He once saved daddy's life."

A tuxedoed man and a scantily clad waitress materialized and the flowers were whisked away. They popped open a magnum of French champagne and two crystal glasses were filled. Leaving the bottle to chill in a silver ice bucket, they withdrew. Angelina examined the bubbly beverage with discernment. She leaned close to Bunny, her voice low. "Hey, I know my memory isn't very good, but I seem to remember something about prohibition. Is this... a... a speakeasy?"

The familiar giggle filled the air. "Well, I'm not so sure daddy would approve of calling the Oasis a speakeasy."

"Your father..." Angelina glanced around, taking in everything, finally understanding. "Oh... then he's..."

Bunny's eternal smile spread from ear to ear as Angelina's ears reddened. "Oh, Sweetie, you are something, you know that!"

"You... you could have told me where we were going..."

"What, and miss that expression on your face?" Scooping up a glass, she passed it across the table. "Drink up, Sweetie. The night is young and so are we!"

The two women clinked then drained their glasses. "That was divine!" Angelina said, catching her breath. "I guess whoever I am I must be accustomed to drinking champagne."

"Just the beginning, Sweetie, wait till you taste dinner!"

As promised, dinner didn't disappoint. During the feast of anti-Pasto, tender veal, angel hair linguini, steamed asparagus and canolis, the club filled to capacity. Two muscular mobsters showed up, planting themselves like cigar store Indians, flanking the ladies' table. Bunny frowned, sticking out her tongue at the stoic pair. "Don't worry about them. They're just a couple of daddy's goons here to *protect* me."

The table cleared, a handsome but skinny young man strolled over. His manner uncertain, he nodded politely to Angelina, and then turned. "You're looking lovely as ever, Maria. How have you been?"

Angelina caught a touch of crimson shadowing Bunny's pale cheeks. Her friend's voice grew soft; serious and unsure. "I'm fine, Freddy. Thank you. How have you been?"

"I've been ok. You know..." He picked at invisible lint on his sleeve, the silence between them growing louder.

"How's your mother?" Bunny asked.

"She's good, doing well." His dark eyes brightened. "She misses you..."

Now Bunny, too, fidgeted, avoiding eye contact. "Tell her... tell her I said hell-o. I'll stop by soon. I promise."

The young man looked as though he were about to speak. Instead, he nodded, turned and left. Lowering her eyes, Bunny sat silent, toying with the linen napkin in her lap. Finally she sighed and sipped her champagne. It was a side of her friend Angelina had never seen. She touched Bunny's wrist. "Hey... are you alright?"

Her infectious smile slowly returned. "Yeah, sure... I'm fine. He's just... just..."

"Another uncle?"

The quip made both ladies laugh. Bunny pointed to the dais. Several of the men were now accompanied by tittering young women. "See the guy to the right of the middle seat? That's daddy's brother Vito... my real uncle. The man next to him with the deep clef in his chin is Frank Nitti. They call him the enforcer. He's Snorky's second in command."

Angelina recognized the infamous nickname. "Snorky... you mean..."

Bunny nodded, delighting in the other's expression. "The man on the left side in the brown suit with the broken nose is Billy Maharg, a gambler and ex-prize fighter. He was involved with fixing the World Series in '19. Next to him is Lefty something or other from Detroit. The guy with the cigarette holder is the boss of Cleveland. I'm not sure about the rest, except the two with Nitti are the ones leaving tomorrow."

Angelina regarded the redoubtable dozen with amazement. These were the kind of men most people only read about in the newspaper. "Gee, Sweetie," Bunny said quietly, "I hope you don't mind. I mean, me bringing you here. I thought it would be fun."

"Are you kidding? This is great, it's so exciting!"

"Oh, I knew you'd like it, Sweetie. C'mon, let's mingle."

Her words were no sooner spoken when a tall, thin man with coal black eyes and a shifting sneer approached the table. He was one of the guests of honor. At first sizing up Bunny, he winked at Angelina. "Well... what do we have here... hell-o there, Doll Face."

Her ears burning red, Angelina demurely looked up. "Hell-o..." Without another word, she rose and followed him to the dance floor. From her seat Bunny beamed.

As the music mellowed, Angelina permitted herself to be taken into his embrace. She became rapt in the redolence of his dangerous aura. "Haven't seen you 'round here before, Doll Face."

"Oh, well, this... this is my first time... I mean..."

"From 'outs of town, huh?" His manner was as gruff as his voice. Angelina found herself drawn to the hardened hoodlum. "Me, too. From Kansas City... 'Dats in Missouri." He grinned, his breath heavy with whiskey. "Ever been there?"

"No... no, I don't think so."

"Well, maybe sometime, huh?" With a firm hand, he led her back to the table. An olive skinned man with squinty eyes was cuddled close to Bunny, the two laughing and talking. They looked up as Angelina and the mobster squeezed into the booth.

"Oh, Sweetie, this is Paulie. He's from Cincinnati. Paulie, this is my friend Angelina."

"Pleased to meet you. I see you already know Nicholas."

❦

The evening flowed with the imported liquor. To Bunny's dismay the central seat on the dais remained empty. The more they drank, the more the two gangsters talked openly. Angelina listened captivated to the pair's yarns of their exploits as hired guns. They had moved up to positions of fear and respect in the organization, coldly eliminating whoever stood in their path.

"Doesn't it ever bother you," Angelina asked with the fascinated naïveté of a school girl. "I mean... to think about the people you've killed?"

"So who thinks? Or cares?" the smug thug replied, eliciting rowdy laughter from his partner.

"Yes, but what about family... friends?"

Nicholas leaned back, an arm sweeping the room. "'Dis is my family," he boasted. "The only family a guy needs." Pulling aside his suit coat, the chrome steel of his .38 flashed. Angelina became mesmerized. He padded the weapon with affection. "And 'dis is the only friend he needs."

Noting Angelina's expression, Nicholas winked at Paulie. Removing the Smith and Wesson, he emptied the revolver, snapped the cylinder closed and set it on the table. "Go on, it won't bite you." The seditious sneer returned. "Not now, anyway."

Tentatively, Angelina touched the weapon. Lifting it by the handle, she giggled impishly. She adjusted her grip. The pistol slipped comfortably into her palm. It felt cold, heavy; good. She became lost in the moment.

Nicholas reached across the table. "I seen looks like 'dat before," he snorted, "only never in a dame." He reloaded the pistol, giving the cylinder a spin, and slipped it back into the leather shoulder holster.

Bunny looked on, bewildered at her friend's actions. "Gee, Sweetie... you ok?"

"Yes... yes, I'm fine."

"Maybe I'll show ya what 'dis baby can do, Doll. When Paulie and me gets back."

Angelina blinked as if returning from a trance. "You're... leaving..."

"Yeah, we has ta be in Chicago." Nicholas lit a Lucky Strike, a grey cloud gathering over the table like a storm. "We gots business on Thursday."

"Thursday... that's the fourteenth... Valentine's Day, isn't it?"

"Yeah, sure, I guess so," Paulie replied.

Angelina looked into Nicholas' black eyes. A shiver traced her spine. They were the eyes of a dead man.

"Don't go."

"What's 'da matter, Doll, you gonna miss me? Don't worry; I'll be back soon enough."

Angelina suddenly felt very tired, as if all the energy had drained from her body.

"No... you won't."

Snatching up her clutch purse, she slid out of the booth and hurried from the room.

Chapter Seventeen

"How late are you, Sweetie?"

"That's the problem, Bunny, I'm not sure. I know I haven't had my period since Potter found me. That was just over two months ago. Beyond that... who knows?"

"Wow... what are you going to do?"

They sat on the sofa in the reading area of the book shop. Angelina shook her head. "I wish I knew."

A breath of crisp air accompanied the door chime as a customer exited the store. Bunny looked up, nodding across the room. "Maybe I know."

Potter stood behind the front counter, pricing some recently acquired books. To his left, a large black cat stretched, looking up from his nap. "Well, Chaucer," Potter said, scratching the sleek feline behind the ear. "It's been a pretty good day so far." He checked his pocket watch. "And it's not even noon yet."

Chaucer fanned an impressive set of nails, yawned, and began to purr. Angelina noted the tender show of affection, "Potter?"

"You said he was some kind of doctor to be or something. Maybe he can help."

With an uncertain shrug, Angelina called to him. "Potter, could you come here for a moment, please?"

Chaucer returned to his nap, nestling into the fold of an open copy of *Canterbury Tales*. Potter took a seat across from the women. "What can I do for you ladies?"

Angelina found herself lost for words. With an encouraging smile, Bunny spoke up. "Potter, Angelina thinks she may be pregnant."

Potter studied the carpet at his feet, his expression blank. Finally he broke the uneasy silence. "I thought it possible."

His words surprised Angelina. "Why... how... how did you know?"

"The night I brought you home… when I examined you…" He moved uneasily in the chair. "I've seen bruising like that before…"

"What do you mean?" She touched his arm. "Talk to me Potter."

With a sigh, Potter raised his head, his eyes finding Angelina's. "Down at the mortuary… on … on women who've been raped."

The breath escaped the lovely blonde. She felt herself fall back into the sofa.

"Oh, Sweetie…" Bunny's own eyes began to well up. The dizzying emotion of empathy was new to the young flapper. Trying to shake the urge to cry, she looked at Potter. "Can you help? Do you know someone…? I mean so we can be sure."

Potter rose and strode across the room without answering. Bunny moved closer to her friend, running an arm around her shoulder. "Hey, Sweetie… it's ok. We'll get through this… together… I promise." The alien feelings won out. She hugged Angelina to her.

Minutes later Potter returned.

"I have a friend… she's a doctor. She runs a clinic." Both ladies looked up, dabbing at their eyes. "It's not what you think," Potter ensured. "She can see you in forty-five minutes. Bunny, were you driven here?"

"No, Ricco is out with daddy somewhere. I took a cab as soon as Angelina called."

"Ok. I'd better take you. I'll get the car."

The Margret Sanger Center for Women was located in a non-descript walk-up, in the middle of a non-descript block. There was no sign, no notices; nothing to indicate the presence of a medical building dispensing birth control information and pre-natal care. The maverick clinic operated on the fringe of several vague, ambiguous, and out-dated laws its pioneering founder was fighting to change.

Potter found a vacant parking spot a half block away. He pointed down the street. "The office is there, the brown building. Ask for Doctor Quinn. She's expecting you. I'd better stay here with the car, this is a rough area."

Alighting from the old Franklin, Bunny and Angelina looked around. The few people they saw appeared as tired as the used up neighborhood. Despite the late winter chill, several dirty faced children played in the street without coats and in torn and tattered shoes. A boy of about seven with a runny nose came up to them. "Got a nickel, lady?"

Bunny reached for her purse. Angelina stopped her with a discreet shake of her head. "Come on, Bunny, its ok."

The waiting room was small, stuffy and overcrowded. Above, a rusty ceiling fan struggled to circulate the stale air. Women of all ages and races, many with small children, sat in an assortment of mismatched, straight backed chairs. In the corner, a girl in a shabby grey dress rested on the floor. Her arms wrapped securely around her knees, she rocked and quietly sang to herself.

Taking in the affecting scene, Bunny felt a strange tightening in her chest. "Oh, my God..."

A woman wearing a nurse's cap appeared. She eyed the two well dressed ladies suspiciously. "May I help you?"

Angelina could feel every eye falling on her. "We're here... I mean, I'm here to see Doctor Quinn. She's expecting me."

"Name?"

"Moira... Angelina Moira."

With a disparaging glare, the nurse slipped into a connecting room.

"Wow..."

"Yeah..."

"Do you want me to come in with you, Sweetie?"

"No, Bunny, thanks. I'll be alright."

Just then a woman in her thirties entered from the other room. Head down, she quickly shuffled past. The nurse called out, "Miss. Moira, doctor will see you." Taking a deep breath, Angelina followed the voice.

Bunny paced the waiting room. She was aware of the others watching her. But her thoughts were on the girl in the corner. Finally she walked over and stooped down. The girl continued to sing and rock back and forth. "How old are you, sweetheart?"

"Almost fifteen," she replied without looking up.

The tightening in Bunny's chest grew. "Where's your mother, your father?"

She only shrugged and continued to sing softly.

Bunny adjusted her position and forced a smile. "That's very pretty. You know, I'm a singer."

The child stopped rocking. She studied Bunny for a long moment. "Are you really a singer?"

She was an attractive girl with a pretty, round face and deep, questioning Mediterranean blue eyes. Her matted, stringy light brown hair reached past her shoulders. The tired house dress hung loose on her needy frame. Bunny sat down on the floor next to her. "Well… actually I used to be one, in a night club. I don't sing much now. But you have a very lovely voice."

Her tender face lit up. "I'm going to be a singer and make recordings and be on the radio."

"What's your name, sweetheart?"

"Maryann. It's actually Marina. I don't like it much."

"Well, Maryann, my name's Bunny."

Maryann laughed, covering her mouth with her hand. "That's a funny name."

"You think so, huh? Well, just between you and me, I think so, too. Tell me Maryann, where are your parents?"

"I don't have a father," she answered in a calm tone. "Mom's never around. When she is she's drunk or with one of her boyfriends, or both."

Fighting off tears, Bunny folded an arm around Maryann and the young girl went back to her singing.

Twenty minutes later, Angelina returned. Bunny tried in vain to read her friend's expression, "Everything ok, Sweetie?"

"Yes... yes, fine, Bunny. We'll talk later. Let's just go."

"Wait... please, just a moment." Summonsing up unknown courage, Bunny turned and marched into the rear office.

"Miss... you can't go in there!"

Ignoring the nurse, Bunny strode into a sparse exam room. A dark haired, middle aged woman in white looked up from the sink where she was washing her hands. She raised an eyebrow, sizing up the young flapper, and then called out. "It's ok, Martha. Please, just close the door." Her drawn face stiffened. "What do you want?"

The pit of Bunny's stomach boiled and she fought to keep her legs from shaking. "That girl in the waiting room," she managed, "Maryann..."

"Marina... yes, what about her?"

"Tell me about her... her condition."

Drying her hands, the doctor moved to behind a beat up wooden desk. "I'm sorry, patient information is private, only for the patient and her parents."

"Have you ever seen her parents?" Bunny shot back.

"That's not the point. I only discuss patient care with family... or guardians."

Bunny snapped open her purse. Keeping her eyes locked on the doctor's, she dropped a hundred dollar bill on the cluttered desk top. "I just became her guardian."

Doctor Quinn glanced at the crisp new bill. "I'm sorry... it's..."

"I can see what you are trying to do here, Doctor," Bunny interrupted. Despite being nervous, her voice was strong and steady. "I can also see that you are understaffed, overwhelmed with patients, and in need of financial help." She gestured toward the desk. "There's more where that came from. And I can raise a lot more for you, more than you can imagine; enough to help every Maryann that comes through your door." Bunny's stomach began to settle and she smiled thinly, speaking with new found confidence, "How about it, Doctor? You help me save one girl; I'll help you save a hundred."

For the first time all day Doctor Quinn relaxed. She settled into the creaky desk chair. "Marina… Maryann is fourteen. She's in her first trimester. Luckily she came to me right away. You obviously know her family situation."

"The father…?"

She shook her weary head. "Maryann says she was attacked by one of her mother's boyfriends. I believe her."

"What are you going to do, Doctor?"

"I've recommended an abortion. I don't normally approve of them. Here at the clinic we try to advise women of their choices before it comes to that. But in Maryann's case, because of her age, and the fact that she was raped… My main concern is she is very mal-nourished. She needs to be stronger for the procedure."

Reaching into her purse again, Bunny laid a card and another hundred dollar bill next to the first. "Make the arrangements, as soon as you think it is safe. You can reach me at that number." Her signature smile returned and she let out a long breath. "Thank you, Doctor Quinn. And don't worry about Maryann. I'll take good care of her."

"Thank you, Miss. Franzesee."

Bunny turned, surprised.

"I know who you are, Miss. Franzesee. And your father," the doctor confided. "That's why I agreed to see you. I was curious what you were doing here. I take it you came in with Miss. Moira?"

"I did…"

"Well, I can't say I approve of the source of your money. But you are right about us being overrun with patients and badly in need of funds. If you are serious…"

"I am…"

She smiled and nodded. "I'll be in touch."

Angelina was waiting by the door. With a wink and a giggle, Bunny held out a hand to Maryann. "C'mon, sweetheart, we're going home."

The girl looked up. Finding Bunny's eyes, she smiled and rose, slipping into a threadbare green sweater.

"Where's your coat, honey?"

"I don't have one." The smile waned. "I'm sorry."

Maryann looked to Bunny like an animal that had been beaten by its owner. She hugged the girl to her. "It's ok, sweetheart, it's ok." They wandered to the door. Angelina read a sense of elation in Bunny's sparkling eyes. "Sweetie, I want you to meet Maryann. Maryann, this is my best friend, Angelina."

As the trio climbed into the back seat of the Franklin, Potter turned, "Well, hell-o there young lady." Starting the motor, he called over his shoulder, "Where to, ladies?"

Angelina and Bunny grinned at each other, answering in unison, "To eat, then shopping."

༄

They sat in a booth at Woolworth's lunch counter. Potter was off running an errand and had agreed to meet them later under the Wannamaker's eagle.

Maryann looked up, letting the straw slip from her lips into the empty glass. "I have to go to the bathroom."

"Ok, honey. It's through those doors. Would you like anything else?"

"Another chocolate milkshake?" she asked with doe eyed innocence.

Bunny's painted lips twitched and her heart melted. "I suppose it's ok."

"Thanks." Grinning, Maryann slid from the booth.

Bunny couldn't help but notice Angelina's glib expression. "What?"

"I go in for the pregnancy test and you come out with the child! I hope you know what you are doing."

"So do I, Sweetie, so do I. But I couldn't just leave her there… I just couldn't. I had to do something."

"So you chose instant motherhood."

"I guess so," she answered, resting her cheek in her palm. "Colli always did say I was the impulsive type."

"Colli, was that your boyfriend?"

"That's him. Collin was so smart. He'd know what to do."

"Did… did you say… Collin? Your boyfriend's name was Collin?"

"Yeah, Collin Crowly."

The glass of Pepsi slipped from Angelina's hand. Bunny reached for some napkins and began to blot the soda. "Gee, Sweetie, are you alright? You look like you seen a ghost."

"Bunny… I… I…"

She understood. "Oh, Sweetie… you knew Colli, didn't you?"

"Yes… I think so." Angelina peered down at the pooling liquid, struggling for words. She felt bad for Bunny. "Potter is sure I knew Collin Crowly. And he has reason to believe I was there the night he… the night of the fire…"

Reading the other's expression, Bunny melted back into her seat. The incredible coincidence was overwhelming. Her forehead furrowed in thought. Slowly she looked up, studying her friend. "You know, Sweetie," she said with a steady voice, "I can see it. Yeah, you're smart and pretty and everything. Colli definitely would have gone for you. He and I… I mean… I kinda figured he had other girlfriends."

"I'm so sorry, but Bunny I really don't remember him or any of this… not at all. If we did know each other…"

Bunny took Angelina's hand. "No… it's ok. Honest, I really don't mind. Matter of fact, you know what? I'm glad it was you." The spunky flapper was back to her bubbly self.

Angelina drew an uncertain breath, squeezing Bunny's hand. "Bunny, do you think that Collin… do you think that he could…?"

She shook her pretty pixie head, her bright expression speaking for her. "Don't even think it, Sweetie. I knew Colli. He was a good guy. He never would have."

"Thanks, Bunny."

As Maryann returned, Bunny's familiar giggle filled the air. "Gee. What a day!"

✏ *Chapter Eighteen* ✑

Spring arrived wearing a scarf and umbrella. The week long rainfall turned main roads into streams and left many side streets impassable. For the first time, the city's Saint Patrick's Day celebration was postponed, then finally canceled. The most recent round of showers, while lighter, brought with them much milder temperatures.

Angelina remained in her room with a cup of hot cocoa. The copy of *The Man Who Knew Coolidge* on her lap remained unopened. Nana was tending the store. Potter had driven Bunny and Maryann to the girl's appointment with Doctor Quinn. The suspected morning sickness Angelina was feeling prevented her from joining them. Now, she stared out the rain streaked window, the past week's events winding through her mind like and uncertain river.

Over dinner one night at the Oasis, Angelina and Bunny had talked at length about Collin Crowly. Angelina doubted she could be as calm and understanding as her friend, were the situation reversed. The unflappable flapper was candid and frank about her relationship with the man she affectionately called Colli. During the conversation it became evident how little she knew about the dashing, mysterious man about town. Angelina was left with more questions than answers.

A soft tickle against her leg stirred Angelina from her thoughts. "Well, old guy, how are you? Catch any mice today?"

Chaucer leaped effortlessly, landing on the arm of the oversized chair. Purring, he nuzzled the crown of his head against her arm. His saffron eyes peered fondly into Angelina's. "You've got the life, you know that, fella? Catch an occasional mouse; keep the place rodent free, and its milk and tuna and napping in your book to your heart's content. You have a girlfriend, huh, guy?" She stroked his silk like fur as he continued to rub against her. "I'll bet you've got several. And I'll bet you hear and know every little thing that goes on around here, don't you?"

Chaucer let out a low, throaty yowl in response. Angelina suspected the clever feline understood everything that was said. Nana was certain he did.

The sound of Nana's cane tapping on the stairs caught Chaucer's attention. He jumped down and hurried from the room. Angelina had been reluctant to speak to the old lady about Crowly, perhaps for fear of what she might learn. This morning, upon awakening, she'd made up her mind.

"Well," she rose, stretching, and then smoothed her dress, "here goes nothing."

Lachesis sat sipping herbal tea, enjoying a program of classical music broadcast by WIP radio. Chaucer was curled on her lap. She looked up and smiled. "Hell-o, Missy, how are you feeling?"

"I'm much better, thank you. I'm not disturbing you, am I?"

"Of course not, I closed the store. Not too much business this rainy day anyway. Please, sit down. It's about time we talked, isn't it?"

Angelina settled uneasily into the opposite chair. "What do you mean?"

The soft black eyes sparkled with understanding. "Come now, Missy. I know you've wanted to talk. What better time for a nice heart to heart than a rainy afternoon, with Toscanini conducting Mozart so elegantly? Tell me, what's on your mind?"

Angelina tried her best to relax. "Please, tell me about the man who purchased my book."

The old woman remained silent, gently petting Chaucer. Finally she spoke. "What is it that you wish to know, Missy?"

"What you know."

"I know only what I see."

"Yes, but you see with your mind; touch with your eyes…"

The shrewd smile Angelina had come to love slid across Lachesis' weathered face. "Yes, but then, so can you, everyone can… or rather could." Her ancient eyes turned thoughtful. "It's a shame, 'What fools these mortals be'. Mankind has lost and forgotten so many of the gifts he once possessed. Oh, they are still there, lying dormant; waiting to be re-discovered, awakened. Man needs only to dream it and believe it to make it so, to achieve Elysium. Only man no longer has time for dreams, does he? He doesn't believe in them." Her thoughtful expression changed into one of sadness, "Or in those who grant them. Well... anyway...

"...the man who came into the shop that day... now he was a dreamer. He possessed unique gifts. But he was troubled; innocent of direction." Nana touched a finger to her lips. "Fate is a fickle Mistress, my dear. One must not squander what is afforded them. Else Fate steps in and withdraws her favors."

"And was I part of his favors?"

She nodded, "In a way, yes. I could see you knew him... in another place, another life, let's say. He was very fond of you, Angelina, in love. For a time you became his muse, his inspiration, his light. You helped him to see."

"But there was someone else, wasn't there?"

"Yes... but I'm afraid his troubles run much deeper. Not unlike your own, my dear. You see, Mr. Crowly, too, is trying to find himself, his place; where he belongs in this universe."

Angelina considered the other woman's words. They felt right, confirming what she already suspected. "He's alive, isn't he?"

There was no need for an answer. "Just remember, Fate will not be denied, my dear. Each of us has a destiny."

"And this is why I'm here... now."

"Exactly."

Angelina fidgeted in her seat, unsure if she wanted to know the answer. "Tell me, Lachesis, what has Fate decreed for me?"

Chaucer stirred, glancing over towards Angelina from the old woman's lap. Nana sighed, knowing her words would find only emptiness. "Follow your heart, Angelina. It will not lead you astray, if you listen. You have powers, my dear, abilities. Use them wisely."

Returning to her room to think, Angelina decided not to tell Bunny that Collin may be alive. It would serve no useful purpose, only complicating matters. If Crowly turned up they could deal with it then. But she still burned to know more about the man with whom she may have had an affair. Remembering Bunny's words the day the two first met in the book store, Angelina had an idea.

The Franzesee manor lay behind imposing iron gates, at the end of a grand tree lined driveway. A rich, well manicured lawn surrounded the stately, ivy covered brick home. The fashionable town of Narberth was home to many of Philadelphia's conservative old money. Its residents successfully blocked Don Philip Sonny Franzesee from purchasing in the area. Unfazed, Franzesee acquired a large plot of land adjoining the neighborhood. He then paid off township officials to approve construction of a street connecting his newly built home with the quiet, exclusive community.

Angelina was shown to a large, paneled den by a woman in a maid's uniform. She found herself pleasantly impressed. Dozens of books, many rare editions, lined the towering shelves. A plush imported carpet added warmth to the manly but stylish study. In fact, the entire home was tastefully done, inside and out, unlike the ornate, tacky Oasis club. The house closely resembled the estate of an English country gentleman.

"Welcome, Miss. Moira. It is long past time we met."

Sonny Franzesee was not what Angelina expected either. Much younger than she believed, the pre-maturely salt and pepper hair added a roguish charm to his rough but handsome features. Crossing the room, the Don emanated a confidence Angelina found attractive. "Maria told me you were beautiful. She did not say you were so stunning."

She permitted her cheek to be brushed with a kiss of greeting. "Thank you, Don Franzesee. It is an honor to meet you. Bunny… Maria has told me a great deal about you."

Counterfeit charm oozed from the Don like rich olive oil. Taking her by the elbow, Franzesee guided his visitor over to a grand Chesterfield divan. "First, you must call me Sonny, I insist. And do not put too much stock into what my daughter relates about me. I'm afraid we are not as a father and daughter should be. But that, of course, is my fault. My work keeps me away much of the time." As they sat, he gestured with a sweep of his arm. "However, as you can see, all that work is not without its compensations."

"Your home is lovely. And I'm sure you do your best with Maria. You must know she cares about you very much."

"As I do her, of course. But ever since her mother passed, rest her soul, we seem to have grown apart." The unexpected, robust laugh echoed through the room. "We are too much alike, my daughter and I. We butt heads at every turn. Like me, Maria is very strong willed."

Angelina found herself relaxing, captivated by the mobster's powerful presence. "Yes, I can see where she comes by her confidence."

The maid entered, bringing a crystal cruet and two pony snifters. As she exited, Franzesee poured. "This is Anisette from the hills outside of my home in Calabria. Trust me you have never tasted anything so superb."

They sipped the tart licorice liquor. Angelina decided she liked the infamous gangster despite his questionable reputation. Or, perhaps, it was because of it, "My, yes that is delicious."

"Only the best," Franzesee boasted. Setting the empty glasses on the coffee table, he turned to the pretty blonde. "Now, please, tell me, what is this I hear about Maria adopting a child?"

The notorious gangster was playing his hand to a turn. Unlike the cold killer she imagined, Angelina thought Franzesee a gentle, cultured man, living with-in extraordinary circumstances. She admired him for his accomplishments. "Well, she's not exactly a child. She is almost fifteen. Your daughter rescued her from a very bad situation. I wouldn't wish to betray Bunny's confidence. Let's just say she is taking good care of her." She searched his steel grey eyes, finding the understanding she sought. "If you will permit me, I think Maria is just looking for the love that is missing in her life. I believe they are good for each other."

The Don sat silent. At first Angelina feared she may have spoken out of place. But Franzesee laid a hand on her arm. His touch was electric. "Thank you, Miss Moira... Angelina... for being so candid. Allow me to tell you what I think. I agree. I believe this is a good thing for my Maria. Perhaps it will help settle her wild nature; give her direction, purpose." His hand rested gently on Angelina as his manner mellowed. "You will keep watch over my daughter for me, yes? Let me know she is doing well."

"Of course, I am very fond of Maria. Naturally I'll look after her."

"And for that I will be forever in your debt." Reclining back into the sofa, Franzesee smiled. "Now, my dear Angelina, I know you did not come here to discuss my relationship with my headstrong daughter. Please, tell me, what is it I can do for you?"

Angelina suddenly felt herself the prey within the lion's grasp. She found the situation oddly arousing. "Well, it was something Maria told me. She said you know a great many people."

"Yes that I do. I am fortunate to have contact with many individuals. Is someone giving you trouble, Angelina?"

"Oh, no… no, Sonny, it is nothing like that. I just want some information on someone." She toyed nervously with the hem of her flowered dress. "I assume Maria told you that I suffer from amnesia. I have no memory of my past." Angelina didn't notice the wry grin that shadowed Sonny's face then was gone.

"My daughter mentioned it to me. Please, do not be embarrassed. Permit me to help."

"Thank you, Sonny. There is a person I wish to know about, someone I may have known. His name is Collin Crowly. Have you heard of him?"

Franzesee stiffened. With the animation of a movie actor, he rose from the sofa, dramatically rubbing his dimpled chin. "Of all the requests you could have made, my dear… perhaps this one is best left unanswered."

Angelina was determined. "No," she replied. "If there is something, I wish to know, no matter what."

Still emoting with flair, Sonny Franzesee nodded slowly. "Then I am glad you came to me. Yes, I knew this Crowly. Our paths crossed several times. Crowly was not a man to trifle with."

"What do you mean?"

"Are you familiar with the name Frank Mc Ginny, Angelina?"

"Yes, Maria told me about him. Why?"

Scrumming back his thick, wavy hair, Franzesee sighed. "Crowly was deeply involved with Mc Ginny and his mob."

"Collin Crowly was a... a gangster?"

"No, no, my dear, Collin Crowly owed allegiance to no man..." His look was deliberate, "... or woman. No, Mr. Crowly was for hire. And Mc Ginny employed him often. My daughter was unaware of his activities. This is why I did not wish for her to associate with him."

Angelina blinked in disbelief. "You mean... you mean he killed people?"

"Yes, my dear. He was a paid assassin; a very good one."

"But I thought he was well respected, a socialite?"

"Can you think of a better alias for a hired killer?" He laughed. "No, Collin Crowly was *demi-monde*."

She thought. This much made sense. Bunny had told her Collin would often disappear for days, even weeks at a time. And she said no one seemed to know the source of his wealth. Angelina swallowed hard, forcing the words, suddenly fearful of the answers. "And where... where did I fit into the picture?"

Sonny returned to the sofa. He took her trembling hands in his. The Don looked very much a father about to scold an errant child. "You were his girlfriend, Angelina, more... his prized possession. And..."

"Yes, go on."

Now Franzesee seemed lost for words. Playing the part perfectly, he turned away from the anxious woman.

"Please, Sonny, you must tell me."

Slowly, deliberately, the amoral mobster peered into Angelina's troubled jade eyes. "You were his assistant, my dear. In certain circles the two of you were well known and feared, by reputation only, of course, and with good reason." He paused, savoring Angelina's expression. "Please, be aware, I can only relate what I know or have heard from my sources. But as I understand, you wanted out. Crowly wouldn't hear of it. After a prolonged argument you left. That was the night..."

Angelina's head swam. She felt her worse fears about to be realized. "Oh, no… no…"

Franzesee caught the swooning woman in his strong arms. He rested her back in the sofa. Pouring from the decanter, he pressed the glass to her lips. "Here, take this… slowly… slowly… easy."

She sipped the potent drink. It felt good as it warmed her body.

"I am so stupid… I am sorry, my dear. I didn't mean to… you must listen to me, very carefully. It was Mc Ginny's men, not you. You were lucky to be out of the house. You must have returned later. Frank Mc Ginny ordered a hit on Crowly in retribution. Crowly had accepted a job to eliminate two of Mc Ginny's top men, including Big Mike Shannon. That was what you and he argued about."

Finishing the liquor, Angelina considered the fantastic facts about her life. She still held no memory of her past. Yet, she found it chillingly easy to picture herself a gun moll. Perhaps even a murderess. Potter and Nana had already attested to the fact she knew Collin Crowly. Potter suggested Crowly was mixed up with gangsters. Her burns and smoke damaged clothes placed her in the house the night of the fire. And there was the first edition book Crowly purchased from the store.

The scene at the Oasis, when she handled Nicholas' pistol, came to mind. It seemed to confirm Sonny's words. She looked to Franzesee. "Is it really true?"

Suppressing a smile, the Don simply nodded.

ೞ

The sleek black Marmon eased down the long curving driveway. The rain was heavier now. The car's windshield wipers slapped in time to the pinball like ricochet of Angelina's turbulent thoughts. Her mind raced from place to horrific place, trying to deal with the impossible details of her life, as revealed by Sonny Franzesee. Stifling her reasoning was the fact she found the illustrious Don exceedingly attractive.

Angelina blushed and touched her face. Her host had insisted she be driven home. A willing captive to his churlish grasp, Franzesee had placed a tender parting kiss to her cheek.

She looked up.

Ricco stared back through the rear view mirror. His pernicious leer sent shivers up Angelina's spine. Adjusting her position, she tried to hide from the icy stare. It did no good. She could feel Ricco's emotionless eyes examining her.

The big car turned onto a deserted side street. Angelina was sure this was not the route her cab had taken an hour earlier. "Where are you going?" she asked, trying to conceal the rising fear in her voice. "You're supposed to take me home."

"Just relax, baby. You're in good hands."

Something snapped in a forgotten recess of Angelina's mind. Panic seized the young woman. Raw, vivid images flashed like lightening. Angelina became dizzy with the sudden down pour of frightening memories. She forced herself to look up. Ricco glared back through the mirror. A sickening feeling of déjà vu overcame the panicked passenger.

The Marmon bounced and shook, rolling to a violent stop in a vacant lot. In seconds the driver was climbing into the rear compartment. He shoved Angelina back into the broad seat. In one swift motion he stripped off her coat, pinning the stunned woman in place. He began tearing at her dress. "Relax, baby, just relax," he hissed, "we gonna have us some fun."

"No!" Angelina tried to resist. Her efforts only incited the hood further. "No... please... no... don't!"

"What's a matter, baby? You enjoyed it well enough last time."

The memory shook loose like a falling rock, crashing into the pit of Angelina's soul. She looked into the face of her cruel attacker. "You!" she cried out in horror. "It was you!"

With renewed determination, Angelina fought back. Her nails found their mark. Several ugly cuts spread across Ricco's left cheek. Tasting his own blood, the hoodlum grinned.

As they struggled, Ricco's blue steel revolver slipped from its holster. It landed on the car's floorboard. In a final, desperate move, Angelina brought up her leg. Ricco twisted in pain as her knee crashed into the gangster's groin.

It was just enough.

Rolling to one side, Angelina slid off the seat. Scrambling through the door, she bolted from the car.

Rain mingled with the woman's tears. It felt cold, refreshing on her skin. She stopped and turned.

Ricco's voice boomed over the storm. "Come back here, bitch." He staggered forward.

Poised, Angelina deftly leveled the gangster's deadly .38.

"What, you gonna shoot me now?" Ricco took another step. "You dumb, bitch."

Two shots were lost in a roll of thunder. For a moment Ricco froze in place. His face contorted. A circle of blood spread across the front of his expensive Italian silk shirt. The bullets had pierced his heart. With a grimace of disbelief, the mobster fell, landing face down in the mud.

Angelina calmly lowered the smoking weapon. As if in a trance, she ambled forward. An inscrutable smile played on the blonde's pretty face. Staring down at the body of the would-be rapist, Angelina became aware of a chilling reality: she felt nothing.

No remorse.

No pity.

No guilt.

Only a spreading serenity.

Another round of thunder shook the ground, shaking Angelina. The pistol slipped from her fingers. Turning, she fell to her knees, violently ill.

Three days later Angelina learned that she had miscarried.

Chapter Nineteen

The trial of Angelina Moira was expected to take at least two weeks. It lasted less than two hours.

After a rushed investigation, Angelina was arrested and charged with second degree murder. The Montgomery County District Attorney told the Philadelphia Inquirer Newspaper he would prove that Angelina and Ricco Fabiani had been lovers. He alleged Ricco spurned the sexy blonde and Angelina had planned revenge. Off the record he bragged Moira would be behind bars twenty years.

Sonny Franzesee had other ideas.

Three hours after her arrest, Angelina was released into the custody of a Philadelphia lawyer who had been retained by the Don. The first thing the slick attorney did was to have Angelina enter a plea of not guilty by reason of self defense. Next, he waived his client's right to a jury. He demanded an immediate trial before a judge. Exactly two weeks after she had been arrested, Angelina Caliopia Moira sat at the defendant's table in a packed county courtroom.

The lawyer had prepared his client well for her role as an innocent victim. Angelina wore a plain but fetching grey dress. Her make-up played down her stunning looks. Two rows behind her Sonny Franzesee sat complaisantly in the spectator's gallery, flanked by a pair of bodyguards.

The preliminary procedures out of the way, Angelina's attorney unexpectedly rose from his chair. "Your Honor, if it pleases the court, I believe I can quickly clear up this unfortunate matter."

"Explain yourself, Mr. Ryan," the judge replied.

"Your Honor, I have an eye witness whose testimony will completely exonerate Miss. Moira."

The DA was out of his seat like a shot. "Your Honor! This is highly unusual! Mr. Ryan will get his turn in due time."

The judge shifted uneasily on the bench. "Mr. Ryan, Mr. Burger has a point. Can't this witness of yours wait for proper procedures?"

Ryan smiled cordially, moving from behind the defense table. "Yes, I suppose under normal circumstances, Your Honor. However, the testimony of my witness will settle any doubts you or anyone may have as to my client's innocence. Not to mention save the county a lot of time and expense." His look to prosecutor Burger was calculated, "And embarrassment."

Under vehement protests from Burger and noisy laughter from the onlookers, the judge's hammer fell. "Very well, Mr. Ryan, I will hear this witness."

The spectators settled and a sonsy young woman was led into the courtroom. As she was sworn in and seated in the witness box, several photographers rushed forward to snap pictures. Angelina thought she recognized her.

Attorney Ryan strutted to the bench. "Miss, would you state your name, please."

She timidly looked across the court and then to Ryan. "Yes, Sir, My name is Jean Newsome."

"Thank you, Miss. Newsome. And where are you employed?"

"Well, I work at the Oasis." She turned to the judge, painting on an effective smile. "That's a very nice restaurant on City Avenue. I'm a waitress there."

The description of the Oasis brought about a rumble of amused comments, causing the judge to rap his gavel for order.

Ryan turned towards the gallery. "Now, Miss. Newsome, please tell the court exactly what you told me in my office."

"Well, Mr. Ryan, Your Honor, I was working three weeks ago last Friday. It was late and most of the customers had gone. Ricco was at a table with three other men…"

"Excuse me, Miss. Newsome," Ryan interrupted, "you are referring to Ricco Fabiani, the deceased?"

"Yes, yes I am."

"Did you know Mr. Fabiani?"

"Oh, no, not personally. But he was a regular customer at the Oasis. I knew who he was."

"So, you could easily identify him if necessary."

"Yes, I could."

Ryan nodded. "Thank you. Please continue."

Jean Newsome demurely crossed her legs, coyly taking in the intoxicating scene. This was her moment. She brushed back a shock of claret hair, wondering how she would look on the front page of the afternoon editions. "Yes, well, as I said, there were only a handful of customers left, including Ricco... Mr. Fabiani... and his party. I was helping the bus boy clear tables. I overheard Mr. Fabiani... he was talking in a very loud voice... bragging to his buddies."

Ryan surveyed the courtroom. It was dead still. Every head was cocked, every ear perked, trained on the woman in the witness box. It was just as he planned. He spoke softly, building the tension. "And what was Mr. Fabiani bragging... err... saying to his friends?"

Right on cue, Jean Newsome flushed fireplug red, straightening in her seat. She raised a hand to her breast as if to catch her breath. "He... he... was telling them about a woman he... he had..."

The judge broke in, his tone patient. "It's ok, Miss. Just go on and say what you have to say."

"Thank you. He... Mr. Fabiani told his friends he had raped a young woman and he was going to... he was going to do it again."

The judge had to bang his gavel repeatedly to restore order. The prosecutor jumped up. "Your Honor, I must object! This testimony is highly irregular. We have no proof of any of this!"

"Sit down, Mr. Burger. And don't let me warn you again! Mr. Ryan?"

"Please, Your Honor, just another minute or two." It couldn't be going better if Ryan had scripted it himself. Newsome was playing to the crowd and the prosecutor was fanning the flames. He switched on his best sympathetic voice. "I know how hard this is, Miss. Newsome. Tell the court, please, did Mr. Fabiani mention anyone by name?"

The witness twisted a handkerchief in her fingers, blotting her damp eyes. "Yes, Sir, he did. He said, 'I'm gonna get that... that snooty bitch Angelina Moira good. Like I did before'."

With that the courtroom erupted. Half a dozen reporters grabbed their notes and hats and bolted for the door. Flash bulbs popped as more pictures were taken of Jean Newsome and Angelina. Among the din, Don Franzesee sat, smugly nodding his head. It took the judge several minutes to restore order.

Ryan opened his briefcase and retrieved several folders. He strolled up to the judge and dropped the documents on the bench. "I have here, Your Honor," he cried out, pointing dramatically, "signed, sworn affidavits of four individuals attesting to what Miss. Newsome has just testified. These individuals were at the Oasis at the time in question and heard what Miss. Newsome heard. Two are Ricco Fabiani's own companions who were seated at his table! These witnesses are here, Your Honor, and ready to testify as to what they heard."

Banging away with his gavel, the judge's voice rang out. "That won't be necessary, Mr. Ryan. Mr. Burger, do you have any questions for the witness?"

The flustered DA mopped his brow. "No, Your Honor. But I reserve the right to question her another time."

The judge's words caught everyone by surprise, everyone but Don Franzesee.

"There won't be another time! This court finds the defendant not guilty! You are free to go Miss. Moira."

The gavel fell with resounding finality.

֍

The victory celebration at the Oasis, which had been planned for days in advance, rivaled that of New Year's Eve. Guests included the judge who presided over the trial, and Potter who agreed to attend at the irresistible urgings of Bunny. Angelina occupied a place of honor between Sonny Franzesee and attorney Ryan.

Another magnum of champagne popped and Don Franzesee rose. The clamor immediately subsided. "My friends, first let me thank each and every one of you for being here, helping to celebrate this joyous occasion." Polite applause quickly died. Drawing on a fat Cuban cigar, Franzesee continued. "Next, I want to propose a toast to the best damn shyster this side of anywhere." He held out a stemmed crystal flute. The others followed suit.

"Don't forget the best judge money can buy!" a voice cried out. The room exploded in laughter.

Smiling, Sonny rapped on the table with an ashtray, simmering the spirited gathering, "To attorney Robert Ryan."

Glasses were drained and hastily refilled. "And now, to the newest member of our family..." Sonny squinted down at the reticent Angelina. Reluctantly, she rose. "And certainly the prettiest," he added, "to Angelina!"

Cheers and whistles flowed like the expensive imported champagne. Ignoring his drink, Franzesee ran his arm around Angelina's waist, pulling her close, kissing her cheek. Breathless and bewildered, still locked in the Don's firm clench, she watched as Sonny called the crowd back to order.

"Thank you, thank you... I have one more announcement to make." A wry grin crossed the Don's face as he looked at his willing captive, his cold eyes twinkling. "I introduced this beautiful lady at my side as a member of our family for a reason." Franzesee's stare held Angelina prisoner as sure as his powerful embrace. "You are all invited to our wedding!"

Everyone jumped to their feet in boisterous celebration, everyone but a shocked Potter, and Maria Franzesee. Finally breaking Sonny's hypnotic stare, a stunned Angelina found Bunny. They exchanged perplexed looks. Before she could speak, right on cue, the band broke into *O Solo Mio*. Now Angelina found herself swept across the dance floor by the determined Don, amid thunderous applause and cheers.

"What the hell is going on?"

"Honestly, Bunny I swear I have no idea!"

After a dizzying twenty minutes of introductions, toasts, well wishes and cheek kissing, Angelina finally broke free of Sonny and signaled to her friend. Now she and Bunny sat talking in a private office.

"You mean to tell me you don't remember agreeing to marry my father?"

"No... yes... no... I mean..." The combination of a long, emotionally exhausting day, too much champagne and too little rest was taking its toll. "Please, Bunny believe me, I have no idea what your father is up to. Honestly! This is as much a surprise to me as it is to you... more!"

"This is so typical of daddy." She crushed out a cigarette. "Whatever Sonny Franzesee wants, Sonny Franzesee just takes."

"And it looks like he wants me!"

"That was pretty obvious from the song you danced to."

"What... what do you mean?"

Bunny shook her head. "*O Solo Mío*? It means *Mine Alone*. In Italy you two would be considered as good as married."

Angelina moved next to the Don's pretty daughter. "Oh, Bunny, what am I gonna do?"

"Marry him... or don't... I don't know!" With a sigh and a sarcastic smile, she turned to Angelina. "There's no way I'm calling you mom!"

Laughing aloud, the two hugged.

Six weeks later, Sonny and Angelina were married in a lavish ceremony at the Franzesee estate.

◞ *Chapter Twenty* ◟

"Italy must have agreed with you, Aunt Angelina. You look radiant."

"Thank you, Maryann. But five weeks is way too long to be away. I'm exhausted."

"You're supposed to be!" Bunny's trademark giggle filled the Franzesee mansion's fashionable bedroom. "You were on your honeymoon."

Angelina flushed red as the three females laughed aloud. "You know what I mean. I really missed both of you. And I couldn't miss Maryann's birthday coming up." She retrieved a box from the spacious closet. "Before I forget, this is for you."

Maryann eagerly accepted the prettily wrapped package. "Gosh, thanks, Angelina." The young girl wasted no time tearing into the gift. A moment later she held a lovely Italian silk blouse. Its deep indigo color reflected the teen's striking eyes. "Oh, it's so beautiful... and so soft!" Maryann cried, pressing the expensive present to her cheek. She threw her arms around Angelina, hugging the older woman. "Thank you, so much!"

"You're welcome. If you go look in your room I think you'll find quite a few more boxes there to open. Just make sure to read the tags, some are for Bunny, Potter and Nana."

Maryann squealed with excitement and rushed out of the room. Bunny looked over at Angelina who was settling across the queen size bed. "You're gonna spoil her."

"Me? You should talk. And I can't believe you moved back home." Angelina hardly recognized the former flapper. Bunny looked lovelier than ever, elegantly outfitted in a chic but modest dress. She wore less makeup, and her platinum hair was noticeably longer, starting to revert to its pretty, natural dark chocolate color. "Let's talk," Angelina said, patting the bed.

Bunny settled down next to her friend. Resting back on the pillow, her elbow struck something hard. "What's that?" Before Angelina could protest, Bunny recovered the shiny object.

"Give it here." Angelina reached out, snatching it up. "It's nothing."

"Nothing? Sweetie, you're talking to the daughter of Sonny Franzesee. If I'm not mistaken, that's a nickel plated, pearl handle, snub nose .32 Colt revolver." Her bemused look spilled over into a full grin. "With a chamois garter holster."

Angelina innocently tucked the small but lethal weapon into the night stand. She tried to shrug off her obvious annoyance. "It was a present... from your father."

"My how romantic!"

"Oh, Bunny... he gave it to me for... you know, for protection."

"Ok, I'll buy that... for now. So, tell me about the trip, your honeymoon; all the details." She eyed the abashed blonde playfully. "Just remember... he's my father."

Their laughter shook the four poster bed, breaking the room's tension. "Not really much to tell, actually. It was a long boring cruise both ways. By day your father often met with some strange men. Most nights he spent in the ship's private club room playing canasta and gin, usually till late." Bunny noticed sadness shade Angelina's face. "As soon as we settled into our villa, your father was off on some business. I spent the first five days of my honeymoon in beautiful sunny Italy by myself."

"Gee, Sweetie, I'm sorry. But you know how daddy can be."

"It's ok, Bunny. And yes, I do know how single minded and stubborn Sonny Franzesee can be. But he can also be very kind and caring. We did spend some beautiful evenings together." The fresh memories tasted bittersweet. Silence fell between the two. Angelina feigned a smile. "Oh, you don't want to hear about an old married woman. Come on, give, what's going on with you? You're not only looking more beautiful, but there is something else about you. You seem, I don't know, happier."

"I am, Angelina, I really am. And, by the way, it's Maria. Bunny's no longer around." A giggle escaped her precious lips. "Well, mostly."

Angelina glanced across the bed with approval. "Ok, Maria it is."

"Well, I'm not sure where to begin. We're planning a big party for Maryann's birthday. She's looking forward to going to school in September. And daddy's certainly been more attentive since you and he returned. Did you see that lovely necklace he brought back for me?"

"I know I helped him pick it out." She laughed aloud. "You should have seen the monstrosity he selected!"

"Sounds like daddy. But I'm doing my best to keep peace with him. That's why I moved back home. I don't think he's pleased with my working with Dr. Quinn. The clinic needs help. And Dr. Quinn wants to open a second clinic on the city's southwest. That will take a lot of money. The happier daddy is, the easier it is to get him to turn loose of his money." She winked at her girlfriend. "Remember that, Sweetie. And as long as I'm living at home, taking care of Maryann and staying away from the clubs, daddy's happy."

Angelina looked suspiciously at the perky young woman. "That's not exactly how I heard it... you staying out of the clubs."

Maria bit her bottom lip. "Oh, that..."

"Yes, that. And don't worry; I know for a fact Sonny hasn't a clue what you've been doing."

"Oh, thank goodness. If he knew..." She let out a long sigh of relief. "I wish you could have been there! The charity ball at Mr. Mc Ginny's Sharkey's Club was the social event of the season. Everyone was there, judges, councilmen, business leaders; even Frank Mc Ginny himself! I collected over $25,000. The best part, no one suspected the nature of the cause; just some needy charity as far as anyone was concerned."

"Good for you." Angelina's tone and expression turned serious. "But you really need to be careful, Maria. There are a lot of powerful people who want to see the clinic closed down; and everyone there thrown in jail. Remember in April how the clinic in New York City was raided and shut down. And you know how your father feels about you associating with Mc Ginny and Big Mike Shannon."

"I know, Sweetie. I'll be careful." Avoiding her friend's eyes, Maria fiddled with the antique blue comforter's lacy fringe. "Tell me, Angelina, seriously, are you happy?"

The question took the recent bride by surprise. She found herself at a loss for a definite answer. "Sure... yeah... yes, Maria, I'm happy. Your father's a fine man; I'm living in a beautiful home; I have everything I could possibly want." Looking around, she sighed absently. "I even like having my own room, separate from Sonny's. It helps me to keep my sense of independence. The same goes for Sonny. Your father and I... we're two of a kind, I think." Wishing to change the subject, she bounced off the bed. "Come on. Let's go see how Maryann is doing."

Maria beamed like a proud parent. "She's really blossomed into quite the young lady, hasn't she?"

"You have a right to be proud. *You* did that, *Maria*, not Bunny. The young woman was there, underneath the dirt and rags and poverty and pain, waiting to be released. But if anyone blossomed it's you. You've really changed. You've grown into the young lady your father hoped you'd become; despite what he may say."

The heartfelt giggle was sincere. "Yeah... how about that."

"Scusa, Signora, Signor Franzesee wishes to see you."

"Thank you, Anna." As the maid exited, Angelina watched Maryann twirl like a delicate ballerina. "That color is perfect for you, honey."

"Oh, Aunt Angelina, I've never seen anything so beautiful! Everything is so lovely... I don't know which I should wear to my party."

"There's plenty of time to decide, sweetheart." Maria began to help the youngster out of the elegant party dress.

"Make sure she tries everything on, Maria, in case they need alteration. I'll go see what Sonny wants."

Sonny Franzesee waited behind his large oak desk as Angelina entered the private study. "Is our young ward enjoying her new things?"

"Yes, I've never seen her so excited. But you really shouldn't indulge the child too much. Maria is afraid Maryann may become spoiled."

"Nonsense... nonsense, this is a wonderful thing my Maria is doing. You cannot put a price on that."

Angelina crossed the room, biding her husband warily. "As long as Maria does this *wonderful thing* here, in your house, isn't that what you really mean?"

The shrewd smile Angelina had come to expect slid across the Don's handsome face. "You know me too well... already. You learn quickly, Angelina, I like that." He dropped an envelope on the desk top.

The young bride eyed the package, then Franzesee. "Train tickets? Oh, Sonny, no, please, we just returned. I haven't even had time to get settled. And Maryann's party is in less than two weeks."

"Don't worry, my dear, this will not take long. And you will return in plenty of time for the child's birthday."

"Me...?"

"Yes. There is something I wish you to do for me." His Spartan expression was impenetrable.

"What... what do you mean?"

Franzesee switched on his well oiled charm. "You leave the day after tomorrow. These tickets will take you to Chicago. You will be met by an associate of mine. He will give you further instructions. There is a man whom I wish... taken care of."

Angelina reeled at the coldness of Sonny's tone. Shaken at the realization of what he was asking her to do, she tried to protest. "Sonny, no... you don't mean... surely you don't expect me to..."

The rumble of Franzesee's meaty fist pounding the desk top echoed throughout the room. "Yes, I do!" he roared. Then, like a skilled trial lawyer, his manner instantly softened. "Of course I do, my dear. It is what *you do*, remember?"

"I don't know, Sonny... I really don't..."

With a casual wave of his arm, Sonny cut off any further objections. His words flowed like summer honey. "This is a great honor, Angelina. Snorky himself asked me to personally attend to this matter. You should be proud."

His stunned spouse stood there in silence.

Easing from behind the desk, Sonny Franzesee pulled his wife to him. "Do this for me, my dear," he breathed to the embroiled blonde.

Blinking back a single tear, Angelina broke from the Don's embrace and walked out of the room.

❦

The next day Angelina sat chatting with Lachesis and Potter. Downstairs Maryann eagerly immersed herself in several books on Greek mythology. The small parlor above the shop resembled Christmas morning. Dozens of presents, many still un-opened, surrounded the three adults.

Lachesis was admiring a delicate hand knitted shawl from Catanzaro. "Missy, you really shouldn't… all of this, it's too much."

"Don't be silly, Nana. You two have taken such good care of me. It's the least I could do. And from now on things will be different around here… better. You'll be able to replace that worn out furniture downstairs. And I've made arrangements to have a new heat system installed. No more cold winter nights… won't that be nice?"

Potter and Nana looked at each other, Potter's tan brow proclaiming his concern. "You know, my dear, everyone was very surprised when you married so unexpectedly."

Her fiery emerald eyes narrowed. "Was it *how* I married… or *whom*?"

The uncharacteristic defensiveness in Angelina's words caught the couple by surprise. Potter started to reply but Lachesis spoke up. "Do you recall, Missy, the conversation you and I had, right here… about Fate… and destiny?"

Angelina bristled at the question. Unable to look at her wise, older friend, she busied herself cleaning up the remains of boxes and paper. "Yes… yes, of course I do. And I see what you are getting at."

"Do you? I don't believe you do. I don't think you *see* anything anymore."

"What do you mean?" The snappy, indignant reply shocked everyone.

Potter motioned to the old woman. His calm manner and tone always managed to assuage the headstrong young blonde. "What I think Nana is trying to say, Angelina, is that you have been through a great deal these last six months; much more than any woman, any person, should have to bear." He forced the unpleasant words. "You've changed, my dear. Perhaps you haven't noticed, but we have. Your friends have."

"Really? I don't think so."

"Yes, Missy, you have. Why, it's even in the very tone of your voice."

"I'm sorry. I just wanted to help you and Potter. I wanted to make things easier on you; to repay you both for all you've done for me."

Nana leaned forward on her cane, shaking her head slowly. "Is that why you married Don Franzesee, so you could repay Potter and me?"

Frustration overcame Angelina, frustration cast with confusion. She returned to collecting the torn wrappings. "Of course not! Sonny is a fine man who cares for me, as I do him."

Potter reached out, catching her by the hand. "Angelina," he asked softly, "who are you trying to convince… us, or yourself?"

Once again the young wife found herself without an answer. She looked around. For the first time she felt a stranger in the home she'd come to love. Don Franzesee's words haunted her: *It's what you do.*

It was true. She and Sonny were two of a kind. "I love the both of you very much," Angelina said, slipping from Potter's grasp.

"We know, my dear. And we love and care about you."

"Yes… I know." Tears marked her determined green eyes as she reached the stairs.

"Where are you going, Missy?"

Angelina looked into the senescent face, realizing the perceptive woman knew the answer better than anyone. She smiled fondly at the caring pair, recalling Nana's advice, "To fulfill my destiny."

Chapter Twenty-One

The proper young lady who alighted from the Capitol Limited at Chicago's Union Station bore little resemblance to Angelina Franzesee. Her hair pulled back in a tight bun, the fiery red head made a careful adjustment to her gold wire spectacles. With a huffy stomp befitting a harried spinster, she looked about the station. Finally, discreetly lifting her prudish gray frock, the woman begrudgingly took a seat on one of the train station's uncomfortable wooden benches.

She didn't have long to wait.

"Damn!" The expletive was followed by an obnoxious guffaw. "I'll be damn," the stubbly faced man repeated.

At first she wasn't sure if she was the cause of the man's behavior. Then the stranger removed his black derby and settled next to her. "Franzesee said you were a knockout. I think the Don needs his eyes examined," he said with a snicker. He continued to study the primly outfitted woman. "You can't be Amanda Carlisle?"

"And just why can't I be, sir?" she replied with a deep southern drawl. "And just who are you to approach a lady strange to yourself?"

"Damn!" He slapped his knee, his bulbous nose red with restrained laughter. "If you're the best old Sonny can come up with he doesn't need his vision checked, he needs to retire!" Gathering himself, he straightened in his seat. "My name's Vincent Tarabborelli. Everyone just calls me Trouble," he announced with a proud swagger.

Amanda continued to stare straight ahead, refusing to acknowledge the annoying man next to her. "Well, Mr. Trouble... if we have some business to attend to, I suggest we... attend to it. And the less said between us the better for both of us!"

Tarabborelli's puffy lips turned south. Rising, he planted the round derby atop his square head. "Have it your way, sister. C'mon, we gots a train to catch."

Amanda rose but didn't move. After a few steps Trouble stopped and turned, eyeing his new charge. She glanced down at the single leather valise at her feet.

"Oh, brother!" Snatching up the travel bag, he doffed his hat and bowed in a mocking gesture. Concealing a satisfied grin, Angelina Franzesee collected her skirt and marched away.

Shortly after noon the Kansas City Chief pulled into the recently refurbished mid-west station. Among the passengers stepping into the cruel Missouri sun was an unlikely couple. The man called Trouble had shaved. He now sported a fresh white carnation purchased from a young flower girl who had boarded in Quincy.

Amanda Carlisle was attractively attired in a fetching silk print dress. Her ruby hair hung loose. The entire trip the disparate pair had exchanged no more than a dozen words. That suited Amanda just fine.

Taking her by the elbow, his other hand occupied with her bag, Trouble steered the enigmatic woman to an old Chevrolet. "Ever been to Kansas City?" She didn't answer. In minutes they were sizing up the stuffy hotel room which had been rented in advance.

"Well," Tarabborelli said, bouncing on the squeaky Murphy bed. "It ain't the Ritz... but..." He patted the mattress and winked, cracking a crooked smile, "We's gots some time to kill..."

Ignoring the overture, Amanda lit a cigarette and wandered to the open window. "Where do I meet him?"

"Oh, all business, huh? Ok, sister, there's a beanery he eats at every day two blocks from here called Smokey Joe's." He sized up his companion who now gazed out the second floor window. "You're probably over dressed for the joint."

"You just worry about yourself. I'll take care of myself," she replied, blowing a stream of blue smoke.

"Whatever you say, sister. The way I sees it is this, we drive over 'bout three. That's when he's always there, the same thing every day, black coffee and a double slice of apple pie. He'll be wearing a snazzy three piece suit, dark – either black or brown – and seated at the end of the counter. You can't miss him."

Well, Amanda thought, at least he *seems* to know his job.

"You go in and make his acquaintance." The crooked smile resurfaced. "He'll go for you all right. Get him to leave with you. He don't have no car. Lure him to the Chevrolet. I'll be hiding in the back seat. Simple."

With that her opinion quickly changed. Amanda wondered how the mob survived with idiots like this joker in their employ. She decided once she returned she'd have a long talk with Sonny about Mr. Tarabborelli.

She turned and stared down at the two bit hood. "Keys…"

"Huh?"

"Give me the keys to the car," she said, holding out her hand, an uneasy edge to her voice.

"What, you kiddin' sister?"

Painting on a broad sexy grin, Amanda crushed out the cigarette beneath a heel. Sauntering over to the bed, she planted a foot on the mattress next to Trouble. The silk dress slid seductively up past her knee. Tarabborelli swallowed hard at the sight of the sexy gam. Stroking his forehead, Amanda suddenly grabbed a handful of the hood's greasy hair. She jerked his head back. In one smooth, swift motion she had the pearl handled .32 out of its garter holster and jammed beneath his chin.

"First," she cooed alluringly, "I only ask politely once."

With a trembling hand, Trouble reached for his coat pocket.

"Easy," she warned, tugging harder on the thug's hair.

Timidly he produced a pair of keys and handed them over.

"That's better. Second… I don't fraternize with the hired help. And third…" she relaxed her grip. "I only work alone!"

Placing a heel to his chest, Amanda Carlisle kicked out. Trouble tumbled to the floor. She tossed the keys in the air, catching them triumphantly. "You can pick up the car later, at the station. Now get out!"

Without a word the frightened gangster scrambled across the floor, snatched up his derby, and bolted out the door. She dropped the revolver on the mattress. Angelina Franzesee stood there for a long moment. Perspiration beaded her smooth brow. As her breath slowly returned, she let out a deep sigh and landed heavily on the bed.

Smokey Joe's turned out to be a dive on the city's near south side. Amanda parked the sedan across the street, studying the layout. To her relief, there wasn't much to study.

For half a block in either direction shops were closed and boarded. A few old cars lazed down the dusty street, along with an occasional truck heading to the stockyards. On the corner, a Chinese laundry attracted some business. Scott Joplin's Maple Leaf rag danced on the hot summer air from a store selling Philcos and victrolas.

Unconsciously, the fake red head patted the Colt strapped above her left knee. She slipped from behind the steering wheel and headed across the street.

The crude eatery was just as run down inside. A few wooden booths lined the walls. A bar like counter ran the width of the building. It was obvious Smokey Joe's had seen better days as a pre-prohibition gin and jazz joint.

A pair of old men in vests and felt hats gazed up from their game of dominoes. Feeling their eyes on her, Amanda realized Trouble might have been right. She was probably over dressed for the tired grill. The only other customer was a man in a dark suit at the far end of the counter. He chatted casually with the lone waitress.

With counterfeit courage and composure, Amanda slinked across the room. She paused at the vacant seat beside her mark, striking an enticing pose. The ruse didn't quite evoke the desired results. The waitress eyeballed her lazily while the man sipped his coffee.

"This here seat taken?" Amanda purred in her best South Carolina drawl, kicking at the empty stool.

"It's a free country," came the dry reply. The man bit into a slice of pie and the waitress snickered.

Put off by the indifferent response, Amanda became more determined. Sliding the stool aside with her foot, she wiggled into position, close to the man in the dark suit. Resting an elbow on the bar and her chin in an upturned palm, Angelina Franzesee suddenly found herself face to face with a man she knew.

"Well, now, look what we have here!" The words paralyzed Angelina. It was Nicholas, the man she'd met at the Oasis. Her mind spun wildly. Had he recognized her? It was too late... she'd just have to see how it played out.

"And what's that?" She managed through a suddenly dry mouth.

"I don't know, Doll. That remains to be seen."

Her breath returned in a rush. Holding Nicholas' eyes in hers, she pulled a cigarette from the pack lying on the counter, rolling it between red painted lips. The hired gunman struck a match on the bar. Now operating on instinct, Amanda cupped his hand in hers, lighting the unfiltered smoke. "And do you like what you see, Sugar?"

"So far, Doll... so far." He dropped the spent match on the floor. "What's your name, Doll? Mine is..."

Amanda placed a slender finger to his lips. "I know who you are, Sugar. That's why I'm here." Her accent was as smooth as a Mint Julep in July.

Nicholas leaned back in his stool, grinning from ear to ear. "Well, now... didn't I tell you I was famous?" Rolling her eyes, the waitress retreated to the kitchen. With a hoarse laugh, the cocky hood turned back to Amanda. "So, what now, Doll?"

"I have a car."

"And I gots a room not far from here."

Consumed by her character, she batted her long dark lashes. "Too hot... too stuffy." She tamped out the cigarette in an ashtray. "I've got a better idea."

Without a word, Angelina headed out the door. This time it was she who was in control.

The unsuspecting gangster wheeled the Chevrolet sedan into the deserted street. "Where to, Doll?"

"Why don't we just head south on Main Street, Sugar, and I'll tell you what to do."

The shifting sneer Angelina remembered crossed Nicholas' face. "I'll bet you will..."

Adjusting her position in the passenger seat, she considered the doomed man. She still found him attractive. She wondered about this. Was it just his profession?

"Turn right on Pershing. Then take your first left," she said, wishing to clear her mind.

Nicholas glanced out the corner of his eye as the car entered Penn Valley Park. "So, where we goin', Doll?"

"To talk…"

"Talk?"

"Sure, Sugar. Talking… gets me… in the mood. Pull over there."

The Chevrolet rolled to a stop. Still very much in control, Angelina hopped out. The thick nappy grass beneath her feet reminded her of the carpet in Lachesis' parlor. She strolled over to a large statue of an Indian astride a horse. Nicholas followed close behind.

Angelina relaxed back against the monument, one leg provocatively bent. There was one more thing she needed to know. "You like to ride, cowboy?"

Nicholas leaned into her.

Their lips met.

The kiss revealed two things. As she suspected, he wore his .38. And she felt nothing for the man. Satisfied, Angelina slinked away.

An ironic smile twisted her pretty face.

She had become him.

"Tell me about it, Sugar."

Nicholas wiped her lipstick on the back of his hand. "You is some strange broad, you know that, Doll?"

"And you are one hot killer, aren't you, Sugar?" She took a promising step forward, offering herself to him… for a price. "Tell me about Chicago."

The familiar sneer returned. The hood nodded. "Ok… sure, why not… it ain't nuttin' everyone don't know already."

"That's right, Sugar. You're famous," Amanda encouraged, wetting her lips.

She had him.

The hired killer's dead black eyes melted in the sunlight. He might have been recalling a past lover; a fond memory from childhood. He wasn't. He was thinking of a cold, calculated mob hit that had stunned the nation and polarized the city of Chicago.

"Damn, it was cold," he began. "God, I hate Chicago in 'da winter. Paulie was worried the Tommys would freeze. No chance in hell.

"Everything had been set perfectly, the uniforms, the fake police car... The mornin' of 'da fourteenth... Valentine's Day..." He laughed harshly. "Some hearts and flowers, huh, Doll? That mornin' the five of us met at an abandoned warehouse. There was only three uniforms so we flipped for it. Me and Paulie lost. Once the others were changed we wasted no time. We cruised over to the Moran garage on the north side."

Pausing to light up a cigarette, the gangster looked at Amanda. "You really into this, ain't you, Doll?"

She said nothing.

Shrugging, Nicholas continued his story with icy detachment. "Everything went like clockwork. We arrived at the garage and the street emptied, just another police raid as far as anyone cared. Man, we waltzed into that place... I thought a couple of 'dem guys would shit 'demselfs." His cruel laugh gave Angelina chill bumps in the hot sun.

"We lined those poor bastards up against that wall... one looked at me, straight at *me*, and says, 'Hey, you guys ain't...'" Nicholas made a gun motion with his thumb and finger, "pow!" He grinned. "That was all he said. The blast from the twelve gauge nearly took his head off. Me and Paulie and Chaz, we had the heavy iron, the Tommys. Three Tommys and a pair of twelve gauge... shit, what a mess!"

Nicholas shook his head. "I wouldn't have missed it for nuttin'!"

He looked up.

"You should have, Nicholas. You should have listened to me."

Angelina wondered if the hood's surprised expression was one of recognition or disbelief. It didn't matter. The rough but handsome features exploded in a jumbled mess of flesh and blood and bones. She watched as the faceless body crumbled to the ground.

Overhead, a pair of blue jays, startled by the three muffled reports of the .32, squawked and returned to their nest.

Angelina slid the Colt into its holster. The petite revolver felt hot against her flesh. Adjusting her dress, she casually returned to the car.

⸎ *Chapter Twenty-Two* ⸎

"What are you doing, Aunt Angelina?"

"Oh, it's just some writing, Maryann." She considered the brown leather book. "Silly, I guess."

The teen settled down on the day lounge, next to Angelina. "What do you mean?"

"Well, Nana gave this to me, it's like a diary. In it you write personal things."

"Why's that silly?"

"Most people write their thoughts; their wishes and hopes." She sighed. "I write my dreams and visions."

Maryann considered the older woman. "Visions, you mean like predictions? Like a soothsayer or an oracle?"

Angelina smiled. "You've been studying those books on mythology, haven't you? Lachesis has you believing that stuff."

"Don't you believe?"

The intimate reading den was Angelina's favorite room in the rambling Franzesee mansion. She rested back in the chenille chase as the crackling fire dispelled the damp October air. "Gosh, Honey, I don't know. There was a time I did, now… I just don't know. Writing my dreams down has become more a habit than anything."

"Nana says people used to rely on oracles and tellers all the time. It was as common as reading a newspaper today." The young girl giggled, "And probably more accurate."

"Well, maybe so, I guess if anyone should know Nana should."

Maryann turned in her seat, her blue eyes bright with questions. "Do any of your dreams ever come true?"

Her first meeting with the ill-fated killer Nicholas flashed through Angelina's mind. There was certainly nothing mystical or magical as far as she was concerned. Considering his chosen profession, a blind man could have seen his death.

But what of the circumstances?

The scene beneath the statue in Kansas City returned. The mastermind of the Saint Valentine's Day Massacre held an unhealthy penchant for talking too much, especially when alcohol and women were around. He had to be silenced in order to protect the organization, and Don Franzesee. "No, no... not really," Angelina replied, trying to shake the memory. "Not yet anyway."

"Wouldn't that be wonderful... to be able to predict the future... know what was going to happen?"

"I know a few gamblers who'd love to have that power."

"Oh, Angelina!" The naïve fifteen year old scrunched up her delicate face. "No! I mean to be able to help people; make things better."

She patted the child's leg. "It's nice to see some of Nana's wisdom has rubbed off on you."

Maryann's expression grew thoughtful. "Yes, she is wise, isn't she? But I want to be like Maria. I think it's wonderful the things she has done for Dr. Quinn and the clinic. She spends all her time there, helping out, doing whatever she can. If it wasn't for Maria there wouldn't be a second clinic. And what would have become of me?"

Angelina thought fondly of her close friend. She knew how Maryann felt. She owed a lot to Maria. Where would she be if Nana hadn't insisted that she remain to tend the store; if she and Maria never met? Later that fateful first day, after Bunny left the shop, Angelina discovered a full tin of coffee. The inscrutable old woman had known. Fate had played her hand. "You are right, Maryann. But I worry about her at that clinic..."

"Tell me, Angelina, what sort of things do you dream about?"

She flipped through the journal. "Most of the time they don't make any sense." Pausing at an entry dated March 15, 1929, she read:

"Everything is dark and gray, even in the middle of the day. Gloomy is a better word for it. Not just the weather. You can read

hopelessness in the hungry eyes of children. And in the sullen despondent faces of adults.

"A blank calendar hangs over a tall building like a shroud. Two of the empty days – a Tuesday and a Friday – are blacked out.

"There are lines everywhere and people wander the streets. Yet, the city seems like one abandoned. No one works. Everyone just roams the dirty, windswept streets searching. But for what?

"In the park, wrinkled men in wrinkled suits and top hats rehash tales of once great companies, and mergers, and take over's, and industrial rivalries.

"Desperation permeates the air."

She closed the volume, her green eyes searching vacant rooms.

Maryann shook her head, "Wow!"

With a cynical laugh, Angelina returned from her reverie. "Yeah, like I said, it's silly."

"No... not at all, Angelina." Maryann placed an affectionate hand to her older friend, "It sounds to me like some sort of financial collapse, like the one in 1893 and 1894. We studied it in school. Only yours seems so much worse. Did your dream give you any indications of when?"

Angelina stared off into the flickering fire. "No. Not really. But the number ten kept appearing everywhere."

With wisdom beyond her delicate years, Maryann replied. "Humm... numbers can represent dates, times, amounts or duration. Like, this is the tenth month. Or maybe ten times, or lasting ten years."

"Well, I'll tell you what, Sweetheart." Angelina flipped one last time through the enigmatic journal. "This book is just about full. Since you are so interested in predictions and such, why don't you take it?" Rising, she handed it over to Maryann. "Maybe you can figure it out."

The teen grinned broadly at the unexpected gift. "Thanks, Aunt Angelina."

Later that evening, Maryann lay across her bed searching the ambiguous writings. A one line entry read simply: *A over C 4 of 5.* She was puzzling over the cryptic inscription when the voice on her radio set announced that Philadelphia won the World Series. The Athletics had beaten the Cubs four games to one.

The astute teen smiled to herself.

Two weeks later, panicked selling of over sixteen million shares of common stock signaled the start of the Great Depression.

By the year's end the financial crisis held a strangle hold on the American public. Between 1925 and 1929 the average price on the New York Stock Exchange had more than doubled. But as the country sank deeper into the economic depression stock prices would lose up to eighty percent of their value. The domino effect was swift and sure. Already over five hundred banks had failed. By 1933 that number would climb to more than nine thousand. As banks closed their doors, companies and factories shut down. Unemployment surpassed one in four in 1933. Unable to find work, family after family became displaced. Some 25,000 families and over 200,000 individuals wandered the country in search of food, shelter and work. Then nature added to the devastation with the driest seasons in over a century. The mid and south west sections of the country disappeared under massive dust storms.

One by one, many of Angelina's dire visions played themselves out. Maryann kept close track. Soon the clever teen discovered she could interpret the Delphic predictions in Angelina's journal. The knowledge gleaned would be of infinite value in the difficult times ahead.

In Washington, DC, the new administration was ill-equipped and of little notion to help. President Hoover believed business, if left alone and without government supervision, would correct the economic conditions. He stubbornly vetoed several bills he felt gave too much power to the federal government. A few token measures lending money to banks and railroads and large industries did little to alleviate the situation.

Meanwhile the country slowly starved.

But not everyone.

Organized crime continued to leach off the American public, as tens of thousands of disenfranchised individuals sought solace in the ubiquitous speakeasies. For the likes of Al Capone; George Bugs Moran; Frank Mc Ginny; Sonny Franzesee, and others it was business as usual.

Potter and Nana fared well thanks to Potter's hard work and thriftiness, and Lachesis' stubborn refusal to invest their money into anything but her mattress. Business at the book store slowed. On any given evening the popular little building more closely resembled a soup kitchen, as its owners refused to turn anyone away. But the humble shop still managed to bring a meager profit to the caring couple.

November, 1930, Angelina gave birth to a daughter. The arrival of Baby Lace did little to repair the strained marriage of Sonny and Angelina Franzesee. The disparate pair had been drifting further apart for some time. But Angelina continued to pursue her dangerous double life. At Sonny's, insistence she reluctantly accepted a contract for a local hit. Unknown to her at the time, the victim turned out to be a popular councilman soliciting to close down the women's clinics run by Dr. Quinn. The murder was only one incident in an escalating string of violence. Lines were drawn on either side of the birth control controversy. The dead man's supporters swore revenge.

Don Franzesee grew bolder in his philandering, openly flaunting his paramours at the Oasis Club. Sonny and Angelina officially separated in the spring. However, the new mother and her fair haired daughter remained at the Franzesee estate.

"C'mon, Maria, it'll be fun."

"I told you, Sweetie, I can't. The clinic is being inspected by the city tomorrow. There is still a lot of paper work to be done. With the state of the economy, city hall is starting to realize the importance of clinics like Dr. Quinn's. Everything has to be perfect if we expect to get the public support we need." Maria Franzesee checked her looks in the full length mirror one final time.

"That's a pretty fancy outfit for office work," Angelina quipped, "very sexy."

Maria pirouetted on her heels, and then turned to her friend. "I should hope so, it cost enough! Freddy's dropping me off at the clinic. Then we're going out later."

"You have been seeing a lot of Freddy Martone. Anything to report?"

Her pretty face drooped. "No… and I don't understand why. I mean, I know he loves me." She let out an impish giggle. "Freddy's been in love with me since I was twelve. Now that he's finally won me over he's dragging his feet."

"Men, they're all the same." Angelina flipped a blue boa dramatically around her neck, approving of the reflection in the mirror. "He's probably afraid of your father."

"Daddy? Daddy's been trying to get me to marry Freddy since I was fourteen!"

"I got it! You and Freddy come with me to Sharkey's Club tonight. We'll get him drunk and drive to Maryland. You two can elope."

Maria pulled the feathery wrap from her friend's shoulders. "Be serious, Angelina. And you'd better not let Daddy know where you are headed." She looked the blonde up and down. "Is that one of my dresses?"

"I figured you wouldn't mind. You never wear them anymore." She gave her toned body an alluring shake, causing the layers of silver fringe to jingle provocatively. "What do you think?"

Maria shook her head. "I think you are playing with fire. You and Daddy may be separated, but he's still Sonny Franzesee. And you know how tensions are strained between him and Frank Mc Ginny. Everyone's scrambling for as much action they can get. I half expect a gang war to break out any minute."

Angelina rolled her eyes. "Oh, don't be so dramatic. I can handle Sonny Franzesee. And somebody's always killing somebody else over nothing. You know that. It's just the way it is." She turned to Maria, her jade eyes sad as a spaniel's. "You sure you won't change your mind? It's a beautiful summer evening. We haven't been out together in ages."

"Not tonight, Sweetie. Maybe another time, I promise. I've a feeling Freddy might finally come through with a ring." They exchanged a warm hug. "And you be careful!" Maria chided. "You hear me, sister?"

By midnight the party at Frank Mc Ginny's Sharkey's Club was in high gear. Gin and jazz flowed and Angelina was having the time of her life.

Across town, a black Buick sedan rolled silently down a deserted street. The sound of splintering glass shattered the still night air. Three sticks of dynamite landed in the empty waiting room. The explosion rocked the quiet neighborhood, completely destroying the three story clinic.

∾ *Chapter Twenty-Three* ∾

The funeral of Maria Concessa Teressa Franzesee rivaled that of the great Caruso. Sections of Broad and Market Streets were closed. The mile long line of limousines and cars solemnly snaked its way through the city. Friends and strangers alike crowded the streets as the procession passed. Over two thousand mourners filled Holy Cross cemetery as the beloved flapper turned activist was laid to rest in the family mausoleum. Philadelphia mayor Harry Mackey proclaimed a day of mourning. In an impassioned radio address, he called for an end to the rising violence surrounding the embattled clinics.

His words fell on deaf ears and the city braced for more killings.

The next day Angelina sat in her room alone with her thoughts. The past two and a half years seemed almost a dream; or maybe a nightmare. She recalled fondly her awakening in the bedroom above the book shop. The memory of her first meeting with the bubbly Bunny Callison brought a smile and more tears. So much had happened in so short a time. So much had changed.

What went wrong?

With a sigh, Angelina realized it was her. But wasn't that exactly what Nana foresaw, the destiny she was to fulfill? Surely there was something more; something else that needed to be done. She couldn't accept the fact that Fate had chose her as the catalyst of Maria's death.

It wasn't fair.

She determined to do something, to make things right; to give some meaning to Maria's murder.

But what; how?

"Are you alright, Aunt Angelina?"

Maryann tiptoed into the room. She spoke softly so as not to disturb the napping Baby Lace. Looking up, Angelina forced a smile. Throughout the difficult last few days, the mature teen showed unbelievable strength. Angelina understood Maryann ached for the woman who opened her home and her heart to the needy youngster. She also knew the girl would be just fine in life, making Maria proud.

"I'm sorry, honey. What did you say?"

"I was concerned about you. You've been up here by yourself all day."

"I'll be fine, sweetheart… I'm just…"

Maryann settled on the edge of the bed, placing an arm around the older woman's shoulder. "I know, Angelina," she said, her blue eyes moist. "I know. I miss her, too. Freddy is downstairs. He wants to see you. He says it's important."

"Ok, honey." She touched Maryann's cheek tenderly. "And thanks. Tell Freddy to come up."

"I'm so sorry, Freddy. I know how much you loved her." She brushed his cheek with a kiss. "Maria knew it, too."

"Thank you, Angelina. Maria was so very fond of you. She looked up to you and talked about you all the time." He looked at Maryann, a thin smile on his drawn lips. "She always said you and Maryann were the best things to ever happen to her." Freddy's eyes grew damp. The once handsome face now appeared old and tired. Maria's death had added years to the young man. He shuffled nervously.

"What is it, Freddy?"

"You've got to stop him, Angelina."

"Who?"

"Franzesee, he knows a couple of Mc Ginny's hired goons were responsible for the bombing. His men are gathering at the Oasis right now. He's sworn to avenge Maria's death."

"Good!"

Freddy looked up, his voice anxious. "No… no, Angelina, no! Don't let Maria's death be the cause of a bloody vendetta. Please. Maria wouldn't want it that way. You know that."

Angelina's pretty face grew sullen. "Why should I care what Sonny does?"

He couldn't look her in the eyes. "Because, Angelina... he... Sonny... he was the one."

"What are you talking about, Freddy?"

"The night of the fire... in '29... it was Franzesee... not Ricco..."

Angelina reached out, turning the young man's face to hers. "Tell me..."

Freddy swallowed hard, forcing the words. "Sonny wanted to teach Crowly a lesson – not to see his daughter anymore. Only Crowly wasn't home. Franzesee and Ricco started the fire, not Mc Ginny. As they were leaving they saw you in the house. Sonny figured you were one of Crowly's girlfriends. Angelina, it was Franzesee... who raped you... in the back of the car, while Ricco watched in the rearview mirror."

Maryann moved to Angelina's side, taking her by the arm, steadying her. "Freddy, no," the stunned woman managed. "You're mistaken."

"I overheard Ricco bragging about it at the Oasis. After Ricco died, I confronted Sonny about what I heard. He told me if I wanted to stay alive and marry Maria I should forget everything. That's where Sonny got the idea to rig your trial. I told Maria but she made me promise never to tell you. She said you'd been through enough. Later she became fearful of what you might do."

Angelina closed her eyes, watching the pieces of her ersatz life crumble. When she opened them, she knew what had to be done.

"Thank you, Freddy."

Angelina pulled two large bundles of hundred dollar bills from a bureau drawer, and then stripped the blue comforter off the bed. Bundling up Baby Lace, she kissed the infant and handed her to Maryann. "I want you to gather up as many of your things as you can as quickly as possible. Take Lace and go with Freddy. He'll know what to do. This is for her." Handing one of the stacks of money to Freddy, she slipped the other into the teen's pocket. "This one is for you."

Fear shone in Maryann's sweet face, fear mixed with confusion. "But Angelina... I don't understand. What about you?"

"Please, honey, don't ask questions." She kissed Maryann, hugging her tenderly. "Quickly now, do as I say. I'll see you soon."

Turning to Freddy, Angelina nodded, painting on a hollow smile. "Take good care of them for me, Freddy. And thank you… for everything."

Chapter Twenty-Four

"Where is she!"

The mansion lay deserted save for two burly bodyguards patrolling the grounds. The sound of Philip Sonny Franzesee's voice reverberated through the house.

Angelina looked up from the oak desk.

She said nothing.

Don Franzesee strode arrogantly to the middle of the den. "Where is she, Angelina! Where's my daughter?"

"It's a little late for you to start acting like a father," Angelina repeated calmly.

The knuckles of Franzesee's clenched fists whitened. "Don't fuck with me, Angelina! Not tonight! Now tell me... where's my daughter?"

She stared her estranged husband in the eye. "Your daughter's dead!" Angelina spat back in anger, matching his tone and volume. "You killed her!"

Sonny Franzesee took a threatening step towards his wife. "Who the hell do you think you are, talking to me like that?"

Angelina could taste the bitter irony in his words. "Now that's the question isn't it, Sonny? Suppose *you* tell me. Who am I, Sonny?"

The Don considered her for a long moment. What he saw in her cold green eyes frightened the normally stoic gangster. He shook it off with a sarcastic laugh. "You wanna talk... we'll talk!" His manner relaxed a bit. "Where shall we begin?"

"How about January... 1929, the night of the fire?"

He nodded, pointing at his wife. "You have been talking to that dandy Freddy Martone, haven't you?"

Angelina glared back. "Maybe, but now I wish to hear it from you."

"Be careful what you wish, my dear," Franzesee replied, shaking his finger. "You may not like what you hear."

"Try me. And, Sonny... this time make it the truth."

He rubbed his chin in thought. "Ok. Just remember... I warned you!" The familiar, deceptive sneer twisted his face, his attitude turning cavalier. "I can't say I enjoyed it much. You were in a daze or something. Ricco pulled you out of the house and brought you to the car." The smirk grew. "You just lay there, taking it, staring blankly."

Her stomach recoiling in disgust, Angelina realized Franzesee was bragging. The bastard was actually proud.

She hated him.

"What about Crowly? Weren't you afraid of what he would do?"

This time Sonny laughed out loud. "You stupid bitch! Do you actually think I was afraid of Crowly?"

"But... you told me he..."

"Crowly was a nobody! A nothing!" Don Franzesee swaggered around the room. She'd asked for this. He was more than willing to oblige. "For all I knew he could have been a school teacher. The first time I saw or heard of Collin Crowly was that night, at Mc Ginny's club. He was with Maria. Ricco and I followed him but he disappeared on us. Burning that house was a pleasure. I hope the bastard fried!" The coldness of his words caused Angelina to shutter. "You were just an unexpected diversion."

Chaos ruled Angelina's thoughts. She tried sorting it out. "But... you said Crowly and I... that I was..."

Sonny turned sharply. "I made you what you are... not Crowly! I didn't even know your name till Maria mentioned you. Not that it mattered. You were just ten minutes in a back seat. That's all you've ever been! A toy... a play thing... a puppet; someone to do my bidding!"

Angelina felt the breath knocked from her. Suddenly she was back in Nana's bedroom... awakening.

Once more she was without an identity.

Once more unaware of who she was... what she was...

Sonny started across the room. "Now, tell me! Where's my daughter? Where's Lace!"

Angelina sprang from her seat. "Where you'll never get your filthy, lying hands on her!" she cried out. Tears streaked her cheeks.

He raised a menacing hand, poised to strike.

"You made me, Sonny... but you should have left me to burn with the house. I would have been better off."

Two .32 caliber bullets at close range were enough to stop the big man. Franzesee staggered. His face knotted in an attempt to speak. Then the Don crumbled to the floor.

Wiping a tear, Angelina moved from behind the desk. She glowered at the lifeless body. "That was for me. This... this is for Maria," she said quietly, pointing the revolver at the back of Sonny's head. "*Ultimo insultare.*"

The exit wounds would be un-repairable. Don Franzesee's funeral would have to be closed casket.

It was the final insult.

Sonny taught her that.

Angelina didn't know how long she stood there. When the two bodyguards burst into the den she was expecting them. Slowly she turned and looked up. The pair leveled their machine guns.

Angelina knew her weapon was empty. She also knew the threatening hoods were unaware of the fact. She thought of Maria. And Maryann. And little Baby Lace. She thought of the old book store and Potter.

And of Lachesis.

"To fulfill my destiny," she murmured, and raised the gun.

A moment later the bullet riddled body of Angelina Caliopia Moira Franzesee lay next to her husband's.

In the bedroom above the book shop, Lachesis clutched at her chest. Potter caught the collapsing figure.

"Nana... are you ok, what's wrong? What is it?"

The ancient woman looked up. Slowly her breath returned. "I'm… I'm ok. Just a dizzy spell. Give me a minute."

Potter and Freddy helped her across the room. She settled down on the bed. "Maybe we should take you to the hospital. Just to be sure."

A smile splintered the withered face, as a single tear marked her cheek. "No. No, Freddy, no need. It's alright. Come here child…"

Maryann placed Baby Lace in the woman's strong arms. Folding back the antique blue comforter, Nana peered down lovingly at the infant. "We'll be fine… just fine. Won't we, Little Missy."

Marsha's Story

*The universe lives and abides
Forever; to meet each need,
Each creature is preserved.
All of them differ, from one
Another, yet none of them has
He made in vain…*

*Book of Sirach
42:24-25*

Chapter Twenty-Five

My life so far: Me...

Tuesday October 31, 1995

For Angie

I was about ten when they began. I remember because it was a week before my birthday when I had the first dream.

I suppose I always had some sort of idea, no... not idea but feeling... yes, feeling that something was different. Looking back I can see that until then I wasn't quite old, or rather, mature enough to understand... understand that things were different for me. Not strange, or weird, or unusual... just different, comfortably different. But everything also seemed natural; natural in the way that I realized I was the normal one and everything and everyone else was different.

I'm probably not making a lot of sense. Some will note that none of this makes sense, not to them anyway. They will be the ones to quickly dismiss me saying, "She was obviously sick... needed help... the poor girl." Everyone will shake their heads in mournful agreement thinking they understand. It's that very human need to categorize, compartmentalize and label everything so they can understand. Then they will be able to point and say with contentment and self-assurance and, most importantly, peace of mind, "That's all there is to it, so let's understand, label and forget, and get on with our normal lives."

But I need to be very clear on something from the start: thought I am no longer here, this is *not* a suicide note!

Nor is this the ramblings or flights of fancy of a disturbed eighteen year old girl who couldn't cope anymore – "The poor girl."

As they say, I am of sound mind and body.

No, this is simply an explanation, a recollection, a re-telling of the facts. The facts which I have come to realize and learn and understand and accept, about myself... about the way things are.

Elysian Dreams – B.J. Neblett

This is the real story... such as it is... that needs to be understood and accepted by those who knew me... who *know* me. Because I am very much alive and happy, very happy with the way things were... and are now.

This is my story: Marsha H.

It was October 24, just a week before my tenth birthday. I was born on that most misunderstood and controversial dates, All Saint's Eve; or, more specifically, Halloween. And, like most kids my age, I was looking forward to the night. This year mom promised I could go trick – or – treating on my own, or rather, with a group of friends... boys and girls.

The day started like any other Saturday at my house. It was one of those autumn days when you swear you can see the leaves changing right before your eyes: green to gold to red to rust. A day when the very air gives you energy and the smell of apple cider and hot molasses spice cake is everywhere. That is if you live where I do, a picturesque nothing of a town with the impossible name of Honeybrook.

Honeybrook, Pennsylvania, which is located a little outside of Downingtown; which is out past Radnor; which is a main – line suburb of Philadelphia. Honeybrook is in the heart of the Pennsylvania Dutch Amish country, which is precisely why nothing ever happens here.

Mom's a teacher at nearby Downingtown High School. If you look carefully you can catch a glimpse of the school in the old Steve McQueen flick *The Blob*. There are also a few brief scenes of Honeybrook, too. That's kinda cool.

Mom inherited our home, an ancient three story wood and brick cracker box, from an obscure great uncle named Potter, the town's undertaker... err, funeral director... sorry Potter. Spacious, drafty and kinda spooky, the place is nothing if not great for Halloween. Especially since Uncle Potter's funeral pallor is on one side, an old Gothic looking stone church is on the other, and an ancient cemetery sits directly across the street.

More than a few old timers swear to have seen the ghost of some Revolutionary War solider, as they clatter past in their creepy black horse and buggy. I did mention this is Amish country, right?

Elysian Dreams – B.J. Neblett

I am an only child. Mom and I are what long time residents refer to as *the new Honeybrook*, i.e.: transplanted city folk. The *city* mom comes from has maybe 9,000 people.

We live alone, with Max our 135 pound freckled Great Dane; an assortment of cats who came with the house; and Herbie, a grey mouse who shares my bedroom with me. From a cartoon–like hole in the wall, Herbie often pokes his cute pink nose and his beady red eyes, looking for cookie crumbs and pizza bones. I've caught him stealing my hair ribbons as well.

I never knew my dad. To hear mom explain it she didn't either. The house; a secondary education teacher's certificate; the teaching job, and I were mom's rewards for four long years of academics at West Chester State College. My grandparents died when she was in junior high and she was raised by Uncle Potter.

I interrupted mom's sophomore college year, the result of a wild party at a frat house. To this day the only recollection she has of that night, or admits to, is wandering out to a secluded nearby hill in the winter chill to watch some *twinkling lights playing off the glistening snow*. When asked if her vision that night may have been chemically induced, mom pleads the fifth.

Of course, now I know better.

But Saturday, October 24, 1987 started out for me with blueberry waffles and fresh whole country milk, and a trip to pick out my Halloween costume.

The Downingtown Farmer's Market is the Amish equivalent of the shopping mall. Take away J.C. Penny, the chain stores, the fancy big building, and the van clogged parking lot; throw in an attached flea market, and you have the idea. But it's nearby, has a dandy little food court, and the fashions are only months, not years behind. And it's a great place for people watching, something that always fascinates me. This Saturday, under a cool blue sky speckled with clamshell clouds, the assortment of people darting in and out of the myriad of connected stores was especially intriguing.

October is harvest time. The area surrounding Downingtown is farm country. From late August through Christmas the market comes alive with fresh produce and hand crafted goods. It is during this time men in bib overalls and long beards and families dressed all in black rub elbows with couples from Philadelphia and the suburbs who are taking in the fall colors, following the covered bridge tour, or looking for that special unusual gift. It's a time when Beamers and Chryslers vie for parking spaces with pick-ups and the ubiquitous horse and buggies.

Being an in-betweener… not belonging to either extreme, just a local… affords me a unique perspective for people watching. Even at a young age I enjoyed watching and comparing; and learning, always learning: taking in the enigmatic human spectacle being played out before me; digesting the rainbow of information gathered, sorting and cataloging, indexing and cross-referencing. But beyond that very human compulsion to understand everything, it seemed as if I knew someday all of this data would become important to me.

Sharing a waffle cone with a double scoop of homemade peach-vanilla ice cream, mom and I weaved our way through the crowds. By the way, mom's name is Angela, after her grandmother. Its Ms. H to her students thought most people call her Angie. So do I. It was the first word I said as a baby. She complains sometimes about my calling her by name, but I can tell mostly she likes it.

"Have you decided what you want to be this Halloween, Marsha?"

"Humm… I'm kinda torn between a witch and Bonnie Parker."

Mom… Angie… almost choked on a peach slice. "Bonnie Parker, as in Bonnie and Clyde?"

"Yeah, but not the Faye Dunaway Bonnie you and I watched the other night. The real Bonnie Parker… the homely one who smoked cigars and swore. We read about her in history class. She was kinda cool."

Angie closed her eyes and took a deep breath before she spoke. That always means trouble. "I don't think my almost ten year old daughter needs to be hero worshiping a depression era bank robber, much less dressing like one."

I smiled up at her. "I knew you were gonna say that. I just like to watch your ears turn purple when you're not sure how to handle something I just said. I've already decided to be a witch."

Elysian Dreams – B.J. Neblett

There it was... another reason I do things like this to my mom... that frustrated look she gets when she's been bamboozled by her *oh, so precocious* – her words – daughter. It's a real Kodak moment.

Angie shook her head causing a carefully clipped strand of hair to come loose and fall across her still tanned forehead. "Ok, ok... you got me... again." She looked around as a man, who more closely resembled a scarecrow, made his way past us leading a brown Guernsey on a rope. That's the Farmer's Market for you.

"I think there are some shops over this way that might have what you need," she said as I finished off the waffle cone.

Except for my reddish, cerise colored eyes – more about that later – and my somewhat darker hair, people say we look alike, Angie and I, almost like sisters. I should be so lucky. Mom is beautiful: tall, willowy, graceful, and very young looking, a cross between Madonna and Veronica Lake.

Yeah, I like old movies.

Angie and I spend almost every Friday after school at Blockbuster. Then the VCR and the popcorn churn late into the night. Old movies intrigue me, as does history, although I didn't know why back then. More of the human need to understand things I figured. Mom says that's a good thing and more people should be as inquisitive as I am. If only she knew...

Inquisitive is a good word... inquisitive. In junior high one time we had a writing exercise in English class: what words describe you best? Mine included inquisitive; funny; enigmatic; confused; lost, and love. The stupid teacher got mad. She said I shouldn't use words I don't know the meaning of. I told her she spoke in dangling participles and if she were more inquisitive as to the nature and abilities of her enigmatic students she wouldn't have said that. Like Angie says: precocious.

But it's more than that. I've always been bright... no, smart... intelligent past my years. School comes so easy to me. It's like I've been through all this before. A teacher will say, "Today, class, we are going to talk about World War Two," and all of a sudden some dusty file cabinet in my brain opens and out pops Hitler, and the Battle of Britain, and December Seventh, and Anzio, and D-day, and the Atomic Bomb, and all sorts of stuff. I like the way it works. I once thought it was like that for everyone.

My principal suggested to Angie she have my IQ tested and consider placing me in some school for gifted kids. "Gifted," he said... as if I'm not normal. I explained to him that I was the normal one. Anyway, mom and I talked about it then watched *The Paper Chase*. Angie decided that it didn't matter what my IQ might be, I needed to be a kid more than a genius. I agreed and stayed happily where I was, taking a few advanced placement classes. I understand now we made the right decision... and why.

The half dozen shops we visited in fact did have some things I needed. Angie picked up theatrical make-up to give me wrinkles and make me look older. Plus a woman selling beauty supplies – beauty supplies in Amish country? – sold us some rinse out grey hair dye. We wandered through the flea market and I talked mom into turning loose of ten bucks for VHS copies of *Bell, Book and Candle* and *The Next Voice You Hear*, a neat little sci-fi drama.

That's something Angie and I share: the old movie thing. I'll pick out a couple of flicks that seem good, staring Lana Turner or Humphrey Bogart or Lon Chaney or Lizabeth Scott or whoever. It's always fun because the movies are as new to mom as they are to me. Angie likes the film noir romances and mysteries. I do, too. My favs though are the slick, often corny sci-fi and space operas from the '50's. But sometimes I get the feeling of having been there, done that.

I don't like the term déjà vu. It's not like that. I know I haven't sat with Angie eating popcorn and watching this same movie before. It's different.

Once we were watching *The Angry Red Planet* and there was this scene of a city with spires and towers reaching high into the red colored sky. I told her the only structures on the surface were small domes, and everyone lives underground, and that the sky was actually a reddish-orangey rust color. She looked at me and said, "That's nice, Sweetie." I was eight at the time.

She says I have a super imagination. It's really the file cabinet thing.

Angie pulled our Plymouth into the gravel driveway, stopping by the kitchen door. Our housekeeper's car was parked out back.

"Tell Elvia I've gone to the IGA. Why don't you check the store room? There's that old trunk up there of my grandmother's, plus some of Potter's stuff. Maybe you can find something for your costume."

"Ok. And don't forget the popcorn."

Mom never forgets the popcorn. And I never forget to remind her. It's another one of those things I do to her on purpose. Instead of the, *you don't have to remind me* mother response, Angie frowns and wiggles her nose like Samantha on Bewitched. Sometimes I feel like a puppeteer pulling her strings, making her do as I want. It's fun. Angie kinda likes it, too, I can tell.

Our house is pretty cool. My room is on the third floor. Actually, I have the whole third floor to myself. My bedroom, the room I share with Herbie, is in the front. Two tall windows reach almost to the floor and lead out to a balcony overlooking the front yard, the street, and the cemetery.

The room is large with polished hardwood floors and area rugs. My favorite is a big, red, plush, hand-woven antique affair. The rug has strange burgundy and yellow and blue and cream colored patterns and designs, and fringe at opposite ends. It sits at the foot of my bed, between my great-grandmother's cedar hope chest and my 1940's art deco dressing bureau with the big round mirror. The baseboards are wide white moldings where Herbie has his inverted U shaped hole. And there is fancy triple-crown molding. Uncle Potter restored the whole house years ago, but Angie and I painted the walls in my room this really pretty red rust, and the ceiling a deep inky mid-night blue.

Self sticking moons and stars and planets and galaxies, from a neat little kiosk in the Exton Square Mall, pepper the ceiling. Sky gazing is one of my most favorite things to do. I arranged them so they map the sky, including most all the constellations, plus the planets and moons in our solar system. For some reason I put seven stars in the Pleiades. I guess I didn't know any better at the time. Anyway, at night, with the lights off, the ceiling disappears and they glow in the dark, keeping me company as they sparkle and twinkle. It makes the room feel homier.

I also have my own fireplace and private bathroom, and a walk-in closet. A smaller attached sitting room is where I have my desk and TV and books and toys and stuff. At the back of the third floor is the room we use for storage.

"Lunch will be ready shortly, Missy."

"K... Angie en el súper marcado."

"Bueno... your Spanish is improving. I hope Señorita don't forget the popcorn," Elvia said, giving me a wink and stirring another dollop of Miracle Whip into the tuna. I like my tuna wet, without onions.

Elvia is a naturalized citizen from somewhere in Central America. She took care of Uncle Potter and came with the house, along with the cats. Her English is good, but it's still funny to watch her and some Amish gentleman go at it over the price he is charging for squash or melons. She lives with her husband Ramos, a fixer of anything. He runs a repair shop in town, helps out at the funeral pallor, and does maintenance for us and several other families. With the loving care of a grandparent, he also takes meticulous care of the old cemetery across the street.

There's a small room off the kitchen where Elvia stays sometimes when Angie goes out, which is not often enough. I already told you she's beautiful. And intelligent. Much too good for these goober farm boys. But there's this really dreamy teacher who makes history dance. He also makes Angie blush when they talk. I've been trying to fix them up forever.

In the ninth grade I invited him home to dinner for a parent-teacher conference. Angie was furious. But, with that *I've been hoodwinked by my daughter* look of hers, she wiggled into a curve hugging, silky dress that mirrored her emerald eyes, lit some candles and dimmed the dining room lights. Unfortunately, he left at a very proper 9:45. Since then they've been out a number of times, including a play in Philadelphia at the Walnut Street Theatre, and to some teacher functions. They are working on a relationship, but at a snail's pace. I'm not looking for a dad, but Angie needs someone... and to have some fun.

"I'll be upstairs, Elvia." Chaucer, a huge all black Tom with large butter yellow eyes, followed me upstairs. He's the undisputed ruler of the cat clan and one of only three felines that have run of the house. Even big old easy going Max shows him respect.

Chaucer is a terrific mouser who keeps the cemetery vermin free. Interestingly enough, though he often sleeps on my bed or stands watch in one of my windows, he and Herbie have struck up a pact of peaceful co-existence. They give each other curious passing glances and Chaucer even tolerates Herbie drinking from the water bowl I keep on the bathroom floor. Elvia, who is in her seventies and has been keeping house here for over forty years, says she can't remember a time when Chaucer wasn't around. There must be something to that nine lives theory.

I flipped the light switch and entered the dusty store room. At my feet, Chaucer let out a low, throaty howl and hesitated.

"What's the matter old guy, too spooky for you?"

He looked up at me as if he understood my words – I'm sure he does – and padded obstinately into the room.

෴

An orange flame skated atop the bundle of logs that alternately glowed red, amber, blue and yellow. The corner fireplace emitted comforting warmth and provided the only light, save for two scented candles. The all brick basement den is probably my favorite room in the house. It's my and mom's hide-a-way from the world. It was after midnight and we were hiding in flannel night shirts, beneath a big blue quilted comforter, and curled up on a thick fur rug. On the TV a black and white James Whitmore tried to figure out several mysterious disappearances in the New Mexico desert.

"Do you think such things can happen?"

Angie tossed a handful of buttery Orville Redenbacher popcorn into her mouth. "What... you mean giant ants?"

"Well... yeah... you know, mutations, like from atom bombs and stuff."

Chaucer stretched a long slender paw, fanning his formidable nails. He seemed annoyed by my question. His expression, as he yawned and adjusted his comfortable position next to Max in front of the fireplace, said, *of course it happens.*

"What makes you ask?" Angie reached for a cup of hot cocoa on the old steamer trunk doing double duty as a coffee table.

I shrugged. "Just wondering, this is a documentary, right?"

She stopped in mid-sip. Her hair, the color of a new tennis ball, was pulled back in a pony-tail and I could see her ears taking on a lavender tint. A second later we both laughed.

Between slices of extra cheese and pepperoni pizza, and mounds of Bryer's Cookies and Cream ice cream, we had already helped James Stewart win gorgeous Kim Novak – despite her witch's pedigree. Then we watched the people of earth tune their AM radios to listen to Godly sermons that seemed to originate in outer space. The giant ants were mom's idea.

Earlier, Chaucer and I found a treasure chest of goodies in great-grandma's trunk, including a long, deep navy, pleated skirt and a cream colored silk peasant blouse. I've always been tall for my age. With some minor alterations, a scarf, layers of costume beads, grey hair and a few well placed wrinkles, I would easily transform into Meliva, the old gypsy woman from *The Wolfman* come Halloween. I thought about asking my friend Tommy to dress as a werewolf.

The store room also held several dust covered boxes and another trunk which looked intriguing. I made a mental note in my file cabinet to check them out some bored Sunday.

Angie and I jumped and momentarily hid under the blue comforter. A fifteen foot ant had grabbed James Whitmore in its pinchers.

"I hate it when the hero gets killed." Angie bravely turned back to the flickering TV.

"He's not the hero, Matt Dillon there is."

"You mean James Arness. And what makes you think he's the hero?"

"Simple, watch… he'll get the girl."

Sure enough, several ant exterminating minutes later they emerged, the hero and the girl, arm in arm, victorious.

"See, the hero always gets the girl."

Mom punched *stop* and then *re-wind* on the remote. "And I suppose you believe in frogs becoming Princes, and living happily ever after, too."

I grinned back at her. "Of course I do! Don't be silly. You know what Snow White said to the Fotomat clerk, don't you?"

"No... what?"

"'Someday my Prince will come!' get it... Prince... prints..."

Angie sighed and rolled her eyes. "Yes, and I wish I didn't." She slid the popcorn bowl in front of me. "And what kind of Prince are you holding out for?"

"I don't know, tall... cute for sure... but someone special. Maybe someone on a noble mission, like to save the world or something."

"From giant ants?" Angie quipped. I tossed some popcorn at her and we both laughed again.

"You know what I mean. And I'll be there with him, helping him, inspiring him."

It is interesting how prophetic those innocent words were.

"A hopeless romantic. I'm raising a hopeless romantic." Angie stretched and started gathering up dishes.

The VCR clicked stop. I switched off the TV and collected the tapes, making room for the newest additions to our growing collection of movies. The jacket artwork of *The Next Voice You Hear* caught my eye. The movie never really makes it clear if the voice coming from space is God's. It leaves the viewer to decide for them self.

I like that.

The fact that some writer somewhere came up with this story just strengthens my belief not only in God, but in life on the other planets. Not the strange little Grays that seem to come and go as they please, undetected. And certainly not the monstrous aliens bent on taking over the earth that is the staple of most sci-fi.

No, I agree with the theme of the movie. I believe humans are not alone. That there is a universe wide community of planets, home to other races not unlike ourselves. These beings share the same hopes and dreams and frailties as us. They love and hurt and cry just as we do. And we all share common ties and links, bonded together by God for His grand purpose.

I guess that's why I love to star gaze so much. To me the sky... the universe... is a very welcoming and friendly place.

After helping mom clean up, I slipped outside to walk Max and steal a few minutes with the heavens. It was a moonless autumn night, the air sharp, the sky gloriously overbooked. From my backyard I counted three shooting stars and could just make out the dim reddish-orange glow of Mars rising over the distant trees. Loosing myself in the sky, I thought of my friends and school and our old drafty house; and of God and giant ants; of Max and Herbie and Chaucer and his gang, and of course of Elvia and mom. My life was almost perfect.

Almost...

Why almost?

Settled into my bed, Chaucer beside me, Max curled up by the door, and that question – *why almost?* – on my mind, I fell into a deep, peaceful sleep.

That night the first dream appeared.

"I have often wondered if the majority of mankind ever pauses to reflect upon the occasionally titanic significances of dreams, and of the obscure world to which they belong."

H.P. Lovecraft

☙ Chapter Twenty-Six ❧

Dreams...

I don't have nightmares. Well... ok, I do have nightmares, but not like you may think. Let me explain.

By nature nightmares are bad, scary things, right? You know: your life's in danger; wake up screaming; a cold sweat. Whether you are being chased by a hungry lion, attacked by mutant space monsters, or falling from a high place, nightmares are something to avoid. After all, who wants to be suddenly and rudely tossed from a nice restful sleep?

So, do I have these dreams, what we call nightmares? Oh, baby, do I! Night of the Living dead, blood splatter, T-Rex gonna have you for lunch nightmares. But... they don't scare me, not at all. Never have, never will. You see, I *lucid dream*.

When I am sleeping and dreaming, I am aware that I am sleeping... and dreaming. Something in my brain says, "Nothing to worry about or be frightened of, nothing can hurt you, you are asleep, it's only a dream." It's as if Dorothy turned to her companions on the Yellow Brick Road and said, "Don't be afraid of those flying monkeys. I'm asleep and all of this is just a dream." That's lucid dreaming.

I know, it sounds kinda boring. But think about it: no being scared out of your wits, or waking up not knowing if you are alive or dead. Just relax and sleep and bring on the monsters... like watching a movie.

I've been lucid dreaming for as long as I can remember. Dreams are another of my favorite things. In fact, I have learned to control my dreams, to a certain extent. I can often wake up and then go back to sleep and pick up a dream where it left off; or close my eyes and draw a favorite dream out of my filing cabinet and dream it over. And I certainly don't mind being chased, even caught, by the unspeakable. It's just a dream. It's really a very cool thing to be able to do. And yes, another one of those things I discovered about myself that not everyone... very few actually... are capable of doing.

Nights in my big comfy sleigh bed, with the moon tiptoeing across the room, and the wind playing in the lace curtains, are peaceful and restful. As I grew older they became downright intriguing. But that first dream affected me in ways none had before, and set a pattern for dreams that followed. It pulled at my emotions.

※

Angie stared out the big bay window, surveying the remains of our flower bed. She nibbled on toast dripping with gooey orange marmalade. Mom's a good, albeit skeptical listener when it comes to anything out of the ordinary, including dreams. She's much too practical an individual, if you ask me. I think it comes with being a parent, especially for moms.

I awoke with vivid images frozen in my mind from last night's dreams. Sunlight warmed the breakfast nook where we usually eat when it's just the two of us. Outside, the skeletons of yellow rose bushes we planted last spring stood ridged and proud. Angie was already dressed in jeans and a soft blue sweater. Sipping from a oversized mug, her yellow hair long and loose about her shoulders, her legs drawn up beneath her, she reminded me of Kim Novak in last night's Bell Book and Candle.

"Good morning, pumpkin. How did you sleep?" She dropped two slices of whole wheat bread into the toaster. "Any ants chasing you?"

Still dressed in my long nightshirt and pink bunny slippers which Max loves and Chaucer hates, I slid into the booth beside her. "No... no ants, you know me better than that."

"Yes, I do know you. That's why I asked."

"Well..." I covered the crisp bran flakes and pump raisins with whole milk. Angie and I have no secrets, none. But for some reason I hesitated, questioning the necessity of telling her.

Necessity... now there was an interesting word. Why would it be *necessary* to tell my mom about a dream... or not to tell her? I am no stranger to weird dreams, not at all. Mom knows this. And this one topped the chart. But what was I afraid of? Her passing off my visions as nothing more than pizza, pop corn and ice cream induced nightmares, or just the opposite?

"Hey, earth to Marsha... anybody home?" Angie waved a slice of lightly toasted bread before me like a magician holding a watch. "Hello..."

"Sorry. Maybe this should wait till after church."

Our wide front porch stretches from one side of the house, gracefully wrapping itself to the other side. A waist high railing runs its entire length, broken by square columns supporting a flat overhanging roof. The porch, along with another smaller one out back and the balcony off my bedroom, were added about fifty years after the house was completed.

Angie and I sat in matching Bentwood rockers, sipping coffee and hot chocolate, enjoying the mild late morning breeze. The only traffic on the street was an occasional horse drawn buggy, its rhythmic clop of steel shoes on pavement echoing across the lawn.

"Do you believe in pre-destination?"

Angie squinted over the rim of her jumbo sized mug. "A philosophical question tinged with religious overtones... appropriate for a Sunday morning." She thought for a second. "I suppose there are some things that are set down for us... certain paths, destinations... but not everything in life."

"Me too... do you think we can see the future?"

"If you are talking about dreams, I think we have had this discussion. Dreams are just that, dreams... random thoughts and images. Now, c'mon, give, what's going on in that way too complicated for an almost ten year old mind of yours?"

I don't agree with her, not at all. I have always believed we can learn from our dreams, that there is some message for us. Not all dreams of course. Many... most dreams are simply entertainment. Like movies: some make you laugh; some make you cry, and some make you think.

A cool wind stirred up from the cemetery across the street, like a phantom rising. It rustled the oak tree whose sturdy branches used to reach over to my balcony. That is before Angie had Elvia's husband trim them back when she caught me sneaking out to stargaze. I pulled a crochet blanket over my shoulders and sipped my coffee. Several brown leaves tumbled in the air, a last dance before dying.

"It wasn't like normal dreams..."

"Sweetheart, your dreams are anything but normal. Go on, I'm listening."

"Everything was red. Wherever I was... I don't know. But I was surrounded by red: the sky, the ground, even the air, like a thin red mist. It was the color of... blood."

Angie's expression changed as she straightened in her chair. It was the same expression she gets when a student in her class asks for help, her serious, mothering look.

"I really wasn't anywhere," I continued, "just sort of floating... in a sea... no, not a sea... but just red. I wasn't scared or anything. It felt kinda warm and natural. But then..." I paused and a file cabinet opened and out popped the details.

"Then I was surrounded by women, dozens and dozens of them. No one I recognized, they were all very striking looking. They were tall and thin with darkish pink skin and beautiful silver eyes. And they were crying. Their silver eyes ran heavy with tears, transparent red tears that glistened against the women's soft pink skin."

"Wow." Mom leaned forward in the rocker, ignoring the mug of cocoa in her hands. She was looking at me, but I could tell she was seeing, or struggling to see, what I was describing.

"There's more..."

Her eyes focused. "Ok..."

"I felt sorry for the women in my dream. Even now it kinda hurts to think about them. And then I was saying, 'What's wrong? What's the matter? Why do you cry?' The women, every one of them, reached out. Each held a tiny pink baby. They were so small, much smaller than a new born. Even smaller than Jane's little sister who was born early; impossibly tiny. And they were all dead. The babies the women held were all dead."

"Oh, honey..." Mom sat motionless. I could tell my dream affected her, troubled her, more than it had me.

The morning breeze became perfectly still. Even the breeze which had come up and tugged at the stubborn leaves was gone. Angie now stared out across the lawn, past the street, beyond the cold marble and granite markers.

I felt bad.

"So..." I said, summonsing up my cheeriest voice. "What do ya think? Weird, huh?"

Angie's expression changed again, from mothering to contemplative to troubled. She scooted her rocker over to mine and touched my cheek with the back of her soft hand. "Honey, I don't want you to worry yourself with this dream. Forget it. Put it out of your mind."

I knew I couldn't even if I wanted. A voice inside me said there was something to this dream, and it shouldn't be ignored. I wasn't going to.

"Ok," I lied. "But tell me first... do you think it means anything... seriously."

Mom bit her bottom lip and tried to smile. "Marsha, if I *had* to venture an opinion, and *if* you were older, I might say you are probably getting ready to have your first period. I myself had some strange dreams before I got mine. But, you are still too young, and it *was* just a dream. Too much pizza... too many scary movies... too wild an imagination, I don't know. But just a dream... that's all... ok, Sweetie?"

She kissed my forehead. "Ok, mom, if you say so."

The breeze returned... a stiffer, colder, serious wind from the north. It rustled the trees and swept the lawn. In the distance several bells tolled. They were answered by the melancholy drone of the church bell next door.

Halloween came. My friends and I invaded the neighborhood: Tommy a chubby Wolfman; Jess a red haired Cinderella; Bobby a short Frankenstein; Melinda a be-speckled bumble bee, and me... an overly serious gypsy woman.

Over the next year my dream repeated itself, nine, ten, a dozen times. Each time I felt as if the women were about to speak, about to explain. Each time they remained mute.

Three days later, November third, three days past my tenth birthday, to everyone's surprise but mine, I got my first period.

Elysian Dreams – B.J. Neblett

The year whizzed by and before I knew it I was starting sixth grade. Being eleven is strange. People don't look at you the same. From your eleventh birthday to your thirteenth you live in a kind of social limbo. You're not a kid, not a teen. Adults have a word for it: 'tweener.' Dumb, huh? As if being eleven or twelve isn't hard enough, you get to wear a label.

And it's hard in other ways. At eleven you're a sixth grader. In my school system that makes you king of the school, top of the food chain. A year later you graduate to junior high and find yourself a bottom feeder.

The worse part of all this is maturity. Seventh graders are 'tweeners in kids' bodies. Ninth graders are teens who look increasingly like young adults. It's maddening. You're trying to shrink your zits and enlarge your breasts. You haven't out grown your baby fat or into your overly tall body. But it does happen… blindingly fast… and seeming overnight. You wake up one morning and your hormones are at war with your emotions and logic has fled the battlefield. And all of this is just a prelude, and overture, to the wildly off key concert yet to come: being a teen.

To add to the fun of my 'tweener years was the fact I started my period at an early age. That meant all of the angst and pressure and confusion and wonders of being eleven or twelve or even thirteen was magnified a thousand fold.

Angie, God bless her, took me to the doctor, several doctors actually, including some specialists. For all their trouble, and tests, and probing, the best any could come up with was a wry smile and: *she's just maturing a little ahead of schedule is all. It's nothing to worry about. Oh, her blood count is a bit high. Breathing and heart rate are a bit slow, but deeper and stronger than normal. And she exhibits exceptional reflexes and hand-eye coordination. She's fine and healthy.*

Maybe if they knew what they were looking for, or even looking at, they would have sung a different tune.

What they couldn't measure with all of their instruments and know how were my emotions and intelligence. If school was easy before, it was a cake walk now. But instead of becoming bored I jumped in with both feet. I couldn't get enough. My desire for knowledge was insatiable.

I challenged my teachers and did tons of reading and extra credit assignments. History fascinated me, and science and space and nature thrilled me. Mom bought me an encyclopedia, and we spent long Sunday afternoons exploring the Rodan and Art museums and the Franklin Institute.

Academically I was in heaven.

Emotionally I was a mess.

Not that there was anything wrong with me. Several doctors, two school counselors and a few visits with a psychologist confirmed that. No, I was just becoming a very sensitive, caring young girl.

Sensitive wasn't the word for it.

When I was seven or eight I would cheer when Godzilla stomped Tokyo or aliens attacked. By ten I looked for the hero to ride off with the girl. But by the still tender age of twelve I found my eyes getting damp at the dumbest things.

One evening mom and I were parked in our favorite spot: under the old big blue comforter, in front of the TV; in the VCR the classic This Island Earth. The benevolent alien Exador was returning the hero – and the girl – safely to earth, knowing his own time was up. Angie touched my cheek, wiping a tear. I wasn't aware I was crying.

"Pumpkin… are you alright? What's the matter, Sweetie?"

Before I knew what was happening I was in Angie's arms, bawling like a baby. "Oh, mama…" (Mama? I never called her mama!) "It's so not fair! Exador was just doing what he thought was right… to save his planet… his people. Now he's the only one left and his ship is going to burn up and crash!"

So much for emotions.

I can't honestly say I didn't like the changes I, and my body, were going through. Quite the opposite. I may not have understood what was happening to me, but I found I liked it. I woke up each morning wondering what new thought or idea or feeling would be unleashed. What overpowering emotion – love, compassion, empathy, joy, or even disgust – would rear its head within me? What scientific fact or law of nature or history lesson waited to be discovered? I was a developing young girl. Only I was developing to the N'th degree.

All of this made me... how to put this... stand out a bit. My friends took it in stride... *that's just Marsha*. My teachers enjoyed having a gifted (that word again), if *different* student in their class. And Angie kept an overly concerned motherly eye on me. I didn't care. Eleven and twelve were years marked by learning and growth; by dizzying changes and exciting discoveries. And by increasingly cryptic dreams.

The crying pink women – mía señoras' rosada – with their silver eyes and tiny pink dead babies, continued to visit me. But they never spoke. A few months after my eleventh birthday they were joined by a second dream.

In this one the eerie red fog continued. The women were gone, and I found myself atop a low hill. The ground was a dusty reddish brown in color, like a desert of rust. A steady wind swirled the loose dust gently at my feet. It caused my hair to sway. Yet it was so slight, so thin, it couldn't be felt.

All about me the barren landscape was dotted with low, metallic looking cubes protruding from the ground. Instinctively I knew they were headstones. I was in a vast grave yard which stretched for miles. But something was odd. It was the dates.

Each of the markers bore the same year, every one. It was as if some widespread, cataclysmic event, a war or sickness or famine, wiped out an entire population over the course of one year.

But the event hadn't taken place yet. The deadly year etched deeply into the metallic headstones was some thirty years in the future.

I knew I was right... dreams are important, and indeed hold a message. But what was it?

Standing there in the stark stillness and silence common to cemeteries everywhere, tears rolled down my cheek. I touched one. It glisten a vivid red in my hand, the same transparent red tears of the señoras rosada.

I never told Angie, there didn't seem to be any reason. Like the other dream, it repeated itself over, a school lesson, important and to be remembered.

Elysian Dreams – B.J. Neblett

Something told me there would be more dreams, more visions, and more messages. A new file cabinet appeared. It was labeled *Dreams*. Perhaps it would provide the answers and meanings I sought. I would just have to be patient till it opened.

The two dreams persisted, at irregular intervals, along with visions of strange buildings and weird landscapes, all in shades of red. Then they stopped. As abruptly as they began, the dreams ended. I was thirteen.

But my emotions continued to run rampant, thought I learned to control... no, not control... to deal with them. Silly sappy movies still elicited tears, but at least I was able to wait till the really sad part rolled around before the flow began. And things I never cared about before now made me mad, really mad. Ecology and the rain forest ranked high on my list. I became determined to do my part to save the planet. I just needed to figure out what my part was.

Mom, as always, remained patient and encouraging. I joined every club and service organization that would have me. I worked in soup kitchens; picked up trash along the highways; volunteered at a pet shelter; handed out pamphlets for Greenpeace; dragged Angie to lectures on global warming and hazardous waste. She joked that by fourteen my resume was more impressive than her own.

My attempt at being a vegetarian lasted exactly two days. Vomiting the soy substitute was bad enough. But the three days of itching from hives was unbearable. Free range chicken and humanely raised cattle would have to do.

But I was somehow going to find my niche in the world, my curriculum vitae.

The Christmas I was fifteen brought an unexpected and life changing gift. Angie bought me a ridiculously expensive and very powerful telescope. I took to the intimidating instrument like a mad scientist.

I joined the science and astronomy clubs at school and even subscribed to the NASA newsletter. Pictures of Lowell and Hubble, together with star maps and charts replaced the adolescent posters on my walls. Evenings found me bent over the telescope's eye piece, focusing in some distant star cluster, or identifying the craters on the full moon. I discovered the old cemetery across the street ideal for my nocturnal heavenly eavesdropping.

Even my fascination with sci-fi took a more serious turn. Tapes including War of the Worlds, 2001: A Space Odyssey, and The Man Who Fell to Earth, plus a PBS series on the universe, and George Pal's religiously over toned space trilogy found their way among our ever increasing VHS library. I toyed with the idea of becoming the first woman – the first person – to set foot on another world. But deep inside, I still held the dream of saving humanity from itself.

Then came Flaco.

One hot, humid evening, after several hours of watching Saturn arc across the summer sky, I settled down to what I hopped would be a dream about discovering new planets. Instead, shortly after drifting off, I found myself on the surface of the moon.

Decked out in a soft form fitting blue suit made of very supple rubber like material, and wearing a comfortable light weight helmet, I stood on a plain near the base of steep lunar mountains. A blue dot appeared on the near horizon. It approached using that comical bunny hop step of one-sixth gravity. With the intuitive knowledge of dreams, I pictured him in my mind: a man of maybe twenty-two or twenty-three, tall and thin with a reddish complexion. A second later the two of us hopped off towards the gray horizon.

The next night brought a different dream. But once again I was accompanied by the tall figure. This time he wore a simple charcoal jumpsuit, and I could see his hair was straight and jet black. He never spoke but stayed with me, a guide, or perhaps protector, through wherever my dreams led.

My silent companion appeared to me often after that, at least three or four time a week. Regardless of the situation, being chased by dragons, driving mom's car on the sidewalk, or picnicking among the flowers, he was there. We explored together; danced; dined; laughed and cried together. And he was gallant as a knight, opening doors, taking my arm, clearing the way, even defending me.

I dubbed my nocturnal friend *El Flaco*, the thin one, and found I actually had developed a major crush on this ethereal visitor. He became the gauge by which I judged the males in my life, including the ones who asked me out. Very few came close.

Angie laughed and said I was hopeless.

For the next couple of years I lived in three uniquely different worlds: the fascinating universe revealed through my telescope; the comforting security of my dreams, and the emotion driven bewilderment of reality.

Chapter Twenty-Seven

Reality...

This past summer I hit a low spot in my life. I should have been enjoying the summer, being a typical irresponsible, fun loving, slightly mischievous teen. Instead, the roller coaster that is my emotions was racing wildly out of control, till it finally crashed and burned. A combination of depression and frustration set in.

September I would be a senior. October I'd turn eighteen. It was time to make some serious decisions, including college and career: time to grow up, whatever that meant. I really didn't mind growing older. I looked forward to making my mark in the world; doing my part to save it. But how? In what way? Did the world even wish to be saved, or deserved to be? More and more I looked to the sky, idling away hours on end, lost in the universe through the lens of my telescope.

Can an astronomer or an astronaut, a space traveler, really make a difference? I was torn; confused. Not exactly an unknown state for a teenager, I realize. But the beliefs and ideals which I treasured and trusted seemed to be on a direct collision course with reality. Why were things so damn complicated?

It was a warm, rainy Saturday evening in June. Elvia and her husband were at the new Latino night club over in Plymouth Meeting. Angie was off to Atlantic City with her history guy for some teacher conference. I sat in my room cleaning out my closet.

"It looks like it's just you and me tonight, Max."

The old dog looked up from the chew toy he had been worrying for the last twenty minutes. His rope like tail beat twice against the hardwood floor.

"What's wrong with this picture, huh fella?"

If Max had an answer for me he kept it to himself. Instead he nodded his head in his doggy way, offering up his own, unique comfort, and returned to his rubber slipper.

A soft scratching sound got my attention. In the corner, two beady eyes peered up.

"Here ya go. You might as well eat. Even extra cheese pizza with pepperoni can't get me out of this funk." I tossed a thick arch of pizza crust across the room. Herbie Jr's tiny nails tapped a path to the pizza bone. A second later he, and it, disappeared into his ancestral mouse hole.

"Enjoy... you've probably got a date, too," I muttered.

My social life was never anything to brag about. It's hard being the strange, moody but attractive girl with the high IQ. Honeybrook doesn't exactly offer a choice selection of eligible young men, nor does Downingtown High. Being taller and a lot smarter than nearly everyone in my class doesn't help either.

I've gone on a few dates and to my share of parties. Somewhere between eighth and ninth grade my long time buddy Tommy lost weight, gained height and turned into a junior hunk. A promising, budding romance died a painful tragic death when his family moved to Seattle at the end of last year.

I missed him; and what seemed like the simpler life. Before high school and global warming and rising oil prices; before Desert Storm and spotted owls and *read my lips* and starving kids in Africa; before life got complicated.

Even my dreams were changing. My old friend and secret crush, the mysterious Flaco, had vanished on me. Most nights I found myself dreaming about him, rather than with him. I missed him, too.

Outside a crack of thunder announced a new round of showers. My beloved telescope sat in the corner, the two of us prisoners to the weather.

Michael J Fox had the right idea: a DeLorean time machine. That's what I needed. If I couldn't save the world at least I would be able to choose in which decade to live.

I had enough.

Enough of sorting clothes and trying to sort out my life. Snatching up the still warm pizza, I bounded down the stairs, followed by Max with his arthritic hip, poor old guy. Stopping in the kitchen for a fresh Hires Root Beer and some Milk Bones, Max and I made our way to the basement den, my personal fortress of solitude. Before long, Doc and Marty and Max and I were heading Back to the Future.

So went my summer. I didn't need an amusement park; my emotions provided all the excitement I could handle.

Working a week at a camp for children with cancer was rewarding but hard on the eyes. I cried myself to sleep every night knowing most of these kids wouldn't be around for camp next year. I decided I wouldn't return either.

In August, three girlfriends and I spent a few days in Wildwood, New Jersey. By day we enjoyed the sun, sand and surf. By night we enjoyed the company of college guys from Princeton, Penn State or Villanova. I couldn't wait to get back to my telescope.

When school resumed in September I was determined to concentrate on my final year and apply to several local colleges. The idea of dorm life didn't appeal to me, certainly not one so far away that I couldn't come home on weekends.

My emotions had settled down, as much as they ever settled down. I looked forward to my senior year and chemistry and astronomy classes, and field trips to the Feld's Planetarium. The only question that remained was what should be my major. I still wanted to save the world. But I still didn't know in what way I could save it. Very shortly these problems would become meaningless.

Three days ago, October 28, 1995.

Saturday.

Angie was out again with her history teacher. Maybe there was hope for her after all. A nice guy from Drexel University had asked me out. I would have accepted but Mars is at its regular twenty six month cycle close to earth right now, and conditions promised prime viewing. I considered inviting him to join me. But, he's kinda cute and I didn't want to geek him out.

So, around ten PM, I filled a thermos with hot cider, tucked fresh batteries and Mozart into my Walkman, donned a light jacket and hiking boots, and schlepped my telescope across the street. The ancient cemetery is one of my favorite places to visit. Far from interfering lights and obstructions, it affords a peaceful, quite surrounding in which to observe and meditate. Deep inside I found a level spot atop a hill. It was next to a small, old family plot. The inscription on a weathered marker read:

Martin

Jonathan Beloved Husband and Father

April 3, 1706 – March 28, 1733

Becky November 28, 1729 – April 2, 1733

Robert June 15, 1727 – April 10, 1733

John Jr. August 17, 1731 – April 19, 1733

All Taken By The Fever

Rebekah Beloved Wife and Mother

December 26, 1709 – September 21, 1769

As I set up my equipment, I thought about the woman, Rebekah, at rest in the ground next to me. My emotions kicked into high gear. It was hard for me to imagine what she must have gone through, the feelings of helplessness as her family was taken from her one by one. I recalled my dream of the red graveyard and the metallic markers all bearing the same date.

Shaking off the urge to cry, I aimed the telescope skyward, zooming in on a tiny dot barely visible to the naked eye. A shimmering orangey red ball came into focus, filling the lens, and filling my mind, as always, with wonder.

I had been studying the planet in the lens for about thirty minutes when a rustling sound pulled me from my thoughts. Looking up I saw a figure approaching. It was a man, a young man perhaps in his early twenties, dressed in jeans and a black turtleneck. His movements were fluid, graceful as he appeared to float across the dry grass and dead leaves. He paused not five feet away.

"Hello, Marsha."

The face was familiar. "Hello…"

Noting the telescope, he looked up, surveying the sky. He was tall and thin, easily six foot three, with coal black hair. A crescent moon was rising, but even in the dim light his face glowed a beautiful, shimmering reddish brown.

"It is a lovely night, isn't it?" he said.

He was the most handsome man I had ever seen.

"I know you, don't I?" The words came on their own, as if my thoughts could speak.

I did know him. We never met but he was familiar to me: the handsome stranger from my dreams, Mi Flaco.

He turned, a warm smile on his thin lips. His eyes were soft, his voice low, melodic.

"Yes… in a way you do. And I know you, too, all about you… and your father."

"My father…"

"Yes. He was a great man in my land."

As in my dreams he was easy and comfortable to be with, not a stranger at all. I found myself talking with him as I might an old friend. "Where is it you come from?"

The reassuring smile widened. His eyes paused momentarily on the telescope, and then moved to the sky, tracing a path to the distant planet it was trained on.

I understood.

"Oh…"

The ease and calm with which I accepted the fact didn't surprise me. I don't know why but I trusted my instincts… my feelings… about this striking man. It wasn't just that he mentioned my father. My filing cabinet was frantically issuing memos warning me this man was important; that his being here and what he had to say, strange as it may sound, mattered.

I knew it was crazy… insane. If Angie were here she would never understand. I didn't care. Something inside… a force… an emotion… I never experienced before was in control.

"Tell me about my father."

He continued to study the sky, his voice whisper quiet in the still air. "We are not all that different," he began, "the two of us. My people are slightly more advanced scientifically... only slightly. We share the same emotions, feelings, needs, even the same jealousies and wonder, searching for answers... meaning."

He reached out as if plucking an apple from a high branch. "We reached your moon barely five years ahead of your Apollo missions and set up a small base concealed in the mountains on the far side. It became obvious that your people would, in time attempt to move on, to the other planets. A decision had to be made."

The visitor began to pace as he spoke, his hands cupped together behind him, a professor lecturing. And I, his eager student, listened, and understood, and believed.

"Years ago three men, including your father, came to Earth. They were to observe and study, learn everything they could about Earth and its people." His smile returned showing a flash of startling white teeth. "Marshal... your father... was the youngest. He enrolled in one of your colleges. That's where he met... and fell in love with... your mother. He knew better. He knew he couldn't stay, that assimilation was strictly forbidden. He kept his feelings hidden from her best he could. But, one evening, while they studied together... their feelings... their love... well..."

I could see him blush as he struggled for words.

"How come Angie never told me?"

"I don't know."

My heart suddenly felt heavy. "He never told her did he?"

"No... they remained close. But a couple of days after you were born it was time for him to leave. It was then my people made their decision. We would let Earth discover us, if and when it happened, in their own time. There were more pressing problems which needed to be addressed at home. Space exploration was terminated."

I stood frozen, my eyes focused on the telescope, my mind racing, fixed on a tiny dot in the heavens. Sure, mom was a college coed... and dad was... was... no way! The past eight years flashed through my brain like a tape in fast forward: the dreams; my fascination with space and sci-fi; my IQ and thirst for knowledge; the color of my eyes; even my wild emotions. And this man... it was crazy... but why not? Could it really be? What did that make me? Who was I...what was I?

I wasn't sure.

Incredibly, I discovered I liked my new found identity. It seemed to fit. I had been right all along... everyone else was different.

I looked at the visitor, "And my father?"

He sighed heavily. "Marshal died six months ago, testing a new space vehicle. He was coming back for you, Marsha. And your mother."

As always, my emotions were peaking. I didn't fight the tears. This wasn't right! I found, and then lost again, the father I never knew. It wasn't fair. My heart felt as if it were breaking. "Why did you come here? Why are you telling me these things now?"

A troubled expression crossed the visitor's face. His hands folded together, one long, slender finger pressed to his lips. He stood there in quiet contemplation, an explorer who traveled across space bringing news of my father and... and what?

"Do you believe in a Creator, Marsha?"

The question took me by surprise. "Yes... yes, I believe in God."

My answer seemed to satisfy something within him. "Some time ago our doctors discovered a virus which caused infertility. It had spread undetected for many years among our women. Today less than one in six can bear children. The few females who aren't still born are usually themselves incapable of conceiving."

Transparent red tears glistened on his cheek. "My people... your people, Marsha... are dying. The most optimistic estimates say in less than thirty years there will be no more births. After that..."

I felt light headed, dizzy. My God... my dreams... the women crying for their babies... the graveyard... the metal markers all the same! "Oh, my God, can't something be done, anything?"

He shook his head. "We've tried everything. The virus was destroyed but it left our DNA weakened. There's not enough time for it to repair itself naturally. What is needed is…"

"Is fresh, strong, healthy DNA… that's compatible with yours…" The anger and sorrow and self pity I was feeling over my father left me. My favorite movie, The Next Voice You Hear came back to me. Of course… One God… one people… sharing common ties and links, bonded together by God for his grand purpose.

"My DNA…"

"Yes," the visitor replied. "There is no guarantee. But our scientists are hopeful. They say there's a better than fifty–fifty chance." He looked at me. "We hope to meld your DNA with that of our infertile women. There will be no pain or discomfort to you. The decision is entirely yours."

The impact of his words slowly sank in. It was so incredible. And yet somehow it made sense.

He could see the confusion in my eyes. "I know this is a great deal for you to handle all at once. You need time to think, to process everything. But it is your decision to make, Marsha. Take your time. Either way I must leave on the thirty first."

"My birthday…"

"Yes, I know."

We packed my telescope into its case in silence. There was nothing more to say. I glanced down at the marble marker at my feet. Rebekah Martin had been helpless to save her people. I wasn't.

As I started towards the house, his voice touched me. "You look like her, you know… your mother. But you have your father's eyes."

I turned.

The visitor handed me a photograph. Nineteen year old Angie sat in a rocking chair on the front porch of our house. Next to her stood an exceedingly handsome tall man with a dark ruddy complexion and my cerise eyes. In his arms he held a sleeping baby wrapped in a big blue comforter.

I felt the tears return.

Chapter Twenty-Eight

L ife...
Sleep was impossible. I didn't even try. What I needed was to put the evening's remarkable events on temporary hold; lock them away till later. Then I could pull each one out and assimilate the information.

Assimilate... that's the word... I realized I didn't even know his name. That's the word Flaco used: *Assimilation was strictly forbidden*. But Marshal... dad, did assimilate... with mom. And I was the result: half human... half... my God... half... Martian!

A hybrid...

A space seed...

A freak!

NO!

"Not a freak... I'm not a freak!"

"Are you alright, sweetheart?"

I awoke in the basement den, huddled in a fetal position under the big blue comforter. Chaucer lay curled up next to me, purring. There was snow on the TV screen.

"I'm... I'm ok," I replied, wiping sleep from my eyes. "I was just dreaming... can we talk?"

"Honey, you look like you've been crying." Angie took off her jacket and slipped out of her heels. She looked radiant. Her hair was attractively pinned and she wore a green silk blouse and tweed skirt. But it wasn't her clothes. Something about her was different.

"Did you and history guy have a good time?"

She settled into a pillow on the floor next to me. "Oh, yes. He took me... oh... oh, my God..." Mom reached for something on the steamer trunk. "Where..." Her voice trembled. "Where did you get this?"

It was the photograph.

"I... I found it... in the store room... among Potter's things," I said with my best poker face.

It had been real!

"That's dad, isn't it?"

Her eyes glazed. She ran a finger over the figures in the photo as if trying to touch them. Slowly she nodded. "Yes..."

"I'm sorry, mama. I didn't mean to upset you."

"I know honey, I know. I should have told you a long time ago. It's just..."

"Tell me now, please."

Angie relaxed back against the sofa. She stared into the fire. It cast a reddish-pink glow on her pretty face. "It was my first year at West Chester State. Marshal... your father... he was so incredibly handsome... and intelligent. But there was something about him, something I couldn't quite put my finger on. I fell in love with him the moment we met."

I smiled to myself. I thought I knew the feeling.

"We became friends, close friends," she continued. "I knew he cared for me, even loved me. But he never really showed his true feelings. As though he were afraid to, or couldn't for some reason." Angie shook her head slowly. "I didn't care. I was in love. I resolved to give him as much time as he needed... to wait for him."

"What happened?"

"College," she said with an ironic laugh. "College... we were in the middle of mid-terms, doing a lot of cramming. One night... well... you know..." Angie closed her eyes and smiled at the tender memory.

With a deep sight she went on. "When I discovered I was pregnant he became a mother hen. Marshal took such good care of me, fussing over me, driving me to doctor's appointments, making sure I ate right. He was there the day you were born." She picked up the photo and studied it again. "Elvia took this picture the day I brought you home from the hospital."

My eyes grew damp. "He sounds like a great guy."

"Oh, he was. Your father was such a wonderful person."

I moved close to mom, stroking her arm gently. "How come you never told me?"

Angie rested her head back on the sofa, staring up at the ceiling. "Oh, honey, shortly after you were born Marshal said he had to leave, some family emergency back home. But I never saw or heard from him again. I was hurt, felt betrayed. I didn't want you growing up thinking… knowing your father had abandoned you."

A closed file cabinet opened… the one marked *dreams*. "Sometimes there are good reasons for leaving the ones you love," I heard myself say.

Mom turned to me smiling. "You remind me so much of him, always seeing the good in people, in life. You wanna know something, pumpkin?"

"What's that?"

"This is silly, I know, but… inside I've always felt that someday your father would come back."

"He's not coming back, mama." The words hurt. I know they hurt her. But she laughed.

"I know that, honey. Over the past few months I've come to understand and finally admit it to myself. Kinda late maybe… but not too late." Holding up her left hand, she looked at me, her face glowing. She reminded me of a young girl who just experienced her first kiss. Her slender third finger sported a delicate gold band with a most unusual diamond. "I've even decided it's time to get on with my life."

My heart jumped in my chest. "You mean… your history teacher?"

Angie grinned and nodded excitedly. I threw myself into her outstretched arms. "Oh, mama, I love you."

"I love you, too, baby."

The next morning Elvia had scrambled cheese eggs and bacon ready. I slept soundly, peacefully, undisturbed by dreams, or visions, or questions, or decisions. It was a beautiful, crisp day and I couldn't wait to attack it.

Mom, too, looked rested and refreshed, more beautiful than ever. Being in love agreed with her... with both of us.

Later, as we drove to church, she looked over to me. "Hey, kid-o, you wanted to talk about something last night, didn't you? There was something on your mind?"

"It's ok," I replied. "Everything worked out perfectly."

She patted my knee. "That's good. You know the day after tomorrow is your birthday... your eighteenth! We need to do something special."

"Anything you like, mom, as long as it ends with pizza and ice cream and movies."

"You got it, honey."

I gave her a high-five. "Do you think we can do it tomorrow night, though? I won't be around on the thirty-first."

"Sure thing. You've got some big plans for your birthday, I suppose."

Relaxing back in the seat, I wondered if they have extra cheese and pepperoni pizza, and cookies and cream ice cream on Mars. *Yeah... you might say I have big plans,* I thought. *I have a planet to save.*

M Marsha

Angie's Story

ℐ Chapter Twenty-Nine ℐ

Marsha...
Friday June 23, 2000

I was aware of how still the night had grown. A great horned owl no longer marked my progress through the old cemetery with his questioning cries. A dozen other sounds lingering in the background at once became obvious by their silence. It was as if someone had switched off the soundtrack to a beautiful warm June night.

The object appeared out of nowhere. With an almost imperceptible whoosh, like a rush of air through a door suddenly thrust open, a slivery orb slipped from the heavens. It came to rest barely inches above the freshly mowed grass, hovering in an eerie, yet strangely reassuring silence.

The craft was perfectly round, maybe ten feet in diameter. Its surface, smooth, reflective and mirror like, made it difficult to distinguish the object among its surroundings. I stood frozen, uncertain if I were dreaming or hallucinating. Then it opened.

A tall, thin human figure stepped out. Dressed in a charcoal color jumpsuit, he approached, one arm outstretched. Before I could think, and without fear, I accepted his offering. The visitor smiled and nodded, his soft red eyes narrowing into slits. An instant later he returned to his ship. With a gentle whoosh of hot air it disappeared, as if shot from a gun, into the clear summer sky.

I looked down. In my hand I held a large white envelope. It was inscribed with my name in red ink. I recognized the handwriting. It was a letter... a letter from Marsha.

The day my daughter disappeared was the worst day of my life. For all the volumes that have been written – the research, the discussions – the sudden loss of a loved one, especially a child, is an experience that defies description. Your life truly changes, and nothing, not even the simplest things, is ever the same again. When that loss takes the form of a disappearance, the lack of information, the lack of closure, eats away at you like cancer. You never stop wondering or praying. Each time the phone rings; when a stranger knocks at your door, your heart beats faster, your mind races, and the hopes... and fears... the nightmare... begin all over again.

    Marsha is the greatest person in the world. Of course I would say that, I'm her mom. But we share a very special bond, one that transcends that of mother daughter. She is my best friend and our relationship isn't typical.

    Actually, nothing about Marsha is typical. At birth she more closely resembled a loaf of unbaked French bread, with reddish pink skin and not a speck of hair. I was beginning to wonder if she would ever have any hair when the finest, silky strands appeared. Soon she possessed a full head of beautiful sun yellow locks. By the time Marsha was fourteen it had darkened to light honey and reached past her waist. Then she unselfishly cut it to her shoulders and tearfully sent the remains to Locks of Love.

    The remains were considerable since Marsha has always been tall for her age. Yet she remained graceful. Mother Nature was kind, Marsha filled out into a beautiful young woman. Many say we look alike. I should be so lucky. Marsha is stunning, with perfect skin that retained its soft red tint, and a tall, willowy, lovely figure.

    But her most striking feature is her eyes.

    They say all babies are born with blue eyes. Marsha's were almost colorless. One morning, when she was maybe twelve weeks old, I noticed a red tint to her pupils. As you can imagine, I panicked. Scooping her up, I broke several traffic laws getting her to the hospital. The doctors were intrigued but not concerned.

    Over the next several years her eyes were tested regularly. The only surprises were better than perfect sight, and night vision rivaling that of a cat. The red coloring brightened, and then deepened, leaving Marsha with remarkable cerise eyes.

    Doctors have always been intrigued and a bit baffled by Marsha. For a time her reddish pink skin was cause for much discussion. Then, as she started school, a classmate spread his measles to about half the first grade. The childhood illness hit my daughter harder than the other children. Marsha was laid up well over a month.

Elysian Dreams – B.J. Neblett

At one point her pediatrician became concerned about Leukemia. Marsha seemed to have an abnormally high white blood cell count. Other tests showed no signs of the cancer, thank God. It was finally determined that a high count of white and red blood cells was normal for Marsha. Her response, after suffering through the battery of exams and tests, was typically Marsha: *I could have told you that!*

By the time she was declared healthy it was after Thanksgiving. For the next six months I home schooled her. The following September, Marsha returned to the first grade, a little late but at the top of her class.

The greatest thing about my daughter is her heart. She has an unlimited capacity for love, and sensitive feelings that border on empathy. I swear she can feel my emotions.

Marsha's wit and playfulness are unceasing. She can find joy and humor in any situation. And she knows exactly which buttons of mine to push to elicit just the desired reaction. It drives me crazy sometimes but I like the way she oh, so innocently bamboozles me.

Marsha was blessed with a high IQ. She has an unquenchable interest in nearly everything. She spent years searching for her niche, as she calls it. It pains her to see suffering, injustice and human stupidity bent on destroying itself. Marsha is determined to somehow, somewhere make a difference. I believe now she has.

It was Monday, October thirtieth, five long years ago. Elvia, our housekeeper, had breakfast waiting. We live in a ridiculously small town in an old relic I inherited from my great uncle. For all its small town inconvenience, there are worse places than Honeybrook to raise a kid. And Philadelphia is just an hour or so away when the need for urban culture strikes.

Two nights earlier, Saturday, I had been out with a brilliant and sexy teacher at nearby Downingtown High School, where I teach English. When I returned from my date, I found Marsha in our basement den. Marsha's emotions fluctuate more than the stock market. She handles it well. But curled up in a fetal position under her favorite comforter, crying alone, is a bit over the top, even for Marsha. That evening we shared one of those mother daughter heart to heart talks. You know the kind. The kind that makes you feel great about being a parent and turns everything right with the world. That's how I felt this Monday morning.

"Good morning, sweetheart."

Marsha bounced into the sunlit kitchen. "Buenos días, mi madre bonita y señora Elvia." She kissed my cheek and slid into the chair across from me. "It is a beautiful day, isn't it?"

"That's the optimistic, chipper Marsha we all know and love," I replied. "Elvia has your favorite, cinnamon raisin wheat toast and honey. Have you settled on movies for tonight?"

"You decide, Angie. Tomorrow I turn eighteen. That means you have put up with me for eighteen long years. Tonight's your night as much as mine."

That's another thing about Marsha, the way she often calls me by name. I get on her about it sometimes... just to exercise some parental authority. But it makes our relationship special for me. Angie... actually *Angly...* was the first word Marsha spoke as a baby.

We share this movie thing: old movies, pizza, ice cream and pop corn. Discovering old movies is our bonding time. We spend as much time gossiping and talking girl talk as we do watching the screen.

One evening, when she was maybe six or seven, after putting her to bed, I headed down to our basement for some TV. Cable was a little slow getting to Honeybrook, but the local channels provided decent fare. About half way through Key Largo I found a tiny hand amidst the butter pop corn. Unable to sleep, Marsha had slipped under the big blue antique comforter we keep on the sofa. Like mother like daughter I guess. We talked and laughed till dawn, even sharing tears over Humphrey Bogart and Lauren Bacall's bittersweet relationship.

Ever since then, most every Friday or Saturday night you can find us in front of the fireplace, under the comforter, watching some film noir or B movie classic. Marsha loves the cheesy sci-fi and monster movies of the fifties.

This evening we were celebrating Marsha's eighteenth birthday. She was actually born on the thirty first, Halloween, but she said she had plans of some sort. So, with a gallon of Bryer's Cookies and Cream, a giant pepperoni and extra cheese pizza from Mario's of Honeybrook, and

Chaucer the cat and Max our old Great Dane for company, Marsha and I prepared for a night of movies and bonding.

I chose the George Pal trilogy – When Worlds Collide, Destination Moon and Conquest of Space – knowing they are among Marsha's favorites. She was pleased at my selection.

But we spent most of the evening talking at length about my future plans with my teacher boyfriend. He asked me to marry him and I said yes. Marsha was excited and happy for me. Yet, tonight she seemed a bit more serious and a lot more affectionate than usual.

I felt proud of the caring, sensitive young woman sitting next to me. I had no idea it would be the last time we would be together.

❧ *Chapter Thirty* ☙

Me...
I was born towards the end of the baby boom. Dad, like so many other vets fresh out of the service, took advantage of the GI Bill. He and mom settled into one of those cute, albeit cookie cutter tract homes which seemed to be springing up everywhere. Ours was in a sleepy community west of Philadelphia called Marple Township.

Dad landed a good job as service manager at the local Dodge dealer. Mom taught English. When I came along in the summer of '58, Elvis was in the army; Ike was in the White House, and the Russians were in space. An only child, I lived among the playgrounds and shopping centers and community swimming pools and back yard Bar-B-Q's that marked suburban culture. I did well in my classes, attended Sunday school, and was destined to fulfill the American Dream of a safe, secure life in suburbia.

The '60's were a strange time to be a kid. The world was changing. Nearly every day brought a new set of rules, values and morals. The decade teetered between great social reforms and extreme violence; peaceful boom times and a hopeless war; between great achievements and costly failures.

For a young child, the mixed signals generated by a decade of disorder and confusion were near traumatizing. I was too young to comprehend the changes that were taking place. I grew distrustful of the very thing that would mark my life: change.

1971 I was a happy eighth grader when my parents were killed. One night their car was struck head on by a speeding drag racer in the wrong lane. I was sent to live with my only relative, a great uncle I barely knew.

Mom's uncle Potter, actually not a true blood relative, lived in a spooky old house in the country town of Honeybrook. He was a mortician and the town's most eligible senior bachelor. Tall, trim and rugged, he had quite a reputation as a lady's man. An angry, bitter and confused thirteen year old girl was the last thing he needed. His patient, kind, loving and understanding nature was exactly what I needed.

I never knew any of my grandparents. Potter would sometimes relate tall, dubious tales of my grandmother Angelina. I accepted them as just so much entertainment and family lure. The death of my parents hit me hard. For a time I lost all interest in just about everything, even in living. I wouldn't talk; I barely ate anything, lost a dangerous amount of weight, and just managed to get by in school. I do not remember Potter ever raising his voice to me or losing his temper. Evenings, over cups of his special hot chocolate, he would sit and talk with me, patient, loving, as an adult. I listened and understood. And I knew he was right. It did little good. I went from a mute stubborn introvert to well on my way to becoming a juvenile delinquent.

Smoking, drinking and even drugs marked my life. Night after night I would sneak out of the house, shimmying down the old oak tree whose sturdy branches reached up to the small balcony outside my third floor bedroom. I was gaining a reputation in the area as a wild child, and becoming well known to the ever so understanding Honeybrook police. A clear path of self destruction lay ahead.

Potter's housekeeper was Elvia. She and her husband Ramos fled Central America during a revolution. Ramos was a strong, particle man who proudly clung to his Mayan heritage. Making their way to the US, they somehow found themselves living in Honeybrook. At first neither the Amish people nor the newly arrived immigrant couple quite knew what to make of each other. Many evenings I listened to Elvia's funny tales of culture clashes as they made their home here. Her love and strength and worldly wisdom helped pull me through some difficult times. I came to look to her as a surrogate mother.

One spring evening before my fifteenth birthday, Potter took me to his funeral pallor next door to our home. He had just finished preparing a woman in her thirties.

"Tell me what you see," he said. I approached the coffin cautiously. I had never seen a dead person. My parent's service had been closed casket.

"She... she looks like she's sleeping," I managed to reply, "so..."

"Peaceful?"

"Yes, so very peaceful." I found myself staring. She was pretty. Her light honey hair reminded me of my mother's.

Potter placed a hand on my shoulder. "Do you know why she is at peace, my dear?" He didn't wait for my answer. "She knows she's done the best job she could raising her children. She knows that even without her around, they will be just fine."

That evening, as I lay in bed crying, missing my mom, I understood what Potter meant. With his unfailing strength and support, I turned my life around. I found life worth living again. Years later my uncle's words would once more help me to cope with loss.

~

The quiet pace of life in Amish country was beginning to agree with me. My junior and senior years were extremely happy times. Throwing myself into school work, I was determined to make my mom proud. I quickly learned I had inherited grand mom Angelina's love and talent for English and literature. A counselor at school told me good English teachers were always in demand at Downingtown High. My path seemed settled.

I entered West Chester State College in the fall of 1976. It had a good reputation as a teacher's college and was close enough to home to commute. I had come to love our old drafty house, and I clung to the security it, Potter and Elvia provided. Freshman year barely got underway when events conspired once again to change my life.

I was never much of one for dating. A few guys drifted in and out of my life, one more serious than the others. But I was comfortable on my own and found myself pretty much a loaner. Maybe it was a deep seated fear of being abandoned again; some left over baggage from my parent's death. I don't know. So it was all the more surprising and confusing when I fell head over heels in love.

Marshal strode into US History 101 the first day of class and my hormones went on full alert. He was tall, with a thin, lanky but muscular build, and carried himself with grace and confidence unlike any man I ever known.

He sat down next to me. "Hello…"

"Hello..." I felt myself blushing. Trying my best not to stare, I fumbled for my text book. It landed on the floor with a loud, echoing thud.

"On that note... shall we begin?" The teacher, an older distinguished gentleman with a three piece suit, round belly and thinning hair, squinted up at us. "I'm Professor Connolly, and this is of course US History 101."

A devilish smile crossed Marshal's face as he retrieved my fallen book. "He looks old enough to have *lived* history," he whispered.

Professor Connolly provided the introductions. "First order of business is usually assigning work and study groups. Let's see... perhaps you... Miss... err..."

"Hunt, sir," my voice cracked as my ears flushed, "Angela Hunt."

"Yes, Miss Hunt... perhaps you and your friend there would care to pair up?"

Marshal jumped to his feet. "Marshal Walker, Professor." His voice softened and he looked at me. "It would be a pleasure, sir." My already red face and ears glowed brighter.

As class ended, Marshal snatched up my books. "Well, seems like we'll be working closely together this year. Hi, I'm Marshal."

His hand was warm, his touch electric. "I'm... I'm Angela Hunt." It was then I became aware of his eyes. They were red: the soft burning red of an autumn sunset. I became lost in them, mesmerized.

The rest of the day I found myself doodling his name over and over, day dreaming of those beautiful, hypnotic eyes. I was a school girl, a silly school girl with feelings that soared beyond a mere crush.

Marshal and I became fast friends. We were close and spent as much time together as possible. Our friendship grew. I knew I was falling deeply and dangerously in love. I did everything short of screaming, "I love you," to let him know. Marshal remained affectionate but aloof. I didn't care. Something told me he felt the same. I would wait, give him time, all the time he needed.

The holidays came and went. Marshal presented me with a lovely antique gold locket. New Year's Eve we shared an awkward, tender first kiss. Marshal continued to shield his feelings. But I was winning him over slowly, I could tell.

We were often together, spending long hours studying. The close quarters and sometimes intense cramming were beginning to take their toll. One evening, as we lay across his bed, preparing for the next day's test, Marshal closed the book and looked at me. Those gorgeous, mysterious eyes seemed to soften even more. Before I knew it I was in his arms.

When I discovered I was pregnant I wasn't sure how Marshal would feel. I should have known better. Marshal turned into a doting mother hen, taking it upon himself to see to it I ate right and followed doctor's orders. He referred to the life growing inside of me as *our little miracle*, and insisted on being with me when I broke the news to my uncle.

Potter, God bless him, smiled thinly, attempting to maintain parental authority. He looked at me and listened carefully, then shifted his attention to Marshal standing proudly at my side. Finally, he turned to Elvia.

"Well," Potter said, sneaking the housekeeper a wink, "looks like we'll need a nursery."

Marsha was born on Monday, Halloween night, 1977, Marshal in the delivery room with me. There was never any question as to her name.

I was madly in love and set to spend my life raising my daughter with the man who loved and cherished me.

I was mistaken.

Chapter Thirty-One

L ost...
A couple of days after I brought Marsha home from the hospital Marshal left. He said there was some sort of family emergency and he had to go. I had no reason to doubt him. We kissed and he was gone.

Forever.

It's almost funny to think about now, but I didn't even know where he was going. A town that's very far away, *so small even Santa misses it,* was his pat answer whenever asked where he was from. I guess I was just naïve, or in love, actually both. It wasn't until a week or two later that I began to suspect something was wrong.

I was putting away some papers and came upon Marsha's birth certificate. I hadn't noticed before but for some reason the space for the father's name read *unknown*. At first I thought it was a mistake. It wasn't. Marshal reassured me in the hospital the certificate was taken care of. At that moment I knew he was gone.

I was devastated. It was the first time I'd given my trust, my love, completely to another person. That trust had been broken. I determined never to let it happen again, and to protect my daughter as well. It was better Marsha grew up thinking I had made a mistake, been careless, stupid, than for her to know she had been abandoned by her father. Elvia and Potter respected my decision and kept the secret of Marshal.

Of course, I realize now how wrong that decision was. Perhaps I unconsciously punished myself for trusting in another person. I shut down, didn't date, and wouldn't let anyone close. Several guys tried, nice guys, but I pushed them away. I even fooled myself into believing that Marshal would return one day.

School and Marsha became my life. I graduated and headed back to Downingtown High School, this time as an English teacher. The kids took an instant liking to Ms H, as I did to them. I love being an educator.

Barely through my first year, Potter passed away.

His death shook me. Once again one of the most important people in my life was taken. The man who was so understanding and patient when I lost my parents; the man who saved me from myself and the self-destructive path I chose, was gone. I never properly thanked him, told him what his strength and caring meant to me.

We scattered Potter's ashes in the old cemetery across the street. He loved to take long walks there by himself. I remember him telling me when I was maybe fourteen that the dead continue to give off their energy for a long time. And that energy contains their knowledge, their wisdom, and the essence of their lives. That's why people are drawn to the grave side of their loved ones. They can still feel their energy. Potter said he gathered strength and wisdom from his walks in the cemetery. I didn't believe him at the time.

Potter left the old house to me in his will, along with a fair amount of money and some investments which continued to pay dividends. He also took good care of his friend and long time housekeeper. Elvia could have hung up her apron and retire. But she refused to leave me and Marsha. She argued that after all these years she couldn't leave the old house. I knew better. Elvia and Ramos had no children of their own. It was her way of saying we were family.

It was just as well Elvia stayed. My hands were full between the old house, my teaching, and raising Marsha. It seemed like no time at all before she started school. I think the words inquisitive and precocious were invented just for Marsha. To say she was a handful is an understatement.

Life wasn't always easy. Every day that passed Marsha reminded me more and more of her father. She has Marshal's smooth complexion, hers a light pink, and his long, slender, almost exaggerated features. And she has those incredible red eyes of his, Marsha's tinged with brown. Combined with my mom's soft honey blondish hair makes quite a striking combination. She would have had no problem becoming a high fashion model.

But Marsha also inherited her father's questioning nature and thirst for knowledge, to say nothing of his keen wit and playfulness. That playfulness often borders on devilishness. Marsha isn't the hell raiser I was. She finds inventive ways to get into mischief.

Once she told her seventh grade teacher off, certainly grounds for discipline. Only she did it in such a calm, direct matter of fact and convincing way, it was hard to know how to punish her. Especially since essentially she was right.

We had one of those many mother-daughter talks – the ones that often leave me wondering exactly which one is the mother and which one the daughter. Marsha apologized to her teacher, in her own Marsha way, and everything was fine.

As time went by it became evident Marsha had also inherited Marshal's intelligence. She was soaring past her classmates, but never once became bored with school. After another of our talks, I decided not to have her IQ tested as her principal suggested. Marsha stayed with her class, doing extra credit work and taking a few advance classes. She assured me in her oh, so grown up manner that I had made the right decision.

For a time I became concerned about Marsha's lack of dating. She showed typical teen interest in boys and had male friends. But she seemed perfectly happy to spend her time studying or star gazing or watching old movies with me. Seeing what was going on in the world with girls her age, I kept silent and considered myself blessed.

One big romance in Marsha's life, a long time buddy who went from a toad to a hunk – her words – ended when his family moved. I felt for her. Marsha was her usual overly emotional self for a time, but seemed no worse for the wear.

For the most part things fell into a comfortable routine of school, teaching, old movies and learning about life together as we both grew. When Marsha brought Mr. History into my life I was ready for a serious relationship. I just didn't know it at the time.

As I said, after Marshal left I pretty much withdrew from dating. I didn't need any guy with false promises complicating the nice orderly life I managed to make for myself and Marsha. The few dates I did go on were usually at the insistence of well meaning friends. I don't recall any follow up date with any of the *perfect* guys I was set up with. A combination of fear that I would be abandoned again, and stubborn feelings that Marshal would one day return, managed to sabotage any real chances I may have had of moving on. After fifteen years I was still rooted in the hurt and denial stages of loss. Then one day a new teacher came to town.

Part old world sage, part walking history book, he swept into my life, and that of his students like a zephyr. He had the looks and charm of an old time movie star, in the mold of Bogart and Valentino; the manners of a country doctor, and the patience of Job. And, he was single. Mr. History, as he affectionately came to be known, brought history to life for his eager students, and new life to my personal history.

Our first brief encounters in the halls of the high school rattled me. I was instantly attracted to him; yet, his passing glances seemed to be ones of recognition, as if he knew me. I was flattered. If I hadn't been so caught up in my own self pities, I might have attempted my own connection. Thank God for my precocious, interfering daughter.

One evening I arrived home from work late and exhausted, only to find the dining room table set with my mother's good china and a king's feast being prepared in the kitchen. Elvia said one of Marsha's teachers was coming for a conference and she figured dinner would be nice.

Dinner? The house smelled like a gourmet restaurant. I should have guessed the two were up to something. Marsha, who had set the whole thing up, played innocent claiming all she knew was company was coming. And, oh, by the way, she had a stomach ache and tons of homework and she wouldn't be joining us. Naturally it had been one of those days, and I reluctantly climbed into comfortable slacks and a blouse. Then I heard Mr. History's voice at the door.

If I hadn't needed her I probably would have strangled Marsha right then and there. Instead I sent her down to keep him occupied while I attacked my hair, slithered into a dress, and made myself as sexy as possible in twenty minutes.

Marsha vanished like a magician's assistant the moment I made my appearance. "He's in the library," she whispered with a giggle and disappeared.

"Hello, I'm Miss Hunt," I said nervously offering my hand.

"Yes, yes, I know." His voice was soft as a breeze at dawn. I couldn't help but notice him staring at me, studying me. "I mean... I've seen you at the high school. I'm Collin... Collin Crowly..." He continued to stare. I felt like a school girl on her first date.

"I'm... I'm sorry... where... where did you get this?" he placed a book into my hands, his beagle brown eyes glinting.

"Huh... oh..." The worn leather binding was familiar to my touch. "I'd almost forgotten about this." I turned the pages that had brought so much pleasure. "It was my favorite book as a teen. I think I fell in love with the notion of someone being so deeply in love he spends his life trying to get her back. Silly I guess... especially since she was more of a symbol to him."

"Not silly at all..." Collin's smile warmed the room like a log splitting open in a great fireplace. I could feel my ears flush. "A first edition Great Gatsby, signed by F Scott Fitzgerald... must be very rare."

"I suppose... it belonged to my grandmother. I didn't know her, but I understand it was her favorite also. I've been told I look like her."

"She was very beautiful."

Collin's remark returned me from my thoughts. His countenance melted into one of understanding, as thought he'd come to accept something. I felt something move inside of myself as well. Although at the time I didn't, or wouldn't, acknowledge it.

He moved closer. "You carry her name, too, don't you?"

"Yes... yes, I do. Only hers..."

"Was Angelina..."

"How... how did you..."

"Excuse me..." it was Elvia. "Dinner is ready when you are, señorita."

Collin took my hand. It felt warm, natural. We wandered into the dining room. Elvia managed to slip out the back door after serving the main course. I was alone with a handsome, intelligent man who seemed to like me, to know and understand me. We shared a fun, pleasant evening. I never asked him how he knew my grandmother's name. He never volunteered the information. It didn't matter.

Despite my obvious reluctance and sometimes cold responses to his gentlemanly advances, Collin continued to ask me out. He was either terribly smitten or a glutton for punishment. But I could feel the affection growing. I secretly welcomed the increasing attention he showed me, with Marsha's full approval and encouragement, of course. I found out later Marsha and Collin were plotting together. She constantly fed him information about my likes and dislikes; music; books; even my moods. As it turned out her eager interference only shortened the time to the inevitable.

Collin and I found plenty of mutual ground on which to build a relationship. Over the summer of '95 he broke through the walls of my self-built prison. I even finally released the fantasy that Marshal would one day return for Marsha and me. Three days before Marsha's disappearance I accepted Collin's proposal of marriage. I would need all of his strength and support over the next few years.

☙

Marsha's inquisitive nature includes star gazing. She would spend hours in our back yard quietly staring into the heavens. It became obvious this wasn't just a passing phase. I sold one of Potter's stocks and bought her a very sophisticated and powerful telescope.

Marsha never does anything half way. Before, her interests were scattered, along with her energies, on a host of projects and crusades. From ecology to global warming, from nuclear disarmament to homeless pets, no cause is too great or too humble for my daughter. When the telescope arrived she turned into Carl Sagan overnight. She was finally able to scratch that unreachable itch that troubled her for so long: an astronomer was born.

The old cemetery became Marsha's second home. Like Potter, she found the peace and serenity energizing. Isolated from outside distractions, it was perfect for sky watching. Marsha and her telescope became one. It was an extension of her personality, at once revealing and questioning.

The summer of '95 was a time of change for Marsha and me. I was seeing a lot of Collin Crowly. He remained stubbornly determined to win me over. Finally I admitted to myself what everyone else knew all along – I was in love.

Elysian Dreams – B.J. Neblett

The shroud of pain and confusion that veiled my thoughts of Marshal lifted. It was well past time to move on. I surrendered to the reality that Marshal would never return. And I surrendered to Collin.

We spent a wonderful week together in Atlantic City. I discovered a warm, kind, sensitive man, one who cared deeply for me and Marsha.

That summer, while I rediscovered love, my daughter was struggling with depression. She was headed for her senior year and adulthood confused about the future. I kept a close motherly eye on her. Marsha spent her vacation searching far across the heavens and deep within. Somewhere in-between the two she found herself. By the time school started Marsha was back to her old energetic, demonstrative self.

In October Collin proposed marriage and I accepted. My excitement was tempered as I returned home to find Marsha huddled under the blue comforter, upset and crying. She had come across an old picture of Marshal and me. That evening we talked late into the night about her future plans as well as my own; about life and love; but mostly about her father.

Three days later, October 31, 1995, Marsha's eighteenth birthday, started like any other Tuesday.

"Good morning, sweetheart."

Marsha hugged my shoulders, kissing my cheek as she entered the kitchen. "Good morning, mother, what a glorious day!"

"Mother? My, aren't we formal today? It's Elvia's day off. I poured your raisin bran and the toast should pop any minute. And oh, in case I neglected to mention it… happy birthday young lady!"

Marsha beamed across the table. "I believe you did mention something like that… about a bazillion times. But thank you again. And thank you for last night."

"Thank you, Marsha. You know I'm going to miss our movie nights together. Senior year is always a busy and hectic and exciting time. Then before you know it you'll be in college. Gosh. I feel old!"

We both laughed.

"You'll never be old, mom. Besides, you'll have your history guy. And you won't have to put up with my monsters and outer space anymore. You and your *husband*," she exaggerated the words, throwing in a twisted face for good measure, "can indulge yourselves in all the sappy romances you can stomach. Have you two set a date yet?"

"We were thinking perhaps May, before it gets too hot."

The toaster went pop and Marsha moved to retrieve her toast. I sneaked two small, finely wrapped packages on to her plate.

"You will be my maid of honor, won't you, pumpkin?"

A shadow crept across her smile. "Of course I will, mom... I ... what... what's this?" She snatched up one of the gifts.

"Oh, gee... I don't know. Must be from the birthday fairy."

Marsha glanced at the tag and then tore into a long thin box wrapped in blue foil and white ribbon. "It's from Elvia and Ramos," she explained.

The package contained a lovely gold charm bracelet. Dangling from the delicate chain links were an opal birthstone, a tiny telescope, and dog and cat charms.

"Oh, Angie... look..."

She studied the thoughtful gift, and then eagerly fastened it around her slender right wrist. Her eyes landed on the smaller box covered in pink.

"Let me guess... this must be from Max..." she said, unwrapping it.

"No, silly.... from Chaucer," I teased.

Wide eyed, Marsha held up the antique gold locket and chain Marshal gave to me all those many Christmases ago.

"Oh... it's so beautiful! It..." She found the latch. "Oh. My, God... Oh, mama..."

Inside the locket was a small picture of me at nineteen. Next to it was a photo of Marshal holding his three day old daughter. Marsha's emotions went on full effect. We cried as we hugged, so hard I had to re-do my eye make-up.

That evening Marsha's car sat in the driveway but the house was empty. I was already concerned. Marsha hadn't been at school all day. Several telephone calls home went unanswered. My concern turned to worry. Skipping school was not something Marsha would do. Nor would she leave without telling me where she was going and with whom. Calls to a number of her friends yielded nothing. By eleven PM worry gave way to panic and I phoned Collin.

Collin is a loving, caring man, and at the same time strong and particle. His patience and reassurance that night brought back memories of Potter. With a tenderness I hadn't known for years, he reminded me how headstrong Marsha could be at times. And of the fact it was her birthday. And she had mentioned she had plans. I felt better, but it wasn't enough. After midnight Collin phoned the Honeybrook police. As he set the phone down I tried to read his expression.

"Well..."

Collin took my hand and sat on the sofa next to me. He gently brushed back the hair from my eyes. Still in my school clothes, I had been crying off and on. I must have looked a sight. Collin's face showed genuine love and concern.

"Well... I'm afraid there's not much to be done," he began. "The police seem to agree that Marsha is probably just celebrating her birthday and lost track of the time. The fact that she is eighteen makes her an adult. You'll have to wait at least seventy two hours before you can make any kind of official report. Even then they doubt it would come too much." Frustration showed in his soft chocolate eyes.

"Anything else?"

He frowned. "They did ask if Marsha is on any kind of medication or has been depressed or in any kind of trouble. They wanted to know..." Collin forced a smile, "to know if she left a note."

I felt my heart stop.

"Are you telling me the police think my daughter... that Marsha may have... have committed... oh, Collin, that's... that's just unthinkable!"

Collin touched my cheek. My eyes began to well up again. "Hey, let's not jump to anything. They are just being thorough, trying to think of everything." He held my chin in his hand. "Could Marsha have left a note?"

I tried to think. "I went through the house when I got home. We usually leave each other messages on the blackboard in the kitchen. But there was nothing."

"Humm... maybe the den... on the TV?" Collin patted my leg and helped me up. "C'mon, I'll look down here, you take the upstairs."

I pulled Collin to me and kissed him.

"What was that for?"

"For being here," I replied and headed up the stairs.

A cold chill seized me as I entered Marsha's darkened room. I flipped the light switch. On the bed Chaucer stretched and yowled in protest.

Or was he trying to tell me something?

I crossed the room. Something caught my eye. A large white envelope rested against Marsha's pillow. *Angie* was written in red ink on the front. It was Marsha's handwriting.

Chaucer meowed and rubbed against me, purring as I sat down on the bed. Nervously I opened the envelope. A paper cut stung my finger. I began to read:

Tuesday, October 31, 1995

For Angie

I was about ten when they began...

I don't know how long I sat there. The images of what I read played over in my mind. Slowly, I became aware of Collin. He must have come looking for me. Now he sat next to me reading Marsha's note, his expression intense, his jaw set.

Finally he lowered the last page. A smile crossed his face.

"Thank God she's alright," he said looking off at nothing. "And it would seem Marsha may get her chance to save a world after all."

"Collin, please... how can you joke about this?"

He looked at me. "I wasn't joking."

He was serious.

"You... you believe this?"

"Why wouldn't I?"

That was a good question. "Well... I... I don't know... I mean... Mars? It's just..."

"I know... a little fantastic."

"Yes."

"Angela, I teach history. I love what I do and love history. You know that." Collin turned to face me. His words were soft, sincere, as his eyes found mine.

"What do we tell our kids? They need to study and know about history, understand and learn from it. Yet, what proof do we offer them? A few pieces of broken pottery... some drawings scratched into cave walls... paintings of some strangers supposedly in the act of some noble or heroic deed? That kind of evidence would hardly stand up in a court of law.

"So, how do we know that there ever really was a guy named Columbus? Or Caesar... or Confucius? How do we know about the adventures of Alexander the Great? Or the grandeur of the Pharos of Egypt? Or the wisdom of the Greeks? How? Because somebody took the time to write it down. Even the greatest mystery of the universe, the belief in an Almighty Creator, was given to us through the written word, leaving us to believe."

He paused and smiled reassuringly, holding up Marsha's note. "When the written word is all you have... it becomes your truth... until something comes along to prove otherwise."

Collin kissed my cheek, tenderly wiping a tear. "Can you tell if anything is missing, what she may have taken?"

I glanced around the room. "No, not really. Just her bible. She always keeps it on her nightstand. And maybe a few books."

"Which books?"

"I don't know... is it important?"

"No, not really I guess. But... which books would you take?"

Collin's words made sense. But still I just didn't know. It wasn't that I believed what I read. It was more that I didn't disbelieve it. If what Marsha had written wasn't true that left only two possibilities: Marsha had been taken by someone against her will – but then how and why the long, detailed note? It didn't make any sense. And the possibility that Marsha had taken her own life was just too ridiculous to consider.

No... Marsha was alive, well. She had left of her own accord for some reason. There had to be something to her note. Collin's calm assurances did little to settle my confusion. I remained incredulous. I wished I could feel as certain as he did. I wanted desperately to believe... in something.

Potter's words that spring evening in the funeral pallor before my fifteenth birthday came back to me: *She knows*, he said, *she's done the best job she could raising her children. She knows that even without her around they will be just fine.*

Chapter Thirty-Two

. . . and found.

I refused to believe any harm had come to my daughter. Marsha was fine, wherever she was.

For a while my dreams were peppered with vivid images and confusing symbols. I saw Marsha surrounded by strange alien figures. Sometimes she was taken forcibly, abducted by little green and silver men with big red eyes. Marshal came to me in dreams also. He reached out, trying to speak, but remained mute. As the days passed, a new, frightening reality settled over me.

I must have re-read Marsha's note a hundred times. Collin and I agreed it was best not to show it to the police – it would do no good. But as the shock of Marsha's disappearance sank in, the full impact of her words struck.

If I were to believe my daughter's message then Marshal, her father, the man I loved, was… was from Mars. I stubbornly refused to accept it, and yet, it made sense. Marshal loved me. I knew it, felt it. I never stopped believing it. It was his leaving me that didn't make any sense.

Something Marsha said haunted me. It was the night we talked about her father. "Sometimes there are good reasons for leaving the ones you love," she said. She knew that night she was going to leave. She was telling me so. Now, here was the explanation, one that, as preposterous as it sounded, not only made sense, but answered many questions. Not just about Marshal, but about Marsha as well: her skin; her eyes; her intelligence; her unusual physiology; even her deep interest in space.

It made sense. But it didn't help much. I missed my daughter.

A few days after Marsha left, Collin and I sat down with Elvia and Ramos and read them Marsha's note. Elvia had been emotionally distraught, physically sick with worry for her beloved Niña loco. I worried about her health and mental state. I wasn't sure showing them the note was the best idea. But an odd thing happened.

Elvia and Ramos listened carefully without comment. As Collin finished I didn't know what to expect. The old couple spoke to each other quietly in Spanish for a few minutes. Then Elvia looked at me questioning.

"Señorita Angela, why did you not tell us this before? My husband and I, we have been crazy with worry for Señorita Marsha. Now you tell us she is fine," Elvia said, shaking her head.

Collin looked as uncertain as I. Maybe they didn't understand. He started to speak but was interrupted by Ramos.

"Por favor, escusa. I see you are confused," Ramos began. "Please allow me to explain. Elvia and I, we come from an old people with many old beliefs. Some call them... how do you say... superstitions. Our people studied the heavens many, many years before your telescopes and rocket ships. The idea of others like us living in other places is not new to us. We believe in one power, a Holy Power that set us here, as he set others on other bodies. It is part of our faith, our beliefs, not a question to us."

Ramos smiled; his eyes glistened with the wisdom of ages. "You have heard no doubt of our calendar. Many make a great deal about it. To the Mayan it is simple. December 22, 2012 is an important date in my culture. This Holy Power will return to us around that time. Then the new life, the *tiempo Nuevo*, will begin. That is why our calendar stops. It does not signal an end but rather a new beginning, a time when the power will return for his children, no matter where they are.

"It has been said that our people disappeared... vanished into the jungle. We believe that many were taken up, transported in shining orbs which fell to earth and then returned to the sky in silence."

Ramos looked lovingly at his wife. "So, you see," he tapped Marsha's note still in Collin's hand, "this does not surprise us, no. Señorita loved the heavens... she understood. This tells us that Marsha is fulfilling her destino, as the Holy Power has planned. Your Nina is safe."

"A universe wide community..."

"What was that, honey?" Collin asked.

"Something Marsha told me... a long time ago. We were watching one of her space movies." I tried to remember back. "Marsha believed in a universe wide community, that we are all somehow connected."

I looked at Ramos and Marsha's words returned to me: "Bound together... together by God for his own grand purpose."

Elvia and Ramos smiled back their understanding. "Exactly," Ramos said softly.

❧

Time passed. I survived on faith, faith in my daughter and the loving God in whom she believed. Collin and I married in May as planned. We held a small service in the back yard, under a big, bright full moon. There was no maid of honor. I could feel Marsha beside me.

Life became more bearable, bearable but not any easier. I never stopped listening for Marsha to come bounding down the stairs, or expecting to see her grinning up at me from the breakfast table. Evenings, rocking quietly on the front porch, I could see her moving silently with her telescope among the shadows of the old cemetery across the street. I found myself sky gazing more and more, just as I watched Marsha doing so many times. I began to understand her love of the beautiful heavens and the mysteries they hold.

The first anniversary of her disappearance was the hardest. Reluctantly, I agreed to accompany Collin into the old cemetery. This would be my first time there since before Marsha left. It was time to face some demons; time for some closure.

October 31, 1996 was chilly with a biting breeze out of the northeast. Collin held on to me as we made our way among the rustling leaves and stoic markers. We found the family plot Marsha mentioned. Rebekah Martin lived thirty six years after the loss of her family. I could feel her strong presence, just as Potter had said. Studying the sky, I wondered how many years I would spend missing my daughter.

Collin, as always, remained strong. I know I never would have made it without him. I thought about the night he proposed; how excited and happy Marsha was for me. Knowing I would have Collin must have made her decision to leave easier. Despite Collin's firm belief that Marsha was fine in her new home, I could tell he missed her too. I loved him for that.

In the spring of 1997 Ramos passed away quietly in his sleep. We buried him in the old cemetery he loved and looked after. Elvia picked out a lovely spot on a hill. It overlooked the town they had adopted for their home.

To my knowledge the only time Elvia had been in the cemetery was when we scattered Potter's ashes. Yet she seemed familiar with the sprawling graveyard. When we came upon the chosen hill side she paused to look to the heavens. Then she nodded approvingly and said, "Here, this is the place, *un lugar por dos,* room for two."

She placed a hand to my cheek, looking into my eyes. "You must come here often, at night. And do not be afraid, mi Corazón. It is a friendly, welcoming place."

At the time I thought she was telling me not to be afraid of death.

A month later, Elvia joined her beloved husband.

I have to admit I could never bring myself to believe my daughter was living on Mars. Despite Collin's acceptance and assurance; despite Elvia and Ramos' explanation; despite Marsha's note; despite all the evidence, I found I just couldn't accept the fact.

Yet, I had no explanation of my own. Marsha was safe and well, I felt it, sensed it, and knew it. That was all that mattered.

Months slipped into years. Life settled down to a comfortable routine. It was strange not having Elvia around to look after me. The house seemed empty, barren. Elvia was gone. Marsha was gone. Even Max, our old Great Dane, had quietly passed on. It wasn't so much a home anymore as it once seemed, just a house.

Still, I loved the old place. I stubbornly kept Marsha's room just as she left it. Collin understood. He and I began a wonderful life together and I love him more every day. He seems to embody the best qualities of every man I ever knew: my father's strength and practicality; Potter's patience and understanding; Marshal's tenderness and playfulness; Ramos' wisdom. And he loves me deeper than I ever dreamed anyone would. It's as if fate destined us to be together.

Monday, June 19, 2000, four days ago.

I stood beside Elvia's grave. The night was once again still; silent. The air shimmered, like a mirage. As the slight heat generated by the sphere dissipated, the cemetery came back into focus.

Had it been a dream... a hallucination?

A light breeze stirred up. It was cool against my bare arms and brought goose bumps. It rattled the white envelope clutched in my right hand.

Angie... the red letters were Marsha's. There was no mistaking her personal, elaborate cursive style, the one she used for greeting cards and Christmas packages.

After Elvia's death I found myself wandering through the old cemetery, often alone and at night, just as Elvia had said; just as Potter used to do. It was strangely comforting, energizing.

I visited Elvia and Ramos and Rebekah Martin frequently. Potter had been right. I was drawn there and could still feel their presence, as well as Marsha's.

Looking down at the envelope again, a chill ran through my body. I wanted to tear it open and read my daughter's words. Instead I placed a kiss with my fingertips to the simple marker. "Thank you, Elvia," I whispered, and headed across the street.

Collin was in the library reading Abner Doubleday's *Chancellorsville and Gettysburg.* It was his prized possession, a first edition. I found it at a curious antique book store off City Line Avenue and presented it to him on our first anniversary.

He smiled up at me from his leather chair. "Did you enjoy your walk?"

I just stood there mute.

"Are you ok, sweetheart?"

Slowly I raised my right hand. Collin's eyes dropped to the envelope. He, too, recognized the hand writing.

As anxious as I was, I acquiesced to Collin's gentle urgings for patience. As always he was right. We poured some iced tea and then settled down on the sofa. I relaxed enough to explain the events in the cemetery: the sudden arrival of the sphere; the strange figure with the red eyes.

Collin said nothing. He nodded and kissed my forehead. Then he nervously slit open the sealed envelope. He read Marsha's words aloud, one hand tenderly holding mine.

Finishing the last page, Collin and I sat in silence for a long time. My mind raced. Marsha's letter begat as many questions as it answered. Once again I was torn by extraordinary circumstances and the need to believe. I looked to my husband. He was lost in deep thought. A tear touched my arm. I was softly crying.

Collin looked up from his thoughts and studied the room around him. Placing his hand on my knee, he turned. The smile I knew and loved gave some reassurance.

"Well," he sighed at last. "We have a lot to do."

I didn't understand. Collin read my eyes and let out a laugh, "Before Friday."

"What do you mean?"

With his usual patience and confidence, Collin took charge. There had never been any question in his mind.

"We have to close up the house," he said. "I'll contact Tony, our attorney, and write up some instructions. He'll be glad to look after things here. We should close out our accounts and sell the stocks... sell the cars, too... we'll probably be gone a long time. Of course the school will need to be notified so they can find replacements."

"Wait... slow down. Sell... gone? What are you talking about? Gone where?"

Collin ran his hand around my neck and kissed my lips. He looked at me, shaking his head and grinning. "To see your daughter, of course... to see Marsha."

"But..." The impact of Marsha's letter hit home. "Marsha... Marsha's on Mars..."

His eyes squinted and his smile grew. "Friday night... we have a flight to catch."

Sleep was nearly impossible. The next four days passed in a fog. I went through the motions, barely aware of what I was doing. At times I felt as if I were dreaming. I would suddenly awake to find Marsha here, as if I'd been in a coma or something, like in the movies: Dorothy coming to on the farm after the tornado.

Through it all one reassuring thought kept repeating: I was going to see Marsha again.

Even now, as I read over what I have written, I can scarcely believe it myself. When Marsha went away she left behind a note, an explanation. Thought neither Collin nor I have any family, I felt compelled to do the same. *Like mother, like daughter*, Marsha is fond of saying.

Whoever may read this I ask you please keep an open mind. Try and understand, as I have come to understand. Elvia's words that day in the old cemetery were not about death. She was referring to life, telling me not to be afraid. The universe is indeed a friendly, welcoming place. And we are very much a part of the universe: a community of beings, placed here, and throughout the heavens, by God; all of us connected, bound together, for His own grand purpose.

I believe that purpose can be summed up in a single verse – Matthew 22:39:

Love your neighbor as yourself.

Wherever he may be...

As for Collin and I, we are off to be with Marsha.

Angelia C. 6/23/2000

A Letter Home

༄ Chapter Thirty-Three ༄

Wish You Were Here
3.69 Smedas 027

Monday, April 17, 2000 (Earth time)

Tsenoch Nadir, Elysium (Elysium Planitia)

Dearest Mom,

I pray this letter finds you well and happy. I think about you constantly and pray for you and Collin every day. I also pray that someday you will come to understand the things I have done, and my reasons behind them. If not understand, then perhaps you can accept and forgive my behavior.

Remember our talk that Saturday night when you told me about my father; how, despite his love for you, he had left? Remember I told you that sometimes there are good reasons for leaving the ones you love. I knew that this was something I had to do… my destiny if you will. But I also knew that if I tried to talk with you about it, or even tried to rationalize it to myself, I would falter; I would lose my confidence and never be able to leave.

Of all the things you have given to me, mom, your strength is my most precious gift. It was only through that strength that I was able to come to my decision, the right decision.

I am sorry for the pain and anguish that my leaving must have caused you. I never wanted to hurt you. I take consolation in the fact that I truly am my mother's daughter. And in knowing that you would have done the same. You taught me well, mom. You taught me to love and to care, and to never turn my back on those in need, wherever, or whoever, they may be. The greatest Commandment: *Love thy neighbor*. For that I thank you, mom.

I can't begin to tell you how much I miss you and Elvia and Collin. When I think about the old house my eyes puddle. But my tears are happy ones, tears of joy for the fond memories and wonderful life you and I shared. It's those poignant memories which get me through the difficult and lonely times.

At night, if you listen carefully, you can sometimes hear the hollow Martian wind as it sweeps the sullen landscape. It's an empty sound that carries with it ghosts, ghosts of warm yellow sunshine, and steel horseshoes on blacktop; of Elvia's cinnamon honey wheat toast, and bright harvest moons, and Trick or Treating with friends; of snuggling under the big blue comforter, and extra cheese pepperoni pizza, and of all our night talks. It's when I miss you the most, mom.

Yet, I have been blessed. I have found a new home here, a new home and a new life. It's a life more full and challenging and crazy and rewarding than any I could ever have imagined in any of my wild dreams. It's a life I have come to love.

Often I feel as if I am living a dream; that I will suddenly awake and find myself at home with you and Max and Chaucer, as in a movie. Through it all one thought keeps me going: I never doubt that we will see each other again.

So much has happened that I scarcely know where to begin. By now I imagine you understand things as they are, strange as they are. I know Collin, with his calm, thoughtful, knowing manner, has helped you to accept this is all very real. I know how much he loves and cares for you. I saw it in his eyes, the way he looks at you. The two of you have such an amazing love which seems to transcend time itself. You were truly destined to be together.

I know what you are thinking, Angie. Right now you are shaking your head, saying to yourself, "A hopeless romantic… I raised a hopeless romantic." Perhaps so, but like mother, like daughter. But knowing you and Collin found each other, seeing how strong your love is, made my decision that much easier. I knew I was leaving you in good hands.

I think I knew what my decision would be that very night I met Flaco. Perhaps, in a way, I've known all of my life. Walking back to the house that night I felt a strong sense of purpose. For the first time in my life I could feel myself starting to fit in, to belong. That burning desire to make a difference would at last be fulfilled.

As the day approached, I became comfortable with my new identity. It fit, like a pair of well wore jeans, friendly and satisfying. I looked forward to the adventure ahead. Flaco was waiting for me just after dark. He looked stunning and handsome in his charcoal jumpsuit.

By the way, his name is Braam. In his language it means exalted or charmed. Ironic isn't it? Remember how you always teased me about holding out for a Prince Charming? And now I have found him.

But I am getting ahead of myself.

October 31, 1995, the day of my eighteenth birthday, I awoke with a sense of purpose. My stomach was a battleground of emotions – nothing new for me, I know – confused, conflicting feelings about leaving. And about what I was leaving. It was all I could do to struggle through breakfast, knowing it was the last time I would see you. After you left for school I must have cried for two hours. Sad tears; happy tears; confused tears. There was no question in my mind about going. Yet everything which lay ahead, the known and the unknown, began to come into a sharp stinging focus. I was frightened. So much was at stake. What if I failed? What if I couldn't help?

I finally managed to get my eccentric emotions somewhat under control around ten. I spent the rest of the day finishing the note. It turned into more of a book than the personal note I intended... sorry. But it was good for me to get it all out. It put things in proper perspective for me; made it easier.

Before I knew it, it was time to go. You'd be home soon and I knew if I saw you again I would stumble. I spent the early evening wandering around town, saying my good-byes to Honeybrook, I guess you might say. Around dark I headed over to the cemetery.

It was a cool night. A waxing moon played tag with the wispy clouds in the witch's sky, while little ghosts and goblins played Trick or Treat. I found Flaco, Braam, waiting for me by Rebekah Martin's grave.

"You knew I'd come, didn't you," I asked.

"Let's just say I had faith in you."

Braam's warm smile helped me understand I was doing the right thing. Rebekah Martin's strong presence reassured me I was doing it for the right reasons. "'By faith Abraham obeyed when he was called... and he went out, not knowing where he was going'," I heard myself reply.

Braam nodded and accepted my shoulder bag. "You know your Bible."

His words surprised me. "You are familiar with the Bible?"

"Remember, Marsha, I told you we are not that different."

"You have the Bible?"

"Yes... only we call it *Craedo*."

He took my arm and we began to walk. I felt foolish. Along with my photo album, some clothes, my Walkman and CD's, and a few of my favorite books, the bag contained my Bible, the one you gave me on my eighth birthday, grand mom Lace's Bible. "I guess I should have realized... 'By faith we understand that the universe was ordered by the word of God'."

"Exactly, Marsha. You'll find the names may be strange to you; the stories of our people and their creation may differ from your own. But there is still only one and the same Creator... one God."

Braam's words touched me; encouraged me. I think it was right then and there I knew for sure I was in love with him. It felt right. And I could read affection in his mystical eyes; in his voice; in his touch. I recalled what you told me about dad, how you made the decision to wait; give him whatever time he needed. I made the same decision.

We walked deep into the cemetery, to a beautiful vacant hillside which overlooked the town. Preoccupied with my thoughts, I didn't notice it at first. The shiny, mirror like surface created a natural camouflage. With a hiss the sphere, which hovered silently about a foot off the ground, opened. Braam took my hand and we stepped inside, the sphere closing around us.

It was like being inside a round glass elevator. "Welcome, Marsha. Please, do not be afraid." A tall, slender man, also wearing a charcoal jumpsuit, greeted us. "This is just a small EMV conveyance – an electromagnetic vehicle. It will take us to the waiting ship. Please, be seated and just relax." With that he turned to the simple control panel.

Not sure what to expect, I sat back in a leather like lounge chair and braced myself. Braam settled in next to me, giving the pilot an amused look. I didn't understand. Then I noticed we were already rising rapidly. But there was no sense of motion.

"Zero point energy," Braam explained.

"Isn't that something like anti-gravity?"

He grinned and nodded, "Something. We are able to latch onto the gravitational waves of a planet or other object, pinpointing its exact frequency. Then we send out a similar frequency. The combined waves are dispersive allowing us to manipulate the speed and intensity of the wave. By combining the transverse waves either in-phase or out-of-phase, the amplitude of the gravitational wave is multiplied or attenuated, pushing or pulling our craft to or from the object. The trick is to focus the frequencies and keep them highly directional."

"Earth Vs the Flying Saucers."

"How's that?"

"Oh, nothing… just one of my old movies. Sounds like what they were using."

"I see." Braam's brow wrinkled in deep contemplation. "I would very much like to see this documentary. It must have been greatly advanced for its time."

I smiled, conjuring up visions of the funny stiff legged robots and schlocky saucers of the old black and white B movie. If only he knew. But then, why not? The history of earth science is that of science fact following science fiction. The facts were that I was here, traveling through space using a method dreamed about on earth fifty years ago.

The trip to the moon took about nine hours. And as yet we were traveling relatively slow, I learned. I hardly noticed the time; I was so absorbed with the view. It was incredible, Angie, stars so sharp and brilliant, like precious jewels on a lush carpet of black velvet. It seemed as though I could reach out and touch them.

And the earth receding behind us, so blue and beautiful, and so fragile looking caused tears to well up in my eyes.

"It is a beautiful world, isn't it," Braam said.

He was right. It was a sight I shall never forget. Sometime later Braam presented me a lovely framed picture of our earth taken at that moment as we sped away.

We rendezvous with a large ship hovering in place on the far side of the moon. As we skirted the gray lunar surface, I could make out the Alps to the north. Next the Imbrium Plain – the Sea of Rains – came into view, towered over by the weathered majestic lunar Apennines range. Then everything turned a hazy black as we arrived on the dark side.

A section of the waiting ship yawned open and our tiny transport entered the great sphere. The *Sarlein*, named for a famous Martian scientist, was spacious and comfortable. It was kinda like being on board a jumbo jet, only round, if that makes any sense. I was shown to a small, pleasant cabin with a wonderful view looking forward. It was eerie and awesome to lie in my bunk and watch the stars slowly carousel about me. I took to the journey like a bird on wing. Braam said I was a natural born astronaut.

On board with us was Klaatu, the pilot, who had shuttled us in the smaller sphere; Klrif his navigator and second in command; Yolire who saw to meals and everyday operations; and Vana, an incredibly beautiful young woman with gentle silvery colored eyes and long silky onyx hair. She was the Sarlein's engineer, and delighted in showing me over the impressive vehicle.

Vana explained Sarlein employed the same highly concentrated zero point energy propulsion. We were literally being pulled to Mars at incredible speeds. With Mars at a point fairly close to earth, our trip would take but a couple of earth months. The ship's round shape and plastic-like construction made it invisible to radio, radar and electrical waves, while our speed and black mirror finish made us virtually impossible to see.

During the long, sometimes lonely hours, Vana tutored me on Martian life and basic Pentriux, her planet's language. Easily converted to our alphabet, I found Pentriux not too different from English. While I studied to learn the Martian tongue, Vana told me that English and all things Earthly was the latest fad with her people.

We spent endless hours in the observation deck sharing stories of our families, our homes and our lives. I learned Vana volunteered to be one of the first Martian women to receive my DNA. I was glad for her company and we became close friends.

The approach to Mars is an experience beyond words. A tiny orange-red ball at first, my new home quickly grew in size and splendor with each passing day. It wasn't long before Phobos and tiny Deimos came in to view. Mars' twin moons are little more than oddly shaped rocks caught in the planet's gravity. Phobos does rise and set three times a day. I wondered what affect that would have on earthly poets, song writers and lovers. Vana laughed when I said the two satellites reminded me of a pair of Idaho potatoes.

Soon the dusty rust red surface could be discerned along with windswept sand seas to the north, and high sloping mountains worn smooth by eons of global dust storms. Mars does indeed have an atmosphere, albeit a thin one. Braam likened it to living somewhere on Mount Everest.

There were also numerous ancient craters. Earth's half mile wide depression called Victoria Crater is dwarfed by the equatorial *Valles Marineris*. The massive canyon system is four times deeper, six times wider, and ten times longer than the Grand Canyon. At its western edge stands the awesome *Olympus Mons* extinct volcano. The largest mountain in the solar system, it towers fifteen miles above the impressive *Tharis Bulge*.

Vana explained some of the lines Percival Lowell erroneously interpreted as canals and channels were actually cracks and fissures created by the extremes of temperature on the surface. These temperatures, she said, could range from a pleasant equatorial 70 degrees during the summer day, to a frightening minus 190 degrees at polar winter night. Surprisingly, I found the climate to be much milder.

Our destination was the enigmatic *Sedona Formation*. A full square mile in size, the iconic *face* of Mars was originally fashioned countless centuries ago by a mysterious and long forgotten people. An orange-pink rising sun cast its pall as we descended into the left *eye* of the famous countenance. The planet's small population lives underground in beautiful stone and crystal cities called *nadirs*. Beneath the rugged surface, a balmy temperature is maintained year round. I learned the Martian population, Pentria as they call themselves, derive power from geothermal energy produced by the planet's volcanic system. Also, below the surface there is an ample supply of ground water delivered by a system of rivers and courses. In this way Lowell was actually right.

The beautiful Sarlein, my home these past months, disappeared through a thin layer of fog into the left eye of Sedona. About nine hundred feet below the surface we began to travel horizontally, through a long, winding natural cavern, pulled forward by an artificially produced magnetic field. It was early Martian day yet a great crowd had gathered. As the Sarlein came to rest in its metallic cradle a roar such as I never heard arouse. Braam said the din was for me. I felt my stomach go queasy. It never occurred to me that I would be a celebrity. With Braam's steady arm to lean on and Vana by my side for moral support, I stepped out into a comfortable amber day.

I found the subterranean Martian atmosphere surprisingly rich and sweet. Mars is abundant in andesite rock. The Pentria refine the resource for its silicon which they use in hundreds of products. The process also cleans and treats trapped oxygen, enriching the sub terrestrial living quarters, and adding to the thin surface air. Lush green plants abound underground, supplementing the oxygen supply. My body quickly adjusted to the thinner atmosphere and lighter gravity of my new home.

As I looked around and waved to the multitude of cheering Pentria, the full impact of my mission finally struck. So much was depending on me. So many excited yet sad silvery eyes pleaded. So many beautiful rosy faces full of hope and anticipation smiled up at me. I could almost read their thoughts: *This slip of a girl has come to save us? She is so young... so pale...* I wanted to run away and hide, find solitude under the old blue comforter. My emotions were cresting. I looked to Braam, finding strength and assurance in his calm, genteel ruby eyes and burning smile. Bolstered by his presence, the three of us, Braam, Vana and I, boarded a waiting conveyance of a monorail design. We were whisked away to a delightful, secluded home. At my request Vana stayed with me, helping me with the transition. She told me I could take as much time as I needed at the quiet retreat which had been prepared just for me.

Life at my hideaway was not dissimilar to the serene surroundings of Honeybrook. We were on the outskirts of a small industrial nadir whose populace mainly served the andesite reclamation plant and the nearby Sedona space port. The artificially magnified sun causes the red Martian atmosphere to glow a stunning pellucid amber-yellow below ground, much like an earthly harvest sunset. Pentria actually translates loosely to *Amber People*. Nights are a mystical inky blue, while the geothermal energy maintains the temperature at a constant early spring like feeling. I can't honestly say I didn't miss the feel of the summer sun's warmth on my skin. All Pentrian women have haunting silver eyes with delightfully deep pink skin. My attempts to explain earthling's preoccupation with sun tanning to Vana met with comical, confused expressions.

The Pentria have an interactive form of television. Their programming consists of cultural, historic and news events, with an odd form of slapstick comedy I'm still learning to appreciate. It's something between Inspector Cluesau, the Three Stooges and Monty Python. Vana said the Pentria pride themselves on being a peaceful, intellectual and cultural race. Their raucous comedy provides them with necessary diversion. It reminded me of a quote from a poster of Einstein which used to hang over my bed. The great thinker, who enjoyed reading comic books, said something like, "The higher the intellect the greater the need for simple release." I soon discovered that despite their wealth of cerebral pursuits, the Pentria are not unlike us in their fascination with celebrity. And my arrival was the number one topic of the Martian press and discussion programs. It took me a while to get used to seeing my face on the nightly news.

One night Vana and I sat up late gabbing and munching on *Isentu*, a buttery flavor popcorn like snack. It reminded me of our many nights together Angie, in the cozy basement of our old house. I confessed to Vana the seemingly odd manner in which my brain works, with its neat and orderly file cabinet drawers popping open. I also told her of my strange, predictive dreams. She explained the Martian people are a very strong mental and intuitive race. Not unlike ESP, Pentrian babies are born possessing the sum total of their parents' and grandparents' knowledge and wisdom. Schools are not looked upon so much as learning institutions as they are cultivating places. It is the job of the teachers to bring out, or unlock, the information and knowledge the students' possess, like my internal file cabinet. Each student is of course unique in the type and depth of his or her knowledge. Teachers fill in the gaps and help each develop individual talents and interests.

Children and their parents are also psychically linked, to a limited extent. And it is believed that when a Pentrian finds his true companion, his *soerienm*, their idea of soul mates, they too, form this bond. In this way you were right, mom, about Marshal. He loved you very, very deeply, and never once gave up the desire to return to Earth for you. When dad was killed in the space craft accident a part of that bond was severed, allowing you to realize your feelings for Collin.

Braam, ever desirous to please me, spent his time on Earth trying to learn about my likes and tastes. I was supplied with everything I could possibly need. An extensive library at my temporary home contained classic literature both Martian and Earthly, as well as a vast collection of earth movies on viewing cubes. With the interest in Earth sweeping the populace, it seems Shakespeare, O Henry, H G Wells, Ray Bradbury, and even Anne Rice are the current favorites among the Pentria.

Food here has also taken on an earthly flavor. Xeursi, the woman who ran my first home, learned of my fondness for Mexican and Hispanic foods. She managed to come up with tasty Pentrian versions of pozole, enchiladas, and mild chili topped with bubbly cheese, just the way I like. It wasn't long before her special dishes were discovered and the Pentria developed an appetite for Mexican food. Elvia could make a fortune here running a restaurant. However, with all their modern and advanced technology, the Pentria still haven't been able to perfect a steamy, gooey double cheese and pepperoni pizza from Mario's.

My third night on Mars, Braam and I walked out onto the dusty rust Martian surface. Protected from the numbing cold by special clothing, and aided by the light atmosphere, we took in the velvet sky and billions of visible stars. The stars seemed strangely askew to me, but the Earth had just risen and shone brighter than the other heavenly objects. Over the months and years it has become a comforting beacon, a lighthouse for me in the crowded sea of stars. That night Braam said that shortly the planet Jupiter, with its magnificent red spot and banded atmosphere of many colors, would begin its approach and soon dominate the Martian sky. He was right. Angie, there are just no words to describe the sheer beauty and power of the incredible massive belted world. God's wondrous creations are gloriously displayed in the Martian heavens.

As we enjoyed the peaceful Martian night, Braam told me of his life. "You know, Marsha, I'm not exactly a simple astronaut."

"What do you mean?"

His eyes waxed thoughtfully, as ocher colored Phobos hovered overhead. "I trained for the space core reserve, even though space travel had been suspended since your father's return. At the time Marshal – his name was actually Meagaalo," Braam smiled fondly at the memory, "it means Great One of Destiny. Marshal was chief instructor at the *Trjoniel*, our academy. I admired him tremendously... we became friends. I used to sit for hours listening to his experiences on Earth. I found myself fascinated with the baby girl he left behind. What did she look like? How did she speak and think... and about what? What sort of woman did the daughter of this great man grow into?

"When it was announced we would return to Earth, Marshal... Meagaalo... personally selected me to accompany him. It was the proudest moment of my life. When your father was killed it was a great tragedy for the Pentrian. And it almost ended my chances of meeting you."

"How so?" I asked. Braam seemed to struggle with the answer.

"Our little population is governed by a small but democratic ruling body. But we have something like a Royal Family, not unlike the earth's England. Their power is limited, although they do have a voice in shaping our government. The Family's presence and continuance is important and vital in the minds and hearts of the Pentria."

Braam turned to me. I read a flood of mixed emotions in his handsome face. I believe it is the only time I have ever seen him troubled. "What is it, Braam?"

"Have you ever read The Prince and the Pauper, Marsha?"

"Mark Twain, yes... it's been some time..."

"I'm afraid I haven't been completely honest with you... I'm a prince... posing as a simple spaceman... a spaceman who has grown very fond of a beautiful girl, a brave young lady, a young lady who may not return that affection. Especially when she learns the spaceman is actually next in line to rule over... as figuratively as it may be... the Pentria people."

He stood there in the cold Martian night looking down at me, his eyes adrift in a vast sky of confusion and doubt. Was he kidding? I could love this man no matter what his position or station in life. And then it hit me… I had found him. Braam… Mi Flaco… the man of my dreams, he was my prince… my knight in a charcoal jumpsuit.

    I'm sure the grin which split my face must have confused him. "We have a custom on Earth," I whispered. Reaching up I moved his protective scarf aside. I did the same to my own. Standing on tippy toes, bathed in the mellow mantle of the Martian moon, I kissed him.

    "We have the same custom," Braam replied. Slipping his strong arms around me, my prince held me tight and our lips and our souls met. Vana was right, we had become soerienm.

    My fifth day on Mars I fell into a restless, haunted sleep, my dreams a confused montage of past revelations and future visions. I awoke with an unquenchable sense of purpose, and that old familiar itch to make a difference.

    It was time to get started.

    Vana, God bless her, wasn't comfortable with my decision. She kept asking if I was sure, if I didn't need more time to acclimate to my new surroundings. Over sweet purple Martian tea, I told her of Rebekah Martin. She understood. The next day Vana and I boarded a private boat. Braam had returned to his family residence promising to come back to me as soon as personal and government business permitted. I missed him, but my days would soon be full and hectic, marked by promising advances and anguished setbacks.

    Petrians use the canals and courses as highways. All of their cities… their *nadirs*… are located along the underground water ways. The Pentrian are a naturally curious and explorative people. They love to travel and discover the secrets of their rich and mysterious home. Vana said because of the waning climate and foreboding terrain, only a small portion of Mars is inhabited, and with the growing need for andesite, many remote areas of the planet are just now beginning to be explored.

    Our destination was *Tsenoch Nadir*, the largest city and seat of government for the Pentria. Tsenoch is located in the lush, mystic Elysium Planitia, or plain, just north of the planet's equator. It is in the foothills of the sacred Elysium Mons (Mountain), the Pentria holy land. With a very mild, for Mars, climate, the dazzling city of golden paths and beryl canals, walls of jasper, and emerald and amethyst buildings became my adopted home.

I was set up in a lovely *muzien*, or single home, of my own. It was at the center of the busy learning and medical hub of Tsenoch. Here I would spend many long hours and days at the hands of the skillful, patient Pentrian doctors and scientists. To my surprise and joy Vana was my neighbor. And Xeursi, whom I'd come to depend upon as I once did Elvia, again was here to cook and manage the house and take care of me.

I must admit I felt at times like a guinea pig, or a lab rat. Early each morning I was escorted to an advanced research facility next to my home. The Pentrian scientists and researchers were delighted to have a human subject to study. I was given an endless battery of tests and a complete, exhaustive examination. It turned out Earthlings and Martians share near identical physiologies. The most obvious differences are the result of the climatic disparities of the two worlds. Also, the Pentria have attained a higher plateau of intellect and learning, a level their scientists believe mankind is destined to ascend to in the near future. No evolution at work here, just the miraculous hand of an Almighty God.

Sometimes the testing necessitated I remain overnight. Often Vana accompanied me for moral strength and to keep me company during the long periods between tests. I had brought a deck of cards with me from Earth. Vana took to rummy like a fish to water, soon winning every hand. It was time to teach her a new game.

The experiments, often scary sounding when explained, turned out to be mostly simple and benign. The advanced technology of the Pentria, and the thoughtful, caring doctors made the procedures as painless as possible. I surrendered bottles of my blood; squares of skin; slivers of my liver; a portion of my appendix; a measure of muscle tissue; bone marrow, hair and even fingernail fragments; and a spattering of saliva.

The idea was to map my DNA; isolate the curative and reproductive segments; meld it with the Pentria DNA, and treat the damaged areas of the infertile Pentrian women. Staunch believers in the sanctity of life, the Martians developed a safe, simple method of retrieving regenerating cells from adult donors. It was these cells, not unlike stem cells, that they hoped to stimulate with the aid of my DNA.

Time dragged torturously by as my samples were tested, experimented on, re-tested and studied. For what seemed like an eternity, the Pentrian people anxiously awaited news from the researchers. Finally a breakthrough was announced. The first Pentria subject, a lovely, quiet, unassuming young woman of twenty four earth years, was brought in for the procedure. We had the opportunity to talk privately for a time. Like all of the participants, she was a volunteer. She had been selected to be first based on her health, age, family genetics and other factors. Tears puddle in my eyes as I wished this heroic woman all of the Lord's blessings. I wondered, if the situation were reversed could I be as brave.

The populace of Mars held its collective breath; prayed in silence. A few weeks later the results were confirmed.

The procedure had failed.

I was devastated.

The researchers and scientists and doctors took the failure in stride, as did the first volunteer. I went to her the evening the news was to be made public. I don't know how much comfort I gave. It turned out I found myself drawing on her strength. With a genteel smile and a twinkle in her silvery eyes, she helped me realize that even this setback put her people closer to a cure. I returned to the lab the following day nervous but ready for the next round.

It was during this time Braam returned. The new set of tests were more vigorous and I insisted on being in on the least little experiment whether I was directly involved or not. The rigor of the pace often left me tired and stressed, even irritable. I discovered the patient and caring, affable nature that marked the Pentria. Braam took care of me, tucking me into bed and fixing *otcuila*, a sort of Martian equivalent to chicken soup. Many a restless night I awoke from one of my dreams with a start. I'd find Mi Flaco sitting attentively at my side reading or listening to music.

I remember the look that always came over you, Angie when you spoke of Marshal. I remember thinking how much dad meant to you, how much you loved him. And I remember wondering if I would ever know those feelings. Now I understand, mom. The emotions that Braam and I have come to share are beyond describing. But I know you understand.

Sometimes, when a particularly disturbing dream kept me from falling back asleep, Braam and I would play rummy and talk till perfumed amber rays of morning danced across my bedroom. Braam shared his dreams and his hopes, even his fears for his people's future. We talked and laughed and planned out our own future like two youngsters unfettered by the realities of the worlds around them. Braam confided in me that his family, the Royal Family of the Pentrian, had slowly and reluctantly come to accept me and our love. Like an intergalactic Romeo and Juliet, we stubbornly refused to allow neither family nor planetary politics to deter our feelings for one another. Perhaps this was the destiny of both our worlds, a union that would strengthen and benefit both planets.

Before I knew it the year had turned – well, an earth year. Here the Martian year is actually some 687 earth days. It still confuses me at times, although I've come to deal with the long dark terrifying Martian winters. Temperatures in our cozy underground nadir remain pleasant, albeit cool, with artificial lighting supplementing the sun's diminished rays. Up on the surface, however, the CO_2 ice patches can extend well into our Elysium Planitia. These are the ever waning and waxing ice caps so often observed and written about on Earth.

The one year anniversary of my leaving arrived with my emotions predictably troubled. A fitful night's sleep found me dreaming of you, mom. I saw you, Collin at your side, wandering through the old cemetery. It was so real I could smell your shampoo in the cool air. My first birthday without you, Braam and Vana did their best to cheer me, surprising me with a makeshift birthday cake. Missing you, Angie, and the uncertainty of my mission here made the celebration bittersweet.

As the *Acacecn Aloastvic* approached, an ancient Pentrian festival welcoming the returning sun, an excited buzz began to circulate around the research lab. A discovery had been made. The Pentrian Doctors now believed they understood why the first attempt at repairing the damaged Martian DNA failed. As they explained it to me, Martian spermatozoon contains a diluted form of lysine from that of Earthmen. My regenerative genes had done their job too well, repairing the Pentrian DNA in the egg cell's nucleus. This new *super egg* attacked and destroyed the male lysine, leaving the sperm unable to penetrate and fertilize the now healthy egg. An effective balance was needed, one that would repair without damaging. The researchers believed they had it.

On a luminous Martian morning I kissed Vana's soft pink cheek as she entered the operatory. This time the doctors would perform only the repair operation. Vana and her husband elected to put their faith in God and allow His hand to guide nature's course. Four months later the beaming, teary eyed couple announced the procedure had been successful. Vana was pregnant. Imagine the surprise and delight, Angie when the first successful birth to an infertile Pentria woman turned out to be a strong, healthy pink little girl with your green eyes!

As soon as it was announced the procedure was successful with Vana, several more volunteers were prepared. The number was limited to six for fear some unforeseen complication might arise. However, it wasn't long before all six ladies were given a clean bill of health. Soon, Vana and her husband were joined by five other glowing Martian mommies to be. It was later discovered the sixth volunteer failed to become pregnant only because of her husband's low sperm count.

The day Vana was to deliver little Marshanna, the Pentria declared a holiday. It was hardly necessary. I don't believe anyone on Mars went to their office or plant or school that day. A crowd of some 3,000 Pentrian flooded the flaxen streets around the medical center where Vana was to deliver. The rest of the population remained close to the nearest tele-link, intently awaiting the news.

Vana asked me to be in the delivery room with her. Martian pregnancies, development and delivery nearly mirror those of humans on Earth. Pentria women practice a form of breathing and exercise that prepares them mentally as well as physically. When it came time for green eyed Marshanna to arrive, Vana was alert and smiling and seemingly in no pain or discomfort. I on the other hand was riding my emotions for everything they were worth. By the time I cradled my pink namesake in trembling arms, I was a total wreck. In the months that followed, five precious Pentrian babies arrived one at a time. Each was strong, healthy and perfect: three silver eyed, raven haired girls and two ruddy boys with cherry eyes. One eventually sported my light honey hair.

With the arrival of the last miracle baby, the Pentrian government declared the procedure safe and effective. A portion of my donated genes was set aside for further study, while the remainder became earmarked to help other women. But one final test still remained.

Over the next year – Martian year – so many incredible things happened. A few days after her birth, Marshanna was presented to the Pentria people in a time honored ceremony not unlike a christening. I was named Marshanna's godmother. Braam became her *leginea* or godfather. Mi Flaco beamed so proud you would have thought he was the father.

The same evening a second ceremony was held, one which came as a total surprise and shock to me. At an official state dinner at Braam's princely home, the Pentria conferred upon me the name Msarah. On Mars the highest honor one can receive is to have their name officially changed by the Royal Family. It is equivalent to receiving a medal or knighthood. My new Pentrian name, Msarah, means *Mother of Nations*.

A few weeks later, Braam and I strolled in one of Tsenoch's rich green places, large expanses set aside to aid in the production of oxygen.

"You know," Braam whispered, holding me to him in the silky night, "the people love you very much."

I looked around. The delicate lacteous leaves glistened with early dew. The golden city shimmered in the distance, a soft iridescence. Above and all around me the crystalline walls of our subterranean world twinkled and sparkled, reminding me of the ceiling of my bedroom back in Honeybrook. I felt Braam's warmth, the beating of his heart against mine. He saw the drops form in the corner of my eyes.

"I don't know how I can be any happier," I said, burying my head in his chest.

"Perhaps I know of a way." He fumbled in the waist pocket of his summer shirt. A silver box tumbled to the aqua colored grass. Braam dove like a school boy chasing a Pete Rose rookie card suddenly caught up in a shifting breeze. His skittish antics made me laugh.

"I'm sorry... I..." he managed breathless, collecting himself and the errant cube. "I..." As he straightened, those incredible florid eyes found mine. On one bent knee, without any words, my prince charming slipped a delicate gold band with a fiery translucent five pointed amber stone onto the third finger of my left hand.

With Vana as my maid of honor, Braam and I wed in an elegantly elaborate ceremony at the home of his parents. The Royal

Family of the Pentria accepted me warmly, and I have grown ever so fond of them. My fairy tale was almost complete.

Cutting short our honeymoon, Braam – my husband – and I rushed back to the medical center in Tsenoch. Vana was already there with one year old Marshanna. Doctors and researchers were anxious to see if her regenerated genes were strong enough to be used in the same way my own had helped Vana. A simple, painless procedure was performed. Once again the Pentrian people prayed. Once again God showed his greatness and mercy. A few months later the recipient of little Marshanna's DNA announced she was with child. It would soon be possible to begin restorative procedures on a planet wide scale.

As you can see, mom my life has been and continues full and rewarding. Many times I resisted the urge to contact you. I wanted to wait till my odyssey came to some conclusion: the happy ever after ending you love to tease me about.

Now it has.

After a long, bounteous reign, Braam's parents stepped down into a much awaited and well deserved retirement. Braam and I moved into the Royal Palace. Braam joyously sees to the affairs of the people with caring and empathy. I'm kept dizzyingly busy with the wonderful duties of a queen.

Best of all exactly five days after receiving this letter, you and Collin will be on your way here. The Sarlein will deliver you to me, mom in time for the arrival of your first grandchild.

All my love,

M Msarah

THE END

About the Author

B.J. Neblett was born in the heart of South Philadelphia. At the tender age of 17 he gained national exposure as a writer appearing in Encounter: An Anthology of Modern Poetry. An avid writer, he authored dozens of short stories, poems and articles. After service in the army during the Viet Nam war, BJ fulfilled his childhood dream. Embarking on a 30 year odyssey, he built a career across the US as popular radio DJ Billy James. During this time he honed his writing skills on radio scripts and commercial copy. Known as one of the last true personality jocks, he also helped write the book on club beat mixing. His savvy segues and tempting tempos helped define "thumpus uninteruptus" during the '70's and '80's.

Presently he is hard at work on his memoirs; a book about growing up during the Kennedy era, a short story collection, and a sequel to Elysian Dreams. When not working, BJ can usually be found listening to his extensive record collection, tinkering with his old cars, playing soft ball, or just relaxing in his Seattle home with one of his vintage guitars.

For more information, or to contact BJ Neblett:

Web site: www.bjneblett.com

E mail: info@bjneblett.com

Blog: www.bjneblett.blogspot.com

Publisher: www.brightonpublishing.com

CPSIA information can be obtained at www.ICGtesting.com
Printed in the USA
BVOW06s0538220916

462890BV00004B/8/P

9 781936 587735